The Playgroup

"Daddy and I don't want you to go. Tonight is for staying home. Are you hungry?"

"We don't have time, Mama. Lokomo says it's easier to fly on an empty stomach. Iceman says I can bring Banky with me."

"Little girls don't go by themselves," her mother said, panicking. "Their parents love them too much."

"All right, Mama"—breaking free, her voice neutral again—"Do you take me or do I go myself? I'll give you to ten."

She lay down clutching Banky. For a moment her mother thought she was out from under the strangeness. Then she began counting. "Ten. Nine. Eight. Seven. Six. Five. Four. Three. Two. One." Her eyeballs rolled back in her head until only the whites were showing.

Heidi screamed as she had never screamed before.

THE PLAYGROUP

NANCY WEBER

CHARTER BOOKS, NEW YORK

The lines from the poem "The Lost Children" on pages 130 and 131 are reprinted with permission of Macmillan Publishing Co., Inc., from *The Lost World*, copyright © 1965 by Randall Jarrell.

This Charter Book contains the complete
text of the original hardcover edition.
It has been completely reset in a typeface
designed for easy reading, and was printed
from new film.

THE PLAYGROUP

A Charter Book / published by arrangement with
St. Martin's/Marek

PRINTING HISTORY
St. Martin's/Marek edition published / 1982
Charter edition / October 1984

All rights reserved.
Copyright © 1982 by Nancy Weber
This book may not be reproduced in whole
or in part, by mimeograph or any other means,
without permission. For information address:
St. Martin's/Marek, 175 Fifth Avenue,
New York, New York 10010.

ISBN: 0-441-67070-9

Charter Books are published by The Berkley Publishing Group,
200 Madison Avenue, New York, New York 10016.
PRINTED IN THE UNITED STATES OF AMERICA

*To three magical children—Rose, Lucy, Jenny—
and one decent grown-up, Art Almeida.*

RULES OF THE PLAYGROUP

1. We the undersigned mothers hereby establish the East Sixty-sixth Street Playgroup.
2. The goals of the Playgroup shall be twofold: (a) to encourage our kids to share, cooperate, trust, explore, and have fun with each other; and (b) to give us moms some much-needed, well-deserved escape by pooling and rotating responsibility for said kids.
3. The Playgroup will meet Monday through Thursday from 10:30 A.M. to 1:00 P.M., with mothers-in-charge as follows:

>Monday—Heidi Kahn
>Tuesday—Elizabeth Gray
>Wednesday—Jackie Geritano
>Thursday—Kelly Smith

4. If a mother-in-charge is unable to preside over her scheduled shift, she may hire Mary Girard to take her place. No other substitutes are allowed unless all the other mothers agree.
5. The mother-in-charge will use verbal discipline only.
6. The mother-in-charge will serve a wholesome, appealing lunch, without being so goddamn creative as to arouse feelings of inadequacy in the other mothers.

7. If a mother suspects that her child is coming down with a cold or may be harboring nasty communicable germs, that mother will keep her child away from the Playgroup.

8. Mothers will compensate promptly for any property damage inflicted by their darlings.

9. Mothers hereby agree to hold one another harmless in the event of a playground mishap or other accident, but

10. Don't let anything bad happen to the children.

April

1.

Afterward you think: If only.

Stupid; too late; your child is gone; but your mind has to tick its wretched guilty tocks.

If only I hadn't brought Daisy to New York. If only we'd stayed away from Central Park. If only I hadn't let her drag me to the playground, the one just north of the zoo, nice fenced-in oval playground where everything is painted red and blue.

Terrific paint job. Two red seesaws, two blue ones, blue handles on the red ones, red handles on the blue.

Don't panic if that's where you take your kids to play. The swings are safe again. You can drink the water.

If only I'd snatched her out of the sandbox when I saw what was happening. If we'd run away to some cave.

Useless, indulgent thinking. As though we could spiral back through time to safety.

We were never safe. If we'd stayed in Vermont I might have kept the world at bay for a while, but that wouldn't have changed Daisy's nature.

She was three and a half when I lost her.

Maybe you have a three-year-old, or you remember one, or you have a terrible two and everyone keeps saying, Wait until three. The darling age. They tell you how much they love you. They're small enough to ride on your shoulders, big enough to wear official running shoes and race you down the street. They print their names, draw faces with saucers for ears, help you scramble the eggs, sometimes put their puzzles away, consent to have "Sesame Street" turned soft if you explain that you're hungover, sing songs about pumpkins and blackbirds, tell knock knock jokes, sort of.

"Knock knock."

"Who's there?"

"Daisy."

"Daisy who?"

"Daisy crazy lazy fazy!"

And so gorgeous. Physically simply gorgeous. People would stop us on the street and say how much we looked alike, but all they were seeing were the twin bowl haircuts from Frank Your Barber in Tindy, Vermont. Her skin had the pale plump newness that no grown woman, however lucky or artful, can hope to see in the mirror. Bright little blushy clown cheeks. Eyes that were absolute blue, inky at the centers, set off by absolute whites. Berry-stained summer lips all year round. Her hair was the silvery pale sort of blond that seems to be lit from within. My hair is paper-bag brown.

A typical three. No, really, she *was* a typical three, aside from being a different order of creature from anyone else who ever lived on the planet. She had a cat, Thomas, which she claimed to love but Mommy had to feed it. She liked books about trains and monkeys. She thought clomping around in my shoes was perfect fun. She wanted hamburgers and French fries and ketchup and Coke whenever we ate out. And: Why is the sky blue? And: What is poo-poo made of? And: Where is Wednesday?

The imaginary friends were typical too. That's what the pediatrician in Tindy told me. Even three-year-olds with fathers and brothers and sisters have to invent their own casts of characters. A way of being in control, he said.

Iceman came first. I bought Daisy a yellow plastic push-button telephone she flipped for at Woolworth's (typical exalted three-year-old taste), and suddenly Iceman existed. Mommy, I have to call Iceman and ask him to come for dinner. Iceman wants to talk to you, Mommy. Iceman was sick but he's feeling better now. Mommy, I can't finish my milk because Iceman says it tastes funny.

I liked him most of the time. He felt kind. Now and then when Daisy handed me the play telephone and ordered me to talk to him, I worked up such a babble that she danced with impatience and grabbed the receiver. Once I bothered to brush my hair when she said he was coming for dinner. His minor details changed from day to day but never his resounding maleness. And his favorite color was blue.

I liked Iceman. I didn't like the idea of Iceman. It seemed such a lonely business, making up friends. It seemed like a plea for a life with more interesting facts. I didn't want my girl to need to dwell in the mists.

A few weeks after Iceman first happened, my cousin Larry called. He was leaving New York for six months, maybe forever; he was off to try out at the London bureau of one of the television networks. We could have his apartment on East Sixty-sixth Street, rent free, until he knew if the job was going to jell. I didn't need free rent, but I've always needed invitations. For sure I needed one just then. Outside there was mud, inside there was Iceman. I thought about tall buildings. Maybe New York would fill Daisy's mind with stone reality.

I closed up our house of exile. On a Monday morning in April we drove south to the city, Mommy Jill and her little Daisy and Thomas the big orange cat.

2.

I have always been uneasy in Central Park. Trees and grass are wrong in New York City. Green is wrong. Round is wrong. Open is wrong. New York is about straight lines and right angles, about glass and steel and cement and a hundred shades of gray. Buildings are safe. The grid is good. The park is the dark heart of things, tendrils snaking out at you, holes waiting to swallow you.

Unreasonable fears, unreasonable courage, Jack once said of me.

I was twenty-nine when Daisy was born. I'd thought that the birth of a child would put an end to the fears. I would look unafraid for a child and therefore would become unafraid.

Some fears went away. Pregnancy gave me new faith in my body—no more waking, sweating, in the middle of the night, diagnosing terminal diseases. Other fears swelled to encompass Daisy. I sometimes dreamed that the trees in Central Park were waiting for us both.

We drove to New York on a Monday morning in April. Monday afternoon we walked west on East Sixty-sixth Street, toward the dreaded trees. One glimpse of green and my joy in the city vanished. I tightened my grip on Daisy's hand. My throat swelled. My legs longed to run away.

I told my legs to keep going straight ahead. I thought, Daisy needs to know other tots. (Did I freely think that thought? Or did the brats make me think it? Lokomo, Lokomo, fly me away. Drop me in the deepest sea.) I thought, She needs a place to run and shout. She had lived her whole life in Tindy, in the ramble of a house my parents had left behind. Now her home was a small two-bedroom apartment. There were no other children in the building. My cousin Larry had talked about a playground two blocks away where East Sixty-sixth crossed Fifth Avenue and Central Park began.

"Look, honey." I drew deep breaths to quell nausea. I pointed to the grand old apartment houses of Park Avenue, rising massively just ahead. "Aren't those beautiful buildings? So straight and tall? Golly, what a day this is. I swear it smells better than Vermont. Look at that poodle, Daisy. Its legs. Do you believe it? Someone shaved it—isn't that silly and terrific? You don't know how happy I am to be in New York with you. I used to live here before you were born, for years and years, downtown in Greenwich Village—I'll show it to you someday—and, God, how I wanted you. Don't horns sound better than crickets?"

"Horns sound much better than crickets," Daisy said, but she grabbed hold of my thigh as we stopped for the light and traffic roared by us.

Here, I knew, was what the sensible mother would fear: the crazy cabbies who jumped red lights, the whistle-blow-ing bikers who ignored the lights altogether. I scooped Daisy up. "I love my girl," I said, the magic message to cure bad moments.

"I love my mom."

I drank in the sustaining words. I kissed one clown cheek, then the other. I marveled at her eyes, as though I'd never before quite gauged their intensity. I took fresh pleasure in the silvery hair.

"I love my mom," Daisy said again, "and I love Thomas, and I love Iceman, and I love my mice."

The mice were the latest invention. I sighed. It was too soon for New York to have done the work I wanted it to do, but I'd had my hopes.

"Here's Iceman." Daisy reached into one pocket of her red-hooded sweat shirt. "And here are my mice. Say hi to them, Mom. You can pat the mice, but don't pat Iceman. Iceman's not for patting today. He's my daddy. My pretend daddy," she amended, as she saw my lips compress.

I shifted her. "Hi, mice." I patted air. "Hello, Iceman. Okay, honey, we've got the light." I set her down on her feet and took her hand again. "See how the sign says WALK? W-A-L-K? Isn't that terrific? We always wait for the WALK sign in New York. This is Park Avenue. Daisy, look. Look."

We were on the esplanade, halfway across the avenue. My knees trembled for beauty. Twenty blocks of soaring buildings carried the eye to the urban ultimate—the glinting old gold heft of the Helmsley Building and the sheer icy loft of the Pan Am Building behind it.

"Look, my Daisy."

"How do you spell Park Avenue?"

I bit back disappointment. I spelled Park Avenue.

"And *p* is for pineapple," Daisy said, as the WALK sign changed to a blinking red DON'T WALK and I hurried her across the other half of the avenue. "And *p* is for porcupine, and *p* is for penis."

"That's right," I said swiftly. "And *p* is for playground.

We're almost there. Are you going to slide first, or swing?"

"Iceman has a penis," Daisy persisted. "And you have a vagina, and I have a vagina."

I was sure we'd caught the attention of a brittle blond toting miniature shopping bags—an aqua-and-white bag from Tiffany, a dull gold foil bag from Godiva. Once Jack sent me a hundred bittersweet chocolate hearts from Godiva.

"How do you spell Iceman?" Daisy asked.

"What, baby? I-C-E-M-A-N." Funny, I thought, that she had memorized whole books, rhyming books especially, could do a startling imitation of a person reading aloud; yet she asked to have the same words spelled again and again. Were they all like that at three? She needed to know other tots (came the tricky thought again), and I needed to know other mothers. Central Park would be good.

"Because it's Iceman's birthday, you see," Daisy said. "It's his birthday all day. Sing 'Happy Birthday' to him, Mom."

We were at Madison Avenue. I stared at the pale leather shoes in the window at Charles Jourdan—strappy pistachio sandals, spiky two-tone slingbacks. For three years I'd worn sneakers and moccasins and boots, ugly boots to keep the snow and mud at bay. I wondered if my feet could still walk in Charles Jourdan shoes. Once upon a corn, I would have wanted every pair in that silly window.

"Sing 'Happy Birthday' to him, Mom."

I felt crabbiness surge. "We've got the light. Let's go."

Halfway across Madison Avenue, Daisy yanked her hand free.

"Daisy!" I grabbed her. "Don't you ever do that again! You hold my hand when we're crossing streets, do you understand?"

"I was holding Iceman's hand." Daisy kicked at the pavement.

"You hold *my* hand."

"Iceman's my daddy, and it is too his birthday."

"Dammit," I exploded, "he's only—" I couldn't finish the cruel sentence. Any second my girl would weep. A gray-haired nanny wheeling a high-wheeled English baby carriage gave me a look a child-abuser would merit.

"Girlfriend," I crooned, hoisting Daisy again. I stroked the brilliant hair. "I'm sorry I got so angry. It's very important to be careful crossing streets. Cars come fast in New York."

"I hate New York."

My body felt weighted. "Please don't hate New York. Please, baby. There are so many terrific things here. Look straight ahead. Trees." Swallowing a hysterical giggle, I began to proclaim the virtues of the dreaded park.

Daisy listened. She tested. "Can Iceman be there?"

What was the point in fighting? She would only cling to him the harder. She needed time. "Sure," I said.

"Because I can make him a cake in the sandbox. The kids will help."

I smiled at "kids" from the three-year-old mouth. "That's a lovely idea."

We crossed Fifth Avenue to the park side. The trees were bosomy furies waiting to lull me to sleep. Who would look after Daisy? I detoured by the frieze of infantry soldiers—anything to buy seconds—but Daisy didn't want to hear about doughboys. She didn't want a pretzel from the vendor with the red-and-white umbrella. She could hear children shouting and she wanted to play.

My feet dragged. The trees of Vermont had never troubled me, not even the dense stands of pine that choked off every strand of sunlight. It wasn't rational to dread these trees. What wasn't rational mustn't be.

"Come on, Mom." Tugging. So happy; expectant.

"Daisy—"

"I like New York, and I'll be very careful crossing streets because it's very important. Can we go to the playground now? The kids are waiting." She started running.

I ran after her, and there we were. If only, if only, if only . . .

A girl about Daisy's age, with startling coppery hair, waved from the sandbox.

Daisy waved back. "That's Stephanie." She looked excited.

"You know her?" I asked incredulously.

Daisy nodded.

My mind sifted and sorted. There were always New Yorkers coming up to Vermont, summer people and ski people, but I was sure I would have remembered the little girl's conspicuous hair.

Daisy pointed to a dark-haired boy in railroad stripe overalls who was scooping sand with a big blue shovel. "That's Nick. James is coming later."

I laughed. Daisy was playing a new version of the name game, that was all. Today I'm Donald Duck and you're Minnie Mouse. Mama monkey, do you have a banana for baby monkey? This chair is Boop and that one is Beep. I'm going to call Clink-Clonk on the phone and invite her to come over with her mom and dad. She lives on Blue Street, right near Iceman, isn't that funny?

Then, clear as anything, I heard a real and actual woman's voice yodel, "Stephaneeee!" The copper-haired girl climbed out of the sandbox, ran over to the benches set back against the fence, had an exchange with a woman who shared her vivid coloring, and came back to the sand.

My temples started to beat out the overture to a major headache. I wanted to claw at the air, pull the skin of the world tight again. Daisy patted my leg—a mother's pat, a pat to say that everything would be okay. Christ, how we lie with our pats. I stood frozen as Daisy raced over to the sandbox, her pale hair flying. The coppery girl greeted her. The dark-haired boy handed her his shovel. Daisy sat down to dig.

I pressed fingers to the back of my neck, where the tension lay coiled like an evil snake. Three-year-olds don't share their toys with strangers except at their parents' urging and often not even then. I knew that for a fact, like gravity.

I looked at the bench. The coppery mother was sitting with a dark-haired woman who clearly belonged to the boy in railroad stripes. They were staring intently at the sandbox, staring at me. No anxiety in their stares, though. These mothers didn't have headaches.

Because New York kids were different? More precocious than other kids? I'd read that theory. So the other mothers saw no wrongness in this coziness among small strangers?

The kids were building together now. Mounding and patting sand. I watched the sand take form. The headache reached to my toes. The kids were making a cake.

A little girl pedaled her tricycle over to the sandbox. The boy in railroad stripes flung a handful of sand her way. The little girl yelled, "Nah, nah, nah." She pedaled back to her mother.

"Nick!" called the dark-haired woman on the bench. "Nick! We don't throw sand."

"Nick," I whimpered. I begged the bad dream to end. Stephanie and Nick, my girl had said, and James was coming later.

There was still time. The trees hadn't started moving. I could snatch Daisy up and carry her away. We would find a cave somewhere. In the tallest grayest building of all.

But my girl looked so happy. Relaxed, connected, utterly at home.

The kids joined hands and started singing.

> *Happy birthday to you*
> *Happy birthday to you*
> *Happy birthday, dear Iceman*
> *Happy birthday to you*

I stood on the brink for a moment. I have always known, I thought.

I walked over to the bench and sat down with the other mothers.

3.

The Playgroup will meet Monday through Thursday from 10:30 A.M. to 1:00 P.M., with mothers-in-charge as follows:

Monday—Heidi Kahn
Tuesday—Elizabeth Gray
Wednesday—Jackie Geritano
Thursday—Jill Everts

May

Dear Ken:

It was good talking to you last night. Your mother and I both thought you sounded very happy indeed. We keep reading that bicoastalism is the great new sport and wish you would embrace it—but we're glad the work is going so well and that there's "a woman." Do we ever get to know more about her? You breathe maddening new life into the word "discretion."

All right—enough pater patter. Here is the formulation I worked out for the epidemiology department here.

Given: A male, let us call him Tom, has been sexually hyperactive for 25 years, to the tune of an average of 25 new partners a year, in a city with a population of 7,000,000.

Given: Each of Tom's partners, and each of Tom's partners' partners, has a lifetime average of 5 new sexual partners.

Given: Tom is a carrier of a sexually transmitted virus which is silent in adult males and females but manifests in the offspring of carrier women.

Let us suppose just 3 generations of transmittal, e.g., Tom sleeps with Sally (plus others), who sleeps with Harry (plus others), who sleeps with Sue (plus others), who sleeps with Ludwig (plus others), who sleeps with Agnes (plus others). We get the formula:

$$25 \times 25 \times (1 + 25 + 625)$$

i.e., Tom's encounters with women over 25 years give rise to roughly 400,000 carrier mothers. If we adjust for duplications and women outside the childbearing years, we end up, in the 25th year of Tom's larking, with 200,000 potential mothers of infected offspring, about 20,000 of whom are statistically likely to have children during that year. In a city with a population of 7,000,000, you'll have a birthrate of about 100,000. Therefore the chances of any given baby's being infected are .20.

The epidemiology boys came to me because they are concerned about what may happen when an infected child has contact with another infected child. They asked me to compute the probability of clustering in a steady nursery school population of 20. Here's what we get:

—chances of finding 0 infected children = .012
—chances of finding a total of 1 infected child = .058
—chances of finding a total of 2 infected children = .137
—chances of finding a total of 3 or more = .793

In case you no longer carry Yankee statistics next to your heart, let me remind you that in the Yankees' all-time best year (1927), they won 110 games and lost 44, for a winning percentage of .714. In other words, the chance of there being 3 or more infected children in a steady population of 20 is better than the chance of a fan's seeing the Yankees win on any given day in the 1927 season.

I confess to being at a loss as to how exactly this will bear on your work (and I don't suppose you'll enlighten me any), but I hope my sly inclusion of Yankee data will send you rushing to LAX for a flight east. This might just be the year we top 1927. I'll spring for box seats and all the beer you can drink. We missed being with you on your birthday. Can we lure you here for mine?

                                              Lots of love,
                                              Dad

June

MONDAY, THE NINTH

1.

They had bought the brownstone twenty-eight years ago, when the marriage was new and grand and looked likely to produce a wealth of children. The house was just off Fifth Avenue on West Eleventh Street, one of the splendid tree-lined blocks of Greenwich Village—one of the neighborhoods of choice in all New York. It was a four-story structure, rough-skinned, weighty. There were pale green shutters at the windows, and a white Georgian door, complete with fanlight, which had begun life in Dublin, where Jack Keefe's people came from. The shutters and the door were too dressy for the brownstone, but the house worked—like certain Village women who wore pearls with their jeans and sneakers.

The marriage of Jack and Nora Keefe had endured. By conventional definition it did not work.

It had not produced children. It had not, for a very long time, promoted the happiness of the two protagonists. But happiness is not the only matrimonial glue, as Jack's other women kept discovering to their grief. Sometimes pleasure works as well. Sometimes pain provides pleasure enough.

Nora's pain was plain for all the world to see—as much of the world as she let see her. At twenty she'd reveled in being a beauty, a darling; she'd stuffed the Grand Ballroom at the Waldorf for her wedding. At forty-eight she was a recluse, buried alive in the greenhouse she'd had built onto the back of the brownstone, a bulb in frozen earth waiting for a spring that never came. She dressed in drab. Her stale gray hair snaked over her defeated shoulders. No matter that her contemporaries played tennis and larked and lusted and still had questions in the night. Nora was resolutely middle-aged, her mind all made up.

And Jack ate no fat. He ate veal chops, trimmed, evenings at Broadway Joe, where he traded wit with the famous writers; or poached turbot, innocent of hollandaise, at "21," where he played power games with senators. Lunch was nearly always a Jack Keefe Salad—chicken, watercress, stringbeans, cucumbers, with olive oil and lemon—at O'Rourke's, on lower Broadway, two blocks from the Woolworth Building and the law offices of Keefe and Martinez.

He also drank a little. In public he drank Irish whiskey, neat, water back. In silky bedrooms around the city he drank champagne. He was six feet four, with big blunt fingers, and he felt foolish drinking champagne; but he needed the foolishness. The bubbles distanced him from Nora, let him take his ambitions off the hook.

He was a big deal in New York City. Not quite a brand name, but those who had to know knew. He was the village fixer. If you called him with a problem, he invariably had a favor coming from Just the Person Who. He had no other genius—his clerks were better lawyers; he needed no other genius. The White House was careful to court him when the guard changed. He always watched the World Series with the owners.

When he got the itch to go public with his power, a hundred people knew before Nora. He hadn't kept the news from her, he just hadn't gotten around to telling her—at least that was the party line. Then one hard bright June afternoon, when the dust motes and smudges of life gleamed, he got suddenly straight with himself. Truth was he'd put off telling Nora because he dreaded telling Nora, and that wouldn't do. He opened a folder of letters that needed signing. He reached for the telephone.

"I want to be mayor," he told his wife. There was no pretense that he sought advice or consent. "I intend to force a primary."

Nora's thin shoulders went rigid with resentment. She was in her greenhouse, her sanctuary. Wars, depressions, famines, falling comets, and the bad news of daily life were not supposed to reach her here. She focused intently on the lush pink blossoms of a bleeding heart which persisted in flowering past its season. She drew a steadying breath of the loamy air.

"That's nice, dear." She dragged the words over gravel—cocktail party sarcastic. "If every woman you've fucked in New York votes for you, you'll be a shoo-in."

The man who would be mayor snorted. He was famous for his snorts. They were moist, going for gross; undeniably happy; darling to some tastes.

"Nora, my love, you never disappoint me." He uncapped his pen. He signed letters to Cardinal Cooke, to the young Irish potter Stephen Pearce, to the New York Bar Association, varying his signature each time—Jack, Jack Keefe, John X. L. Keefe. He said, "I suppose I should take it as a compliment that you think they'll vote *for* me."

Nora hadn't visited Jack's office in years, but she could picture it perfectly, could picture him in it. The heavy paneling, the view of the East River; and Jack's thick hair sucking silver out of the afternoon light, his lean length set off by the massive nineteenth-century oak desk he'd bought at auction in Rutland, Vermont. He was doing some kind of paperwork, Nora guessed. He was never hers unshared. Her left hand gripped the telephone so hard that ripples of pain traveled up to her elbow.

"If memory serves me, fucking was always one of the things you were good at. Anything where you can be on top. I suppose you'd make a decent mayor at that." She hated her voice now, acid as Irish tea without milk. "Jack?" she tried more gently. "I don't suppose there's any talking you out of this notion?"

"New York needs me, Nora. We've got ourselves a twit of a mayor who thinks that music in the subways—music!—can save the city. Haven't we gone to enough wakes in our time? Are we going to lie back and watch the heart's blood drain out of New York?"

His crisp voice wore a mantle of brogue now, what Nora called his Big Jack Keefe manner o'speakin'. She envisaged the endless appearances on television during the months of the campaign. Jack's face would do its puckish dance—the light blue eyes crinkling, the nose bobbing upward, the smile making apples of his cheeks. He would look very much the statesman, blessed by a touch of the poet. And each time he was interviewed he would say, as if for the first time, "Are we going to lie back and watch the heart's blood drain out of New York? New York needs me."

"New York needs you," Nora told him, "and New York has you. New York has had you—" bitter again—"for the past twenty-five years." She looked down at the camel's hair brush she held in her right hand—she'd been dusting the leaves of her African violets when the telephone rang. "But it doesn't matter how I feel, does it? So I'll save my breath. I have just one question for you. What's expected of me during the campaign? And after?"

"I ask your good wishes, and nothing more." Jack said the words so smoothly that Nora felt he'd been all too prepared for the question, had somehow tricked her into asking it so that he could say his piece and get the conversation done with. "I promise you that you can go on living your life the way you've been living it. Of course no public appearances, and you'll be completely shielded from the press. Your ways are well enough known—"

"My ways. How dainty we are today."

"—well enough known, and if we have to bolster what's known with a statement from Dr. Howard, we will. I don't think that even the most vigorous reporter would want to tamper with the delicate balance of your health."

Nora flung her camel's hair brush halfway across the greenhouse. It landed with an unsatisfying little plop on a twenty-pound sack of potting soil.

"You'll keep the press from me, and you'll keep me from the press."

"Don't be foolish, my love. I trust you absolutely. You'd like me to be mayor, wouldn't you? You'd have no reason to stand in my way?"

Nora felt a tiny rush of triumph. She'd succeeded in making him anxious. But—Jesus—of all the empty joys—

"What difference does it make to me?" she said wearily. "I won't see any more or any less of you. Or maybe you were thinking I'd get a thrill doing the flowers for Gracie Mansion?"

"Now isn't that a grand offer!" Big Jack Keefe signed the last two letters in his folder. He capped his pen. "A little break for the taxpayers too. My love, I've got a call from Washington waiting. I won't be home for dinner tonight. I'll look in on you later if your light is on."

"Do that."

Nora dropped the receiver onto the cradle. She sat staring at the telephone. A green-black bit of mildew was growing on the celluloid-covered cardboard circle on which the number was printed. She wondered how long the mold would take to eat the telephone. A hundred years. A thousand.

She'd lied to Jack, saying his new plans wouldn't make any difference to her. Then again, she'd lied to herself these past few weeks, thinking she might be able to persuade Jack to retire to Ireland on his fiftieth birthday.

What had possessed her to imagine he had covert longings to get out of the thick of life? What willful blindness had led her to hope something other than guilt bound him to her, and a sea change could restore them to each other? Jack was a fine professional Irishman here in New York, grandly serving up Waterfall smoked salmon on Shanagarry fish plates, waxing sentimental in front of his Jack Yeats watercolors; but the city owned him, body and soul. He would never share Nora's green dreams of stone cottages, ripe rivers, a brilliant garden, fine rains and—above all else—solitude.

Nora got up off her wooden stool. Her body felt cold, chafed, arthritic, though afternoon light was pouring through the wide glass panes of the greenhouse. She was too thin, that was the problem. The leanness Jack had loved had turned into a parody of itself, a kind of antiflesh, dry to the touch and unwelcoming to the eye. She disliked eating. She wished she could draw nourishment by osmosis, the way her plants did.

Mechanically she started to make her rounds along the concrete walls. Nora, Nora, quite contrary, how does your garden grow? She looked, she sniffed, she syringed, she stooped to pinch back a bouvardia plant, to cluck over a flat of young snap-dragons. This was the one nursery she had ever presided over or ever would, and she knew all too well that here was the heart of the matter. Jack Keefe, verging on fifty, had to try to become mayor, to immortalize himself, because he had no children to sing the song of his cells. He had to have the other women because Nora's barren body offended him. With silver bells and cocks and balls and pretty maids all in a row.

She stopped in front of the amazing bleeding heart. According to the books, it should have shed its last pink blossom back at the beginning of May. Nora stood poised between love and hate. The flowers were movingly beautiful, and their longevity was a tribute to her nurturing skills; but today they seemed almost to mock her. They were showy and she was stark. They were fleshy and she was bony. They were sanguine and she was bloodless. They were open and she was closed.

Closed, locked, shuttered, rotting, abandoned.

She was reaching for a pair of shears when the telephone rang again.

2.

"Will I die?" Daisy asked.

June, and New York was a fact of our life. We'd gone from saying "Larry's apartment" to "the apartment" to "home." They were still Larry's lease, beds, Bach, his beige-and-brown-striped manly towels in the linen closet; but there were loaves of maple bread in the freezer, crayons underfoot.

Daisy was perched on the toilet, legs dangling, pink overalls and flowered cotton panties bunched around her ankles. She wore her bright blue Mighty Mouse running shoes with turned-up toes and waffling on the soles. She looked enchanting. I'm not often enchanted in the bathroom. Or disenchanted. You will not hear momentous tales of the bowl from this mom.

"Will I die?"

I was scraping coagulated toothpaste off the side of the sink. My thumbnail kept scraping.

"What do you mean, silly?" I asked, light as dandelions—as though we fooled them for a minute.

"Because die is the first word in diarrhea," she said.

I wanted to laugh, to cry, to wire STOP THE PRESSES to *Reader's Digest*.

"You don't have diarrhea, baby girl. Sweet girl. Anyway, it's not very serious when you do have it."

"I used to have it," Daisy said. "Yesterday. When I was a little girl."

I knew what was on her mind. The Playgroup kids had all had some twenty-four-hour intestinal upset the week before. Jackie Geritano's awful way with food, probably; the "wholesome, appealing lunch" of Playgroup rule number six was beyond her.

"Well, you don't have it now," I said. Scraping.

"Well, I would be very sad to die. So I really, really better have some ginger ale."

At three-and-a-half they're not supposed to understand death—its permanence. When I was a little girl is yesterday, and death closes Saturday night.

"Will I die?"

I had never said, Your daddy is dead, though that might have been the cleanest, kindest message.

"Will I die?"

A few nights before, we'd played an improvised game with Scrabble tiles—pushing letters together and talking about words. I'd joined an *I* and a *T*. Daisy had said: "I know what IT means. IT means dead. Because when a flower is dead, that's IT for the flower."

We all lose our children, and there are losses worse than death. No. Nothing is worse than the death of a child. I'm denied even perfect pain.

I gave her the ginger ale. Of course I gave her the ginger ale. Because she'd earned it, and because we bribe the gods. Try to, anyway.

Tindy, Vermont, is on the Connecticut River, just south of Putney. The summer that Daisy was one and a half, we drove across the river to New Hampshire, and clear across New Hampshire to the Atlantic, every week or ten days. We would walk barefoot in the sand, such a soft warm tumble for Daisy. We would have lunch at a place called The World Is My Clam, near Rye Beach, a big shack, rough, long wooden tables, sawdust on the floors—it didn't matter if Daisy flung my clam shells. I invariably ate steamers, sweet and plump and perfectly free of sand. Daisy ate tiny scallops—God's own finger food. She loved the scallops, loved the event. But one bright noon when we pulled into the parking lot at the World, she began to shriek. "No scallops! No scallops, Mama! No clams, Mama! No!" Her cheeks were purple. Her eyes swam wildly. "No! No!" I took her out of the car seat and rocked her and kissed her and begged for calm. I got it only when I agreed, not without irritation, that we would have lunch somewhere else. I bought early apples and farmhouse cheddar and cranberry bread from a roadside stand, and we had a picnic on the beach. Daisy was hungry. Jaunty. That night I heard on the radio that the Red Tide had hit the coast of Maine and New Hampshire, and a dozen people were in the hospital, several critical, after eating tainted shellfish. Steamers. Scallops.

Is that IT for the daisy?

Here's your ginger ale, honey.

I am the most rational person I know. My parents were stage magicians, brilliant amateurs, and no one is more certain than magicians that there isn't any magic. There are physicists willing to consider that such and such a person can bend metal with his mind; magicians know he uses magnets. My parents died in a private plane crash when I was nineteen, much too soon, but not so soon that they didn't make my mind-set for life.

Coincidence, I thought at first, about Daisy and the Red Tide. She couldn't have known. Such knowing doesn't exist. I went to the telephone. I dialed New Hampshire Information. I got the number for The World Is My Clam. I would call so they could tell me no one had sickened from their shellfish that day. A dozen cases in all of Maine and New Hampshire—most likely they'd been spared. And I would know that Daisy's shrieks had been any old tantrum.

My fingers hovered around the dial, then fell away. I never made that call. I didn't want confirmation, I didn't want denial.

I am, I am, I am the most rational person I know. I have my fears, my hopes, but I know them for what they are. I could no more mistake my personal wish for the will of the universe than expect to find running water in a mason jar of salt.

We didn't go back to New Hampshire. I no longer care for steamed clams.

Daisy drank her ginger ale. "I feel much, much better now." She sipped the last slurp in her straw. "All right, everybodeee—" in the shrill furry voice of Grover, the friendly monster from "Sesame Street"—"let's everybodeee go to Central Park."

Afternoons when the weather was fine, the Playgroup often converged, kids and mothers together, at the red and blue playground near Sixty-sixth and Fifth. Each time we went I had to steel myself to the trees, but we went.

I poured out a tad of milk and swallowed a Fiorinal, prince of headache preventives. Aspirin, codeine, phenobarbital would guard the gates to my temples against the jazzy neon green of June.

Had there really been a life before the Playgroup? It set the rhythms of our day. We knew this doorman, that pretzel vendor, this light, those shadows, because we walked to the park afternoons at three. Daisy seemed to take comfort in the repetitions and echoes. I took comfort in them myself. It's fatiguing, no matter how exalting, to be born anew each day.

Heidi Kahn, the copper-haired woman, Stephanie's mama, was sitting on the usual bench between the slides and sandbox. She waved when she saw us coming. She put her book in her bag.

Heidi was my favorite of the Playgroup mothers. At first her looks had put me off—she wore her dazzling hair frizzed out to here, and she had the exaggerated, almost grotesque, features of a German Expressionist portrait; now I found her face exciting. And she was smart, had politics, had details, had passions. She and her husband, Henry, owned the H. and H. Kahn Gallery on Madison Avenue—mostly German Expressionist paintings, in fact; and she made you feel that your life could be changed if you saw a certain Kandinsky landscape.

Jackie Geritano (dark hair, Nick's mother) cared, by contrast, only about her own guilty soul. She was a cabin attendant for one of the big airlines. Even though she had seniority and was able to limit her flights to lucrative three-day "layover" trips on weekends, when her husband, Bob, looked after Nick, and sweetly, she carried on as if Nick were all but a motherless child. She would cry over him because he looked "touching" eating an ice cream cone. You know how he hated those tears. She assaulted him with presents. There were souvenirs from every trip—awful Eiffel Tower T-shirts, pink and orange piñatas from Mexico City; and rich kid presents too—a life-size super-realistic Steiff stuffed fox that would have terrified a six-year-old. If she had cut up her charge cards, she probably could have afforded to quit her job. Of course she liked being away from Nick—hence the guilt.

As for Elizabeth Gray (blond, with a little help; James's mother): she was sweet and generous and patient with the kids but so manifestly destroyed by her blood-and-money marriage that she really dragged you down. And she was young—twenty-four. Jackie was thirty-two, my age, and Heidi was thirty-seven.

Heidi was definitely my favorite of the lot. You could have a real conversation with her—except about the nature of our children.

Daisy skipped off to join Stephanie on the slide. I sat down next to Heidi. Jackie Geritano had her Nick and James Gray out on the Staten Island ferry so that Elizabeth Gray could have a tennis lesson (and more?) with Bob "the lob" Geritano. Heidi and I would not be interrupted. Maybe today was the day to crack the barrier.

"Heidi, what do you think of our kids?"

She angled her striking jaw. "Glorious! Look at that."

Stephanie sailed down a slide, no hands. She landed hard on the rubber safety mat, seemed to consider complaining, dusted off her fanny instead, and trotted around for another go. Now it was Daisy's turn. She scrambled up the steps. (In my mind she is scrambling still. Every move lives in my mind. I remember the light in her hair, and the way her elbows jutted as her hands grasped the railing.) She sat at the top of the slide and banged her heels against the metal.

She liked the boom-boom-boom and banged her heels again. Then she gave herself up to gravity. My stomach did a dive as her body gained speed.

"And gutsy," Heidi said, laughing at the look on my face.

I shook my head. "They're fearless. We're the gutsy ones. What else?"

"What else, what?"

"What else about our kids? Nick and James too."

"Super kids. I love them all. You should have heard Nick this morning." It was Monday. Heidi had been mother-in-charge. "He was talking about Lokomo, and I could *see* it. The purple wings, the little eyes, everything. That kid is going to be a painter, a poet—something terrific. They all are."

"No!" I cried out. "It's too much! Did Julie—" her eight-year-old—"have an imaginary butterfly? That you could see? That you could *smell*?"

"Yes," Heidi said calmly. "Some imaginary little girl who came over on rainy days. Susan. No, Sara."

"But it wasn't like Lokomo, was it? Or Iceman? Or the others? And when Julie was three she went to nursery school."

"Jill, I don't understand you. You should be thrilled that Daisy is so creative." She reached into a pocket of her purple painter's overalls. She found a flat black-and-silver Art Deco cigarette case and absently offered it to me. I made a face. "I don't know," Heidi said. "Maybe you should give up whole-wheat bread and start smoking cigarettes. Or something." Then, contritely, "I don't know how you do it. It's brain-frying enough to be a mom when you've got a daddy in residence. I think you're the bravest woman I know. Look—" puffing—"I've got an idea. Why don't you park Daisy with us some weekend? Get off on your own? Or not on your own. You know. Read a bunch of mysteries, drink too much, screw an eighteen-year-old boy." She shook her flamboyant head. "I take it back. I'll park Stephanie with you some weekend, and I'll go off. But, really. What do you say?"

"Look at the slides," I said, turning away.

There were two slides, one with blue steps and railing, one with red steps and railing. I counted kids. There were six on the red slide—one about to come down, five nudging each other up the steps. There were two kids on the blue slide—Daisy and Stephanie. I saw a boy, kindergarten vintage, come down off the jungle gym and saunter over to the slides. He stood there checking things out. He started toward the blue slide, our girls' slide, then changed his mind. I all but heard the click. He walked to the red slide and got in line.

"Did you see that?" I asked Heidi. I knew she'd seen.

"See what?"

"That kid in the green T-shirt. He was going to slide on the girls' slide, then he changed his mind."

Heidi's heavy-lidded hazel eyes blinked at me. "So what, sweetie?"

"Two slides. One crowded, one not crowded. This kid goes to the crowded one. *Because he's afraid of our girls*."

"Or just doesn't like girls, period. Or once got hurt on that slide. Or likes red better than blue. Most kids like red best, you know. I'm sure that's a known fact. Mondrian wrote it, someone did. I know I read it."

"Our kids are different," I said.

"Sweetie pie, all kids are different. That's the name of the game. Childhood is weird time. That's why we love them madly one minute and want to strangle them the next minute—hell, sometimes both in the same minute. Isn't it? Because they're so radically different from us? Marching to a different violinist?"

"You don't want to see how *deeply* different they are. Not just from us. From other kids."

"And you," Heidi said, "do want to see it." She pinned me with her eyes. "What do you think, they're four little

Martians who somehow got born in Earthling form? Or you and Jackie and Elizabeth and I ate too many raspberries when we were pregnant? They're four supersmart, supercute, superbrave kids. Isn't that enough?"

"Why did Kelly Smith leave the Playgroup?" I asked.

"Shit." Heidi dropped her cigarette butt to the ground, crushed it with a sandaled foot, then—a concession to me—bent over, picked up the butt, and flung it into a trashcan. "She left the Playgroup because she moved to California." She looked at her cigarette case, then put it back in her pocket. "You're coming to the opening, aren't you?"

What could I do? I didn't want to lose her. I let the children go. I said, "I sure am, if Mary Girard doesn't let me down." An opening at the H. and H. Kahn Gallery was an event, and part of me was ready for events again. I'd booked Mary Girard as my sitter weeks before.

Daisy and Stephanie took a last slide apiece, then, hand in hand, walked over to the sandbox. A little boy in the sandbox picked that moment to decide he wanted out. The kindergarten boy in the green T-shirt moved over from the crowded red slide to the empty blue slide.

"What do you say about that, Mr. Mondrian?" I asked softly.

"I wish I had something to wear tomorrow night," Heidi moaned. "I'm getting so effing fat, I may have to wear one of Henry's old shirts. You know what I had for lunch today? Two rice cakes slathered with peanie boo. And a banana. Washed down by a glass of milk. Whole milk."

"You had the kids today. You're allowed. Anyway, you're gorgeous and you know it."

Heidi's fingers skittered through her mass of glitzy hair. "Gorgeous isn't enough. I have to be skinny. I'm a skinny soul. I like to stab Henry with my hipbones. I like old ladies to stop me on the street and offer to buy me milkshakes." She glared at my plaid cotton skirt. "Is that a Ralph Lauren?"

"God, no. Just something I got at the general store in Tindy."

"Good. I was going to have to hate you. I've been popping the buttons on my Ralphs. How do you stay so damn thin?"

"Anxiety," I said cheerfully.

We sat there in companionable silence. We had our tensions, our barriers, but we did like each other.

I looked at our girls in the sandbox. The silvery head and the coppery head were bent close together. Laughter came piping through the air, then one of their little song-chants; new ones were born every hour.

> *One two three*
> *What do I see*
> *The umbrella man*
> *Is watching me*

The umbrella man. His spokes in our eyes. Would they never stop coming? And Heidi was worried about shirts.

"Mom! Mommy!" Stephanie beckoned from the sandbox. "Come see what we're building."

Heidi obediently got up and went to inspect the latest masterpiece. She came back to the bench and stood looking at me. "Okay, my Jill," she said. She gave a resigned little sigh. "You want something to sweat about? For real? There's a man outside the fence. I think I've seen him here before. He's staring at us. No question. Especially at Daisy."

3.

"Mrs. Keefe?"

"Yes."

"This is Arthur Kojak."

As always, Nora had to suppress an evil giggle. It was

too delicious, too pathetic, that this poor worm of a private detective bore the surname of the famous television cop.

"Yes, Mr. Kojak," she managed. Then, a shade severely because he needed severity, "This isn't your time to call."

"I apologize for breaking routine. I have some information I thought you would want to obtain immediately."

He paused. He had a need, maddening to Nora, to have every statement acknowledged before he produced another.

"Go ahead, Mr. Kojak. Report."

"Do you recall a subject named Jill Everts?" the detective asked.

Nora closed her eyes. "Yes," she said.

"I spotted the subject in New York."

"Yes, Mr. Kojak. Yes. Do you have any further information that would interest me?"

"I believe I do, Mrs. Keefe." The detective's normally neutral voice buzzed with excitement. "I took the liberty of keeping the subject under observation until I could ascertain the facts I thought would be pertinent to your interest."

He took a small vacation after this arduous sentence. Nora heard the turning of notebook pages. She wondered where he was. He had a liking for obscure telephone booths, as if she and he were trading state secrets. She imagined him in the lobby of one of the large commercial hotels or maybe in the back of a Broadway drugstore.

"Subject is living on East Sixty-sixth Street, in an apartment leased to one Lawrence Everts," he said. "Subject is leading a circumspect existence. No men." He coughed—a small, apologetic cough that Nora knew to be the harbinger of unpleasant news. And then there it was—a war scare headline. "Subject has a three-year-old daughter."

The hollowness in Nora's chest became a vast dank cave, her heart's only home.

"A daughter," she said.

"Yes, ma'am. Her name is Daisy."

"Three years old."

"That's right, Mrs. Keefe."

"Daisy. She is—fair?"

"Light blond hair. Silvery, almost."

"I must see pictures. Are there pictures?"

"Yes, ma'am."

Nora smiled. Of course there were pictures. Mr. Kojak liked taking pictures. Such delicious pictures sometimes. She had seen more than a few delicious pictures of Jill Everts. Not a pretty-pretty woman, but arresting, with an abandoned gaiety about her, and the sinewy thinness of a fawn. Long legs. Legs that loved to wrap, to open. Nora pictured those legs straining against the stirrups of childbirth.

"I want to see the pictures today," she said.

"They'll be delivered within the hour."

"Mr. Kojak?" Her right hand strayed to her breasts.

"Yes, ma'am."

"You said—no men?" Rub-a-dub-dub.

"Not so far as I know, and I think I would know."

"You're quite certain she has not resumed her relationship with my husband?"

"On information and belief, no, ma'am."

"This Lawrence Everts? Surely not her own husband? One gathers she prefers to borrow husbands."

"A cousin, I believe. He's gone abroad. A journalist. No indication of intimacy there."

"Nobody's perfect," Nora said gaily. Three men in a tub. "I'm very pleased, Mr. Kojak. There will be a bonus for you."

"Very kind, Mrs. Keefe."

"You can drop your surveillance of the Steinmetz woman. I'd like you to concentrate on Everts."

"Very good."

"If there are men, any men—" The butcher. The baker. His honor the mayor.

"Yes, ma'am."

"Mr. Kojak," Nora said, then stopped.

"Yes, Mrs. Keefe?"

"Would you say she's a fit mother, Mr. Kojak?"

"These things are hard to judge, ma'am."

"Try, Mr. Kojak. Do you have children yourself? No, I apologize, an intrusion, like asking a psychiatrist. Perhaps—well, tell me this. Is the child in one of those day-care things?" Nora felt a cold sweat start. "A stream of babysitters? Does Everts drag the child around to department stores?"

"They spend a lot of time in Central Park, ma'am. There's a playground they favor at Sixty-sixth Street; seems to get a steady crowd of nice children. Mornings there appears to be an arrangement of some sort—the mothers taking turns looking after a small group of children."

"I see," Nora said.

"Some of the pictures were taken at the playground."

"Yes. Tell me, Mr. Kojak, if I'm not delving into professional secrets, how did you come to spot Everts?" She pinched her nipples. Pleasure resonated in her shoulders, her knees, her toes.

"I spotted the subject at the zoo," Arthur Kojak said, "where I happened to be surveilling an assignation. You'd be surprised, Mrs. Keefe, at the number of assignations take place at the zoo."

As if in retribution for his extraordinary chattiness, the operator came on the line and dunned him for a nickel.

Nora said, over the sounds of coin being given and received, "Not any of Mr. Keefe's assignations, I trust."

"Oh, no, ma'am. That's not his style. For Mr. Keefe it's strictly the fine hotels and better restaurants."

"That's good to hear. I have my pride." Arthur Kojak did not laugh—Nora had never heard him laugh—and she said, "I'll look forward to the pictures and your next report, then. Good-bye Mr. Kojak."

4.

The spark that would become the Playgroup had been struck ten years ago, 180 miles northeast of Central Park, at the Rountree School, in the friendship of Elizabeth Dobbs and Kelly Smith.

Elizabeth, who would someday be Mrs. Oliver Wendell Gray and the mother of James, was a quiet girl, but very much of the world. Her father was a ranking diplomat; she knew Geneva as well as she knew Washington, French as well as she knew English. She played a lean, effective game of tennis. She had logged many hours in the great museums of Europe and at fourteen cared about what she looked at; she arrived at Rountree for freshman orientation with an early Josef Albers woodcut, *Together*, ovals and ellipses intersecting and embracing, and bribed her roommate not to hang her sloppily registered posters of rock stars.

Kelly—sixteen and a junior when Elizabeth was fourteen and a freshman—was first and last a writer. She would keep her maiden by-line through two marriages and the birth of a daughter, Megan. She was editor of the Rountree *Record*, the first junior to hold the job. Her father was a banker who owned much of Hartford and had little use for the rest of the world. Kelly hadn't traveled outside of New England, but reading had made her familiar, down to the stones and smells, with the European cities where Elizabeth had lived.

Not exactly twins—but both girls were only children, and both had amorphous mothers, and both were serious students, and both were beauties. Elizabeth was a silky blonde with watercress stalk bones. Kelly was a dark-haired wench with serious breasts and a gothic virgin's telltale cheeks. The girls were devoted to each other. They vowed to twine their lives. They planned to go to the same college. Afterward they would live in New York, where their fathers were merely two more princes; Elizabeth would be a translator, Kelly would write for the *Times*. They would marry men who were friends and have their babies, two apiece, in synchrony. If the sex mix worked out, they would marry off a pair of their children. They would end their days as wicked old widows in Paris, supporting the most outrageous painters, renting the attentions of young men, and sending from time to time for their common grandchildren.

At fifteen, Elizabeth was at school in London; her father the roving troubleshooter had agreed to settle down as ambassador to Great Britain. Kelly, seventeen, was at a liberal school in Vermont; she'd been banished from Rountree for sneaking an editorial into the *Record* advocating that birth-control pills be required eating at breakfast for juniors and seniors. The girls wrote long intense letters for a while, and Kelly spent a February intercession at the American Embassy in London, but the girls formed other loyalties, and the grand friendship faded.

Elizabeth married Oliver Wendell Gray the day after her graduation from Wellesley College. She conceived James on her honeymoon. When she was four months pregnant, she went to a prenatal exercise class on East Seventy-ninth Street and encountered Kelly Smith in a swollen green leotard. The two women went out for lunch after the class. They talked until the café filtre was a cold sludge and their captain and waiter, recently sleek, were leaving the restaurant in their civilian jeans and peacoats. The women met for lunch the next day, and the next, and nearly every weekday after that, until James was born.

Elizabeth's mother, who'd stayed on in London when Elizabeth's father returned to Washington, found the perfect nanny, but Elizabeth didn't want a nanny. James's childhood would not be the chilly thing her own had been. She would breastfeed him, she would tidy his bottom, she would cart him in a pouch so he could feel her breath in his hair and coo to the beat of her heart. Kelly gave birth to a daughter five weeks later. Her memories of her childhood were as bleak as Elizabeth's, her ambitions for Megan as sunny. When one of the women wanted an hour to herself, she left her baby with the other. James more than once nursed at Kelly's breast, Megan at Elizabeth's.

The grandmothers shook their heads. The new fathers shook theirs. Oliver Gray called Elizabeth baby-whipped, would have preferred to hire a nanny or at least a steady sitter, but he was relieved that so little was expected of him. Kelly's husband, her second, a raffish actor named Ben Stephens, spent most of his time in Dublin and the marriage was looking unlikely to last, so his thoughts didn't matter.

One day, when James was two and a half, Elizabeth brought him into the H. and H. Kahn Gallery, where she hoped to find a birthday present for her father, who loved the German Expressionists. Little red-haired Stephanie Kahn was running around the gallery—her sitter had canceled at the last minute and Heidi Kahn had to cover the gallery because Henry was at an auction—and Stephanie and James instantly took to each other. Elizabeth was amazed. She hadn't thought James could play so intently with any child other than Megan. For the first time it occurred to her that James might need more friends. She suggested to Heidi that they meet again and take the kids to the zoo. She bought a Kandinsky cup and saucer for her father.

Soon Elizabeth and Heidi and Kelly were getting together with the kids, sometimes taking turns looking after them.

Kelly took Megan to Dublin to see Ben Stephens, who'd left New York permanently. Jackie Geritano was their flight attendant. She got Kelly and Megan through a patch of turbulence by diverting them with pictures of her Nick. Megan said "Play with Nick" so many times that Kelly decided she had to ask Jackie if they could meet in New York sometime. They met, and it was good for Megan and Nick, and Kelly introduced Jackie to Elizabeth and Heidi, and then there were four.

The mothers decided to formalize their connection, to set up a routine. Kelly put the rules in writing. The Playgroup existed.

James Gray, Megan Smith-Stephens, Stephanie Kahn,

and Nick Geritano played together four mornings a week, and many an afternoon, from the end of September on into March. The second Wednesday night in March, Kelly called Elizabeth and asked her to substitute as the mother-in-charge Thursday morning—she and Megan had to go to Hartford for a couple of days. Family nonsense, she said. That was Elizabeth's last word from Kelly.

When Kelly failed to drop Megan at Heidi's for the usual Monday morning event, Heidi called Kelly's number and learned it had been disconnected. Heidi called Elizabeth. Elizabeth, frantic, called Kelly's mother in Hartford and heard news. Kelly and Megan had gone to California, Mrs. Smith wasn't sure what city. They planned to stay a while, she wasn't sure how long. The trip had something to do with Kelly's writing, she wasn't sure just what. No, Kelly hadn't left a message for Elizabeth. Yes, she would send Elizabeth's love to Kelly, relay her consternation, when Kelly called again, but Kelly rarely called.

Elizabeth's imagination rioted. Kelly had been having a secret affair with Oliver Gray and couldn't face Elizabeth. Megan had some unspeakable cancer and Kelly wanted to spare the other mothers and children. Somewhere in her life as a freelance writer, Kelly had unearthed important secrets, and They had taken her away. Kelly had developed a sexual hunger for women. Kelly had gone cultish; she and Megan were wearing white robes and chanting to the Pacific.

In April, Jill Everts met Heidi and Jackie at the red and blue playground, and the Playgroup had four children again. Elizabeth adored Daisy Everts, and she had no problem with Jill, but they did not begin to fill the void left by Kelly and Megan.

June; and Elizabeth still puzzled and sorrowed over the cancellation, without notice, of her most important friendship. She masked her feelings, for James's sake, and because Oliver had never quite liked Kelly (unless he was covering lust), and because she was, by nature, loath to show pain. One mourned behind closed doors.

This Monday afternoon she felt free to let loose. Oliver was at his bank—the *little* bank, her father liked to tease—James was out of the very borough, on his way to Staten Island with Jackie Geritano and Nick. Betty DuPont, the Grays' live-in housekeeper, who was saving to bring her aged mother up from Haiti, spent each Monday, her day off along with Sunday, cleaning for Oliver's friend Jack Keefe and his wife in Greenwich Village. No need for Elizabeth to close the door.

She collapsed flagrantly into the clubby old green leather armchair in what she and James called the book room and Oliver called the Library, as though it held ten thousand volumes. The chair was Elizabeth's favorite place for sorting out her life. She liked the rest of the apartment—a twelve-room duplex on Park and Sixty-sixth, her father's wedding present; she liked the way its ivories and blues, its graceful arches, showed off her own cool beauty. But the cracked green chair was home—a place where posture might be forgotten, tears might flow.

The proximate cause of her misery lay on the desk—the Rountree *AlumNews*, blight of the noon mail. Her giddy contribution to class notes, written in January, was tauntingly stale.

James continues to be the world's most amazing three-year-old! Latest accomplishments: singing Frère Jacques *in flawless French, getting a tennis ball over the net, deciding that artichokes are "yum," not "yuk," sitting through a whole movie (101 Dalmations). His best friend is Megan Smith-Stephens, also just three, darling daughter of Kelly SMITH (ex-'74). Kelly hasn't changed a BIT—which means she's too busy working to drop a card to the* AlumNews. *You'd need a clipping service to keep up with her by-line—she's had articles in* The New York Times Magazine, Ms., New York, Harper's, *and many other publications—all controversial pieces, natch. And she still flushes and blushes! As for your Correspondent, I've decided to put off my brilliant career as a translator until James is ready for prekindergarten. These are his golden years, after all!*

The first reading had brought tears; a second, steel. Elizabeth sat up straight. She drummed a thin tattoo against the arm of her beloved chair.

Maybe she'd handled the defection of Kelly all wrong, worrying and pondering and feeling abandoned and yet somehow respecting the event, assuming underneath that Kelly would pop up one of these weeks and explain the pain away. Maybe Kelly needed to be found.

Elizabeth probed through space, trying to pinpoint Kelly's mind out in California. It was twenty to four in New York, twenty to one Pacific time. Was Kelly looking over a beansprout, remembering truffled times with Elizabeth? Such a rich network of memories for them both, Elizabeth thought. She felt a pressure low in her back, as if the thousands of details of the friendship had compacted into a rock and the rock was pushing. And she hated being vague with James, actually lying, saying that Kelly and Megan had gone off to be with Megan's daddy, were surely missing James and would be back any day, with presents.

In a few minutes she had to leave for her tennis lesson with Bob Geritano, Nick's father. She was hardly in the mood, but Jackie Geritano had been after her to let Bob do his stuff, and she'd finally made a date and had to keep it. At least she'd have something to chat about with her husband at dinner. Oliver wasn't too keen on her nightly singing of James's wonders. There was time before her lesson for one telephone call.

If Kelly didn't want to be found? Elizabeth hesitated. But Kelly had only to tell her to her face, and she would go away quietly, and stay away, and that would be a clean end to things. She owed James resolution. Hope got to be an awful burden. She would rather deal with Kelly's momentary wrath than more months of James's eager little questions. She dialed her almighty father in Washington.

5.

A headache sprang full-blown to my temples. So much for Fiorinal as a preventive.

I walked over to the sandbox. I stared out at the man staring in. He didn't look sinister, but he didn't look about to go away, either. I said to Heidi, "Keep an eye on Daisy, will you? I'm going to go talk to him."

"Jill, you're not."

"I am. It's bright daylight. What's he going to do, bite my nose?"

"Maybe he's a photographer? Kids' fashions?" Heidi said hopefully, but we both knew he wasn't a photographer.

"Be back in a minute, honey," I told Daisy. "Heidi's right there if you need anything." I didn't want my girl to look to the bench and simply not see me.

I half expected him to take off when he saw me coming, but he stood his ground, he offered a confident smile. For a dizzying moment I wondered if he were someone from my past, from that very different life, one of the people who had fallen or been pushed out of my memory. He was what we used to call cute, with a good rumpled head of khaki hair (and khaki pants that matched—had he bought them on purpose?), but I didn't want to have known him.

I kept walking until there were only inches, and an eight-foot-high diamond pattern woven metal fence, between us. "Why have you been staring at our kids?" I said.

"You're a brave one," the man said, "coming to beard me like this. Or am I about to get a face full of Mace?"

I didn't like his voice. It was too resonant, like an actor's, though I didn't think he was an actor. He emanated campus. He was about my age, thirty-two—maybe a few hours younger. He looked reasonably fit—squash twice a week?

He was wearing a blue-and-white-striped shirt that Jack would have approved of, a silly navy tie with koalas on it, and a lightweight brown-and-gray herringbone sports jacket he hadn't bought on an academic's salary; maybe he also wrote. One of the pockets of the jacket had a sag, probably because he never left the house without a weighty paperback. I could picture him standing up to a lectern, the resonant voice filling the room as he gave forth on the meaning of meaning.

I laced my fingers through the diamonds of the fence. "Please don't try to be charming. I want an answer to my question."

"I bet you do." The brown eyes were trying to broadcast that he very much understood me. "I didn't mean to alarm you and the redheaded mama. I'm a psychologist. My specialty is early childhood. I pass by this playground pretty often—I live a couple of blocks away—" zigging and zagging his fingers—"and frankly, I've been intrigued by your children. I suppose you know that they exhibit a perfectly remarkable degree of interaction for three-year-olds?" He took a brown leather wallet out of his pocket, and a card out of the wallet. "My name is Ken Huysman. Dr. Kenneth William Huysman, if that's more reassuring."

If I hadn't been hanging onto the fence, I would have fallen.

"Hello?" He looked alarmed. "Are you all right?"

"Iceman," I said. The air was buzzing. I wanted to lie down and go to sleep for a hundred years. "Is your name really Iceman?"

"I know. I've taken some guff in my time." He gave me a reassuring nod, the equivalent of a pat on the head. He wasn't going to let me think I'd succeeded in being peculiar, or rude. His nose looked as though it had been broken once. I could see why.

"You don't know." The buzzing was louder. Wings were beating against my ears. "It's not at all what you think. I'm sorry. I have an awful headache."

"*I'm* sorry," he said. "I should have found some more orthodox way to approach you. I'm really not a child molester." He bent his card to make it fit through the fence.

"Right. You're a psychologist." I took his card. It said the usual sort of thing. I tried to find comfort in the spelling of his name, in the good creamy stock the card was printed on.

Ken Huysman said, "I think you'd be happier if I were a child molester. You could yell for a cop and forget about me."

"Dr. Huysman—" I stressed the *H*.

He raised his hand: Stop. "You don't have to tell me. Parents don't like to hear that their children are unusual, even wonderfully unusual." He got me into an eye lock and held me. I wondered if he'd done Esalen or est. Did people still do those things? He said, "I don't imagine I'm telling you anything you don't know. How long have the kids been playing together? I've been aware of them since, oh, maybe a month ago. They shine, don't they?"

Daisy's laugh rang out behind me, one of those pure whoops of delight she let loose now and then. I would have focused on that sound, known it as hers, if a thousand children were laughing in concert, just as my ear always tracks the cello in symphonies. Her footfalls, her snores, her coughs, her hiccups, her weeps—I knew all her music by heart, I know it still, I will carry that score to my grave.

"They're nice children," I said. "They have fun together. Why don't you go away, Dr. Huysman?"

He didn't answer. He didn't have to. We both knew the real question was: Why didn't I go away?

I turned to look at Daisy and Stephanie, at Heidi. The kids were sitting in the sand facing each other, joined at the hands, rocking back and forth, row row rowing their boat. Heidi waved wildly. She was probably desperate with curiosity. I waved back. I wondered what would have happened if Heidi had come to the fence instead of me, and Dr. Kenneth William Huysman had said what he'd said to me, given her those knowing looks. Would she have babbled about the kids' beautiful creativity, about her hipbones?

Not that I was doing much better. I turned back to the good doctor. "Still here? Don't you have a four o'clock client?"

"Canceled," he said pleasantly. "Chicken pox. This is a nice place to hang out. Bet you haven't spent so much time outdoors since you were a kid."

"I hate it here," I said. Pleasantly. "I grew up in the country. I don't like parks."

"But you like the city?"

"I love the city."

He nodded. Such a nodder. The nods went with the resonant voice and the understanding looks and "frankly." He knew what was what, did our Dr. Huysman, at least he wanted you to think he did.

"New York is a great place to bring up kids," he said.

"Oh, yeah? You give it the official stamp? Carbon monoxide and all?"

"There's pollution in Vermont. There's pollution," he added too quickly, "in the farthest reaches of Iceland."

My head found new ways to ache. "How did you know I come from Vermont?"

"Do you? Really? And I was so sure you were from the South. Your warm and trusting nature. Are you going to invite me into the playground? Introduce me to your friend? To the girls?"

"No." The playground was public, of course; a weathered sign restricted the area to children and their guardians, but it had no teeth. A gate swung wide open a few feet from where we were talking.

"No curiosity?" he said.

"No."

"Not about me, I don't mean; about the kids. About your daughter."

"I knew what you meant. I don't need you to explain my daughter to me."

We heard a shout from the sidewalk. A young teenage boy, well dressed, had swiped a pretzel from our local vendor and was running down Fifth Avenue, waving his booty. Poor vendor. All he could do was stand there under his carnival umbrella, yelling and waving his fists and scowling at the sky. Another customer came along, and he shrugged, and went back to business.

Ken Huysman looked upset. Such a sensitive man.

"Don't worry," I said. "He'll make up for it by short-changing a couple of people."

"Shocking," the doctor pronounced me.

I pushed his card back through the fence.

"Keep it," he said. "You might change your mind, Mrs. Mozart, about little Wolfgang and piano lessons. You're sure you want to tell him to run outside and play with the other kids? You're sure he'll forgive you for that?"

My shoulders went right down. "Bastard," I said.

"You need a friend," he told me then. "The other mothers aren't much help, are they?"

"Stop knowing things!" I shouted.

"What about your husband?"

"I'm divorced," automatically. "You knew, didn't you? Do you know my name? Where I live? What we had for breakfast?"

"Wholewheat croissants?" he guessed. "Fresh squeezed parsley juice?"

He was wrong, but he could have been wronger. "Did you buy your pants because they match your hair?" I asked.

"Of course I did. You know what?"

"What?" I said.

"It doesn't scare me in the slightest that you knew that." He gave a little wave. He started back up the path toward the sidewalk.

I put his card in my pocket and thought of lies to tell Heidi.

6.

Jack Keefe took his pleasures; his pleasures never took him. He knew when to put down his fork, when to pull up his pants. It wasn't so much discipline as indifference that curbed his appetites, for which indifference he daily gave thanks. To love pleasure was to be in its power, and to be in the power of anything but God and one's own will was to be a slob, and slobs didn't get to be mayor of New York.

He maddened his women, though he treated them well enough for a married man—never made himself out to be a candidate for divorce, took them out and about rather grandly because hiding them backstreet would have been the one true insult to Nora. The women could not addict him, no matter if they licked his toes and squeezed pomegranate juice to chase the champagne; that was what rankled. Jack so often appeared to be having the time of his life. Then afterward he would go back to the office in the Woolworth Building or the brownstone on West Eleventh Street and might not call for months, or ever again.

Jill had been something else for him. He supposed he had loved her, still loved her, but that seemed an uninteresting way of distinguishing her from the other women, an inadequate explanation of her importance to him. He loved Nora, didn't he? Sometimes he thought he loved all the women, even the windup dollies who turned up and now and then at his office, walking talking thank-you notes from recipients of favors. Jill alone had gotten under his skin. He'd missed her when she'd left the bar to make a telephone call the first night they drank together, twelve years ago, and he missed her now, in the same sharp, physical way, after a separation of more than four years.

When he'd made the decision to run for mayor, he'd asked his law partner, Olivia Martinez, to be his campaign manager. She'd agreed, on the condition that he reveal his vulnerabilities to her—she wanted no surprises in the press.

Had he fudged his income tax one year? Was there an embarrassing brother who might choose to surface during the campaign or might be dredged up by the opposition? And what about the women? Nora was officially a shut-in, happy in her greenhouse, only delighted that Jack had the company of others and, anyway, he was too flagrant a philanderer to be blackmailed; was there one woman, though, who could make trouble? Cocaine or a messy abortion or unfortunate Polaroid shots? Jack considered the question. One woman could make trouble, he'd finally said. Not for the reasons Olivia had suggested but because if the woman asked him not to run, he wouldn't run. "Jill," Olivia said, and Jack nodded, and they'd gone on to other talk.

June, and warm, and Jack was drinking tea. He liked tea at four o'clock, strong and very hot, with a small splash of low-fat milk, no matter what the weather. He drank his tea, as he did every day, and thought about Jill, as he did every day—sweet thoughts instead of the chocolate semicoated wheatmeal biscuits he'd had with tea before his coronary. Jill was the weak link in his emotional chain mail, but he didn't fight his feelings for her. He'd decided that the greater weakness would be to permit himself no weakness. As Nora had said in a moment of acid fondness, no lovelier bullshitter graced the earth than Big Jack Keefe.

Jill had the power to get Jack not to run for mayor, but she wouldn't use the power. She had dubbed him the cosmic magician, the way he could put a building code variance into a hat and pull out tenth-row-center tickets for an evening of Pavarotti. Big Jack Keefe as mayor would be the crowning act. He wondered if Jill got the New York papers wherever she was, if she would know when he declared. He wanted her to know.

He could have found out where she was, whether she read the papers, with whom she read the papers. She had made him promise to let her go absolutely, though; and he'd never seriously considered reneging. They hadn't been perfect with each other, but they'd kept their promises.

They'd met, a dozen years ago, just after his coronary, a year after the death of her parents, both of them rocked by the realization that they weren't the darlings of the universe. They'd offered each other the tonic of pleasure, without disturbing each other's fragile new peace by holding out hope of happiness.

That was her ultimate attraction for him, Jack thought now, sitting at his desk, drinking tea. She alone among the women hadn't presumed to think she could make him happy. You can't make a doomed man happy. You can sing and dance for him, you can sponge his forehead—nothing more.

He wondered if she'd changed any, if she'd deserted their private faith, their private faithlessness, if she'd aspired to grace again. For sure she'd found other beds, had loosed that ribby body, those strange energies, on someone else; and maybe she'd found another love. A man who had not yet had his comeuppance from the heavens could well have made her foolish. Jack knew he ought to want that foolishness for her, but he couldn't bear the thought of her changing so much.

She would hear the news when he announced his intention to run. She would have to let him know that she knew. Even if she'd fallen for some boyo, Jack was certain he still had that much hold over her. When she got in touch, he would find out what she was these days. That was all he wanted, really—to know how to think of her each day as he had his tea.

Olivia Martinez had been urging him to declare within the week. There were signatures to be gathered, petitions to be filed. One didn't just waltz onto the ballot come September. He'd been putting off the press conference, the formal declaration; his style was to put out the word here and there, to drop hints at the bar at Broadway Joe, look mysterious at "21"—declaration by orchestrated leak. Suddenly he was as impatient as Olivia, more impatient. Jill would not shrug off the news. He wondered if he could mount a full-scale press conference for Tuesday morning. Were her legs still as wild? That was all he wanted to know.

7.

Jackie Geritano knew the man was wearing a Burberry even before a tongue of breeze flicked back the hem of his trenchcoat to reveal the red, black, tans, and white of the signature plaid lining. She'd been at the Burberry shop on Fifty-seventh Street that very morning, mooning over the size four coats. A hundred ninety-five dollars was an awful lot to spend on a coat for a kid—but the kid was Nick, and the coat was so cute with its epaulets and flaps, and it did have a zip-in lining that would take him right into winter and out again. Her hand had longed to write the check that would buy the coat, then a small interior voice, the local spokesperson for reason, reminded her that she was flying to London this coming weekend and really ought to check out the prices at Burberry there, the source. The Burberry passion had started in London this past weekend—only yesterday, actually; was it possible?—she really had no more clock at all—when she'd seen a Nick-size boy in a Burberry shrug off the rain at Heathrow Airport. She'd wanted to buy one that minute, but she'd had to check in for her flight, and anyway it was Sunday.

The other mothers would think she was crazy. Jill would say the coat looked too military. Elizabeth would remember the clothes of her own childhood, dresses with stiff lace that scratched her neck and coats she could barely move in, and she would worry that Nick would be afraid to eat an ice cream cone or slide down the slide in that coat. Heidi would tell Jackie that she ought to have spent the money on clothes for herself because kids were naturally beautiful and didn't need a hundred ninety-five dollars' worth of help.

The other mothers wouldn't like her even if she didn't buy Nick the Burberry, so what the bazooly?

More to the point, Bob might be upset—his raincoat was ten years old and hadn't been much to begin with. Maybe she should wait until Christmas and buy two Burberrys, father and son. If she did a couple of runs to the Far East, she could pay for the coats in overtime. She might even find a shop in Hong Kong that sold Burberrys on the cheap.

The biggest question was: Would Nick like the coat? She would point out the man in the Burberry sometime during the crossing and pop a neutral question. Though the coat did look a bit much on a day like today, warm and all but cloudless. The man had to be British. He was carrying the inevitable furled umbrella. The kids had sweat shirts, and she had a cardigan tied around her waist—enough protection for a jaunt to the foredeck, where the wind would assault. Maybe she should ask Nick about the coat on a rainy day.

The ferry banged its way out of the slip. Jackie clutched the boys' hands against the pitching of the boat and the jostling of the camera-toting crowd, against the tendency of three-year-olds to try to escape from grown-ups.

"See you later, alligator," James called out to the receding towers of downtown New York.

Nick made a duckling motion. Jackie yanked him upright. The railing was more air than metal; for one stretch a single strand of chain was the only barrier between them and the watery all.

"Nick Geritano, don't you dare!"

"I want to see the alligators." He peered out at the white spume roiling in the wake of the ferry.

"That's only an expression, and you know it." Jackie spoke in the no-nonsense voice she used at 30,000 feet to fend off two-martini lechers. "You've got to be absolutely good or we go inside, and you'll miss the Statue of Liberty."

"He'll be good," James said confidently.

Nick said, in his most virtuous little voice, "'After a while crocodile' is only an expression."

"That's right." Jackie gave his hand a squeeze to signal peace. "Look at those seagulls. Some view, isn't it?"

A woman caught Jackie's eye and smiled. She was tall and weathery, a midlife bohemian in sundress and flowered head scarf, silver hoop earrings and flat raw leather sandals. She wore several cameras around her neck, lenses, meters—no mere gatherer of mementos, she.

"Such darling boys," the woman said. "Are they twins?"

People asked all the time. Nick was dark, with smoky eyes, and James was blond and showed more chisel in his face, but they were just the same height, and wiry—not chunky like lots of boys their age, and they sported the same longish bangs from the same Madison Avenue scissors. Today they were wearing almost identical clothing—short-sleeved T-shirts and railroad stripe overalls and blue sneakers with racing stripes. The real twinning, though, Jackie thought, lay in their gestures, most noticeably their way of cocking their heads to one side, as though they were straining some far-off sound, a train whistle maybe, through the noise of the immediate world. They'd picked up that particular bit of body language from "Sesame Street," she supposed, the way they'd learned that *agua* meant water in Spanish.

"Not even brothers," Jackie told the woman. "But very special friends."

The woman raised one of her cameras. "May I? I'm putting together a portfolio—'New York Off-Shore,' I call it." She replaced one lens with another. "The houseboats, the cruise ships, the garbage scows, the Coast Guard cutters. You can't have a book like that without a shot of two beautiful boys on the Staten Island ferry, can you? What are they, three? I have a niece who'll be five in February. Melissa, but most people call her Missy. She lives in San Diego. Her father's in the navy."

"What do you say, boys?" Jackie hoped she would never have the woman as a passenger on a long flight. Any moment there would be anecdotes about her next door neighbor's mother's best friend's arthritis. "Let the nice woman take your pictures, then we'll go fore to get the best view of the Statue of Liberty."

The boys let themselves be posed against the railing. They smiled their phony camera smiles.

"Real smiles," the woman begged, clicking.

The boys scowled ferociously. The woman laughed and clicked. "Just one more, over there, please, so I can get a shot of that beautiful tugboat." She raised her camera again and started shooting. The man in the Burberry looked annoyed as her camera swept across his face. Click, click. "Thank you, boys." She turned and pushed through the swinging red doors of the main cabin. The man in the Burberry watched her.

Nick said, "No."

"What, honey?" Jackie said.

Nick made a face. "You know."

"I don't know, honey. Do you have to go to the bathroom?"

He pointed to the man in the Burberry. "Well, I like my slicker better because it's just like James's slicker."

Jackie blinked. Wheels whirred. Had she asked him about the Burberry? She hadn't, had she? Had only thought about asking him? Then what? And how? Well, she must have asked him. Jet lag, thy name is Jackie.

"Okay, honey," she said. "I'm sure not going to force you to have one."

"Brrr," Nick said.

"Brrr," James said.

"Brrr, brrr, brrr," they giggled together.

"You're not cold, are you?" Jackie asked. There was some breeze, but the sun was strong.

"Brrr, brrr, brrr, Burberry!" the boys said.

"Hey, you two ought to be doing commercials," Jackie said.

"But Lokomo doesn't like burrs because they stick to his wings," Nick said.

Jackie instantly tuned out, the way she always did when she heard those made-up names. Nick tugged at her, and she came to.

"James is hungry," Nick said.

"He is, is he? Must be the sea air. Let's see, James. I have raisins, bananas, pretzels. What would you like?"

"He wants a pretzel," Nick said.

"Honey, let him answer for himself."

"He did." Nick had inherited his father's calm stubbornness. "He said he wants a pretzel."

"Maybe you want a pretzel?"

"No, Nick wants raisins," James said.

"See, Jackie?" He called her by her name instead of Mama or Mom when he was feeling especially powerful.

"Okay, okay."

Jackie reached into the bright wool bag she'd bought on her last trip to Athens. She handed James a big wholewheat pretzel—a gritty awful thing by her lights, but Jill Everts had persuaded her of the supreme virtue in rough grains. She gave Nick a small box of raisins, small for small fingers, never mind that raisins cost twice as much in individual boxes as they did in the fifteen-ounce packages.

If Elizabeth Gray liked Bob's teaching style, Jackie thought, she could set him up from River House to Southampton; he could start making the kind of money he deserved to make, that he'd be making now if he didn't hate to hustle. Then she could buy Nick his raisins in sterling silver boxes if she wanted to.

James said, "If I gave this pretzel to the umbrella man, he could sell it for lots of money." He flashed his sweet smile.

Sometimes James looked almost fragile to Jackie, as though he had lots of hurts stored up inside, or maybe it was those white bread genes of his. "Who's the umbrella man?" she asked. "Someone on 'Sesame Street'?"

"He's someone on Blue Street," Nick said.

"He's someone on Prue Preet," James said. The giggles started again.

They lost her. She wondered what Elizabeth wore to play tennis—shorts, or one of those barely there skirts with ruffled panties peeking out. Elizabeth would look good, whatever she wore; she'd been bred for tennis clothes, slim hips and no tits, and blond went so well with white. Bob had told Jackie he thought Elizabeth was washed-out looking, but he hadn't yet seen her in tennis togs. Sometimes Jackie was sorry she didn't play tennis herself. Bob had offered to teach her, but she'd never so much as swung a racket before they met, and starting from scratch at her age seemed too dismaying, no chance of getting really good, so better to let the game go altogether, let Bob have that part of his life to himself. Anyway, with her dark crop of curls, the flashy sweeps and juts of her olive face, the various conspicuous curves, she looked better in black silk than in white cotton and Dacron.

"Lokomo doesn't like the umbrella man," Nick said.

Jackie suddenly wished she had Nick all to herself after her weekend away from home. James was the dearest boy, but he made Nick get so silly, move so far away from her. "Let's go fore," she said. "Let's get all blown around, and see the Statue of Liberty." She steered them toward the cabin.

A mother and small daughter came out through the swinging red doors.

"Megan!" James cried, pointing to the girl.

Jackie jumped. She stared. The girl had Megan Smith-Stephens's shoulder-length glossy brown hair, clipped back with two barrettes the way Megan always wore hers, and she had the same big brown eyes flecked with amber; she even wore the kind of denim jumper Megan owned. But this chickadee looked older than Megan, fully four. She had a curdled look about the mouth that Jackie had never seen on Megan's face.

"No, honey," she said gently to James. "She does look a lot like Megan, but she's another little girl."

The girl reached up for her mother's hand as Nick and James edged closer.

"Megan?" James said hopefully, as though Jackie hadn't spoken.

Jackie went on alert. James's face lost color, seemed to lose its symmetry—he made her think of passengers turning airsick. She put hands on both boys.

"Your daughter reminds them of a friend who moved away a couple of months ago," she said to the girl's mother. The woman didn't exactly look like Kelly Smith, but she had the same air about her as Kelly—wenchy, smart-ass, secure. She made Jackie want to move on, the way Kelly sometimes had done. "Come on, boys," she said. "Let's go see Liberty. I bet we have a lovely view of her now."

The boys did not move. They stared at the little girl. Jackie saw hunger in their eyes.

"What's your name, honey?" she asked the child. Maybe hearing a different name would release the boys from their enchantment.

"I hate you," the girl said to Nick and James. She jammed her thumb into her mouth.

The mothers exchanged apologetic looks.

"Do you want to see my butterfly?" Nick asked the girl.

The girl took a step backward, tried to burrow into her mother.

"Megan loved my butterfly." Nick reached into a pocket.

The girl shrieked. She batted at the air in front of her face. Spittle trickled out of her mouth. Other passengers stared.

"Jenny!" Her mother scooped her up and cradled her. "Baby girl!"

"I'm so sorry," Jackie said. She pulled the boys close to her. "None of us meant—"

"Of course not," the other mother said. Her daughter was sobbing quietly now.

"I'm sorry," Nick said.

"I'm sorry," James said.

"That's all right." The girl's mother produced a cold smile. "I think maybe we'll go back into the cabin and get a drink. Want a Coke?"

"I want to get off the boat," the girl sobbed. "I want to get off the boat. I hate them, Mommy. I want to get off the boat." As they went back through the doors, Jackie heard again, "I hate them, Mommy."

She groped for words to console the boys. The boys beat her to it.

"She'll be okay, Mama," Nick said. "As soon as she has her Coke."

"She'll be oke with her Coke," James said. He added wistfully, "She's a baby. Megan never hided."

"Hid," Jackie said automatically. Then, "What do you mean, James?"

"You know," James said.

She didn't know; and all at once she didn't want to know. She wanted to gulp the sea air and let the wind assault her and trade waves with Liberty. James was right. The girl was a baby. Jackie didn't want to see her again, which meant they couldn't go through the cabin to the foredeck; okay. The view from here was good enough. She led the boys to the starboard railing. They looked out over the water and cataloged excitements. Liberty, and more gulls flying by, and a ferry heading toward Manhattan with lots of people to wave at, and Staten Island coming into view.

Nick said, "Daisy won't go away like Megan, will she?"

"No, honey."

"Ever?"

"Well, I don't know about ever," Jackie said. "But she's very happy in New York, and Jill's very happy here, so I think you'll be playing together for a long, long time."

"But somebody might take her away," James said. "The umbrella man." He sounded infinitely sad.

"The umbrella man! Don't you worry about it, boys." She hugged them tight. "Don't you worry about anything.

Hey, how about a song? How about singing Liberty a song?"

"Do you think she'd like 'Three Blind Mice'?" Nick asked.

"I think she'd love it. So would I. All together now. Let's sing the bazooly out of it. Ready?"

8.

A four-story brownstone needs a lot of upkeep, even if two floors are all but sealed off and the stove is seldom splashed. Nora did the daily rounds herself; her stringent demands for privacy precluded a constant other presence in the house. Once a week, on Mondays, Betty DuPont came to change the linens on the bed, and put a scrubbing brush to the bathrooms, and delete the moldy oranges from the refrigerator, and chase the dust from the unlived-in living room. She was a thin woman in her sixties, naturally given to silence, and she had her instructions: Keep out of Mrs. Keefe's way—out of her ken, if possible. She let herself in with her own key, and some days she and Nora were no more than sounds to each other.

When the envelope from Arthur Kojak sailed through the mail slot and onto the floor of the front hall—missing the wicker letter basket as large envelopes always did—Mrs. DuPont let it lie. Envelopes were strictly Mrs. Keefe's business. She ran an ostentation of water in the kitchen sink so that Nora would know the coast was clear. Nora descended.

It was a nine-by-twelve gray clasp envelope, sealed with brown tape, stiff, addressed in block letters, MRS. N. KEEFE. The envelope bore the printed legend, in red and black, running up the left-hand side, of the Kitchner Karting Company, on the Grand Concourse in the Bronx. Mr. Kojak used imaginative envelopes, a different one every time. Printers' errors, he had once confided to Nora; he bought them by the hundreds on Eighteenth Street. Nora wondered, as she walked back upstairs, if the *K* in "Karting" were the error, or a cuteness.

A hesitation at the top of the stairs; a decision. She would go to Jack's room. Mrs. DuPont did not come to the second floor before noon or after three o'clock.

Jack's room. Jack's bed. Jack's handwoven Irish bedspread, green and gold and purple-blue, all mixed together and muzzy, like fields seen at a distance. She pulled up her skirt and sat on the bed and felt the wool of the spread attack her nether lands. Jack be nimble. Jack be quick. Jack fill me up with your candlestick.

She opened the envelope.

Rubber-banded to cardboard backing were a dozen photographs in color, eight-by-ten, clear, suitable for framing. Daisy on a swing, laughing; Daisy on a swing, looking tentative; Daisy at a drinking fountain, looking wet; Daisy and Jill, striding up Fifth Avenue in their blue jeans, striding down Madison Avenue in their blue jeans, going into a flower shop together, coming out of the entrance to 114 East Sixty-sixth Street, together, together, together.

Nora put the photographs back in the envelope, then took them out, spread them on the bed, looked at them, stroked them, put them back. Took them out again.

The silvery blond hair: so very much like Jack's. The eyes were light blue, like his, and the eyebrows swept and peaked like his, the eternal Irish eyebrows. And the bones, the hollows, the lilting chin . . . only the mouth was different, really: buddish, a radish, a rose. Jack's mouth had a straightness to it, even when he smiled; his lips never parted awfully much. But the bud mouth didn't look to come from Jill, either. She had a very ordinary mouth.

Nora gave a sudden little moan. She ran to Jack's green bathroom. She looked in the mirror over the sink. Yes—it was her mouth that Daisy wore. Her mouth, her lips, sweet lips, sad lips, unkissed lips, alive and pink in the dead face. Hers.

A word flew to her mind: telegony. If you mated a mare with a zebra, she might give birth, years later, after mating properly with a stallion, to striped foals. And Jack had carried her cells on his cock, had shoved them into foreign holes—

The most beautiful child she had ever seen.

Arctic, English, Giant, Blue. Oxeye, Shasta, Transvaal, too. Daisy, Daisy, I love you. Loves me. Loves me not. Loves me. Loves me not. Pease porridge in the prick nine ways hot. Jack and Jill went up the hill to fetch a pail of Daisy. Jack fell down and broke his crown and Jill is going crazy.

TUESDAY, THE TENTH

1.

Little Jill is afraid of the dark.

The Vermont nights were heavy going for me after my long season in New York. Other exurbanites would make much of moon and stars hanging bright in boundless sky; my sullen eyes would dwell on the sucky ink behind the prickings of light. Give me the wattage of big cities beating the blackness no matter the time or weather.

Hey, Mr. Edison, what are you doing tonight? Come on over, I'll show you grateful, I'll turn you on, Mr. Light.

The windows of my bedroom face east. My cousin Larry, whose apartment this used to be, is a kind and generous soul but something of a cave crab too. When I arrived in April I found the bed with its big brass back to the windows. Opaque shades and full-length burgundy velvet draperies masked the light—London observing the blackout during the Blitz. I reduced the shades to tight rolls, tied back the draperies, reversed the bed. I have no trouble sleeping in light—the opposite. If dawn gets me up, I fall back asleep almost immediately and sleep more peacefully for knowing the dark has been vanquished and a fresh day has made it to town.

Tuesday morning I woke at dawn and stayed awake. A new fear had taken root in my belly. Not even the small pink light and the increments of brightness rising behind it could make me brave enough to close my eyes and leave the driving to others.

I lay in bed, staring at the changing sky, clutching my quilts. I need weight on me when I sleep, even in high summer, to keep me from floating to the ceiling. I tried to pretend the feeling in my belly was nothing more than the gas of an indigestible dream. I have learned a way with bad dreams. If I open the door to death, paint peeling from her face, rags dripping down from her shoulders, ice for lips, begging to come into my warmth, I can make myself slam the door, I am not fooled or cowed for a minute. This time dreams were not the matter. Death was a hunter, not a beggar, and she ate doors for breakfast.

I got out of bed. I pulled on my extra-large T-shirt proclaiming NO NUKES. Washington, Moscow, were you watching? I crossed the living room, turning off the lights I burn each night. I paused reverently at the entrance to the small square shrine where I kept my household goddess, a golden icon named Daisy.

She had kicked off her own little quilt and her Raggedy Ann top sheet. She was naked, as she always was in sleep. She had drawn her legs up and apart. She advertised her sex.

In moments of rage I have understood the child abuser, though I never hit Daisy. That morning I understood the child molester, though I did not touch Daisy improperly, did not touch her at all. I was an unholy worshipper, standing there in her doorway in the gray light, loving the simple beauty of her construction, loving my sisterly sameness, loving the men who had loved me and the men who would love her, loving the existence of gender. I was different in degree, not kind, from the celebrant who had to go beyond mere worship, who had to take communion and be one flesh with the Child.

Do you recoil from me, mothers? Tell me, I dare you, that no bath, no changing session, ever turned your tide.

Birds sang to me. Thomas, our big orange cat, appeared and asked my ankles for breakfast.

I went to the kitchen. I filled Thomas's red bowl with his unspeakable nuggets. I made coffee. Caffeine and my adrenals cancel each other out. I calmed down. I went back to Daisy's room. I trusted myself to get into her bed. I held her in a pure maternal cuddle.

"Shhh, baby, everything's going to be all right," I whispered to her, or she whispered to me, or my mother whispered to us both.

I slept. I woke. The telephone was ringing.

I looked at the hickory dickory dock clock. Seven-twenty. Who on earth—?

I ran into the living room. "Hello?"

"Is this Jill?" Deep voice, pleasant enough, unfamiliar.

"Yes. Who's this?"

"Jill, I just want to know, are you safe? Is your door locked? Are your shades down? Are you and Daisy safe?"

The light in the room seemed to change. Everything got too bright. The walls lost their rightness of angle. Help. Help.

"Who is this? Please, who is this?"

"Jill, are you sure the door is locked?"

I hung up. I stood there. I trembled uncontrollably. I could not move. My ears went around the corner and down the hallway, listening for creaking hinges. I had locked the door, I had double-locked the door, but every lock has a key. There are no atheists in keyholes. Help.

He had known our names. It's so much worse when they know your name. The man in the liquor store who was too nice about cashing my checks? The florist who gave Daisy broken-stemmed daisies orphaned from their bunches? Help.

I willed my rubbery legs to carry me to the hallway. I peered down its shadowy length. The door was tight in its jamb. Plumb jamb for breakfast, Mommy? I looked at it forever, then worked up the nerve to walk down the hallway, to put my hand on the door.

Locked.

I went back to Daisy's room. She was sleeping on her side, her mouth slightly open and rounded—she was a cherub from a Christmas card, manifesting perfect peace. A jet splintered the sound barrier, and I ducked, tensing for bombs, but the noise didn't seem to ruffle her sleep, her serenity, any more than the telephone had. In the midst of my panic I felt something like pride. Craven beast though I was, I had not contaminated my girl with my fears.

I sat down in the blue rocking chair I'd used for nursing her, the one piece of furniture I'd dragged down from Vermont. I'd brought my breasts, why not the chair? You never know.

Are you and Daisy safe, Jill?

I pulled the rocker close to the bed. My shoulders ached with a longing so strong and specific, I almost cried out. I wanted a man. I wanted him to come up behind me and put his hands on my shoulders, sealing me, promising me all the things no human being can rightly promise another. The love that does not die. Perfect safety.

He wasn't going to come, any more than Daisy was going to wake hungry for my milk. I rubbed my shoulders until longing turned to simple soreness.

I couldn't erase the deeper longing, though. In my raucous old single days I'd laughed off threatening calls. Not now. One thing to be in charge of your own ass, another to be in charge of the future of the world. I was Daisy's Maginot Line.

I wanted Jack.

The thought was out in the air before I could stop it, like some demon germ escaping Pandora's box. Time twisted. I was Jack's mistress, Jack's pal, Jack's little girl, Jack's darling companion—and he was my all and everything. Memories long held down shouted for my attention. Jack singing to me as we walked through a blizzard, Jack covering the odd bounced check with a loan and a joke, Jack telling me to shorten my skirts, Jack vetting the other men in my life.

"Darling," I could hear myself saying, "I just got the vilest phone call. Do something, will you?"

He would put me on hold; he would call the president of the telephone company, the commissioner of police, the mayor, the White House; then he would invite me to Chicago for lunch, to give me something nice to think about.

I still knew his private telephone number by heart. He could have changed it, of course. . . . Unlikely. Jack was fond of his telephone numbers the way other people are fond of pets. He would not let his numbers be changed.

But I had changed. The woman who'd called Jack darling, who'd called everybody darling—the wench was dead. Daisy was my only darling. I could call the cops myself, dammit.

I called them. They were nice. They also sounded busy. They suggested an unlisted number. When I said it was my cousin's number, they told me to let them know if I had any further trouble. Goodbye and good luck, little lady.

I paced. I thought of calling my cousin Larry in London. He would worry and feel helpless—unfair. I thought about calling the other Playgroup mommies. They would worry, but not for us. They would think about keeping their children far away from Daisy.

I went to the jeans I'd worn the day before and got a cream-colored card out of my right front pocket. I looked at words and numbers. I thought about khaki hair. I was afraid of him but I trusted him. Whatever his notions, his ambitions for my girl, he wanted her physically safe, he would hop out of bed and run to us, flexing his squash player's muscles. I was going to have to deal with him sooner or later. Sooner seemed the better choice. I swallowed a hundred misgivings and called Kenneth William Iceman, Ph.D.

2.

Jack Keefe jogged. Every morning, hungover or hale, with a fine Irish shrug of indifference for the weather, he walked the four blocks down Fifth Avenue to the Washington Square Arch, took a few deep breaths, waited until the second hand on his watch hit high noon, and set off counterclockwise about the square.

He jogged, but he did not think of himself as a jogger. It amazed him, irritated him, that such vast numbers of people so construed themselves. No matter how early he got going these days, the perimeter of the square was a glut of bodies—little fatties, mostly, beaming virtue, in orange and purple shorts and clever T-shirts. There was even a pregnant jogstress who was a regular now, and fast; Jack had more than once been overtaken by her. She had her own special sound, thwacking of her braless breasts as she flip-flopped by. Jack thought she must hate her big body and the beastie in it, the way she was trying to run them down.

Jogging was an embarrassment to Jack; a necessity. He'd been at it twelve years, ever since the heart attack. Jogging, and no cigarettes, and the careful diet, if you didn't count the booze, and he'd found a doctor who said he didn't have to count it as long as he kept his weight way down. All in all he was probably in better shape these days than he'd ever been before. He did his daily four times around the square—a few yards under two miles—in sixteen minutes and thirty, maybe forty, seconds. Not the stuff that marathon records were made of, but not bad for a pussy-loving tippler of forty-nine. He was about as fit for the rigors of a political campaign as a man had any business being.

Seven-thirty, and the day was warm going for hot. Jack walked down his front steps. He was wearing baggy old gray sweat pants, devoid of stripes, insignia, and other fripperies, and a plain gray sweat shirt—and, by God, sweat he would today. The sweat was part of his doctor's recipe, which recipe coincided nicely with Jack's notion that a grown man had no business wearing shorts in public, balls blatant as the balls on a Christmas tree.

He waved at his next-door neighbors, a tasty young mother who wore her pale hair in a single braid, and her nine-year-old son. Jack felt sorry for the boy, who began and ended every day from early September to late June in that foul intestinal tube called the subway because his parents turned up their noses at P.S. 41 and the private schools in the Village. When Big Jack Keefe was mayor, the public schools of New York would be so brilliant that the private schools would have to beg for students. Those poor buggers who had to begin their day in the subway would find them safe and clean and efficient, and they wouldn't cost the earth, by God.

"Good morning, Mr. Keefe. I hope you're well this fine morning, sir. Going to break a record today? So long as it's all you break."

"And a good morning to you, Mr. Lazlo. Any more problems with the immigration people?" He asked the question knowing there would be no more problems because he'd made sure there wouldn't be. A voluble doorman of a big Fifth Avenue apartment building would be a valuable minion come election time.

Jack hailed a man as thin and nearly as tall as himself walking briskly out of the cobblestoned bit of the past called Washington Mews.

"Hello, Dick. Hannah feeling better?"

"Much better, thanks, she should be home by the end of the week. The tulips cheered her no end."

"Nice, aren't they? Nora's own hybrid. Even I can appreciate them, great clod though I am."

And he wasn't too much of a clod to appreciate the sweetness of Hannah Steinberg. They'd had a lovely go at it once, Hannah tremulous with guilt then turning silly, on the green-carpeted floor of her office at New York University, where she taught French literature and Dick Steinberg taught constitutional law. Jack liked Dick. He was a pure old-fashioned Greenwich Village liberal—generous, compassionate, and he wore jaunty bow ties.

"Let me take you to lunch one of these days," Jack said. "Pick your brains. I'm off and running this fall, and I don't mean around the square. Making the big announcement this morning."

"Anytime. Anytime. Be honored. I thought I heard a rumor or three." Dick fingered the bow tie of the day, red with silver ovals. He clapped Jack on the back. "Shrink appointment. Better dash or I'll have to hear a fifteen-minute lecture on avoidance. Happy running."

Down to the square in ships then, the deep breaths, and off. Around and around and around and around—sixteen minutes and thirty-one seconds. Good. Home, dripping, to the scale—a hair under 185. Very good. A morning for singing in the shower—"Nancy Whiskey," hokey, off-key—and soaping the little fellow with fondest fingers.

Hello? What's that? Nora? Could it be?

A definite sound of water running into a tub came from Nora's bathroom, adjoining, which bathroom was usually not used for serious ablutions until noon, when Nora, protesting the early hour, bestirred herself from her Irish linen sheets.

Such deviant behavior called for celebration. He rapped out shave and a haircut on the pale green tile of the shower stall. To his astonishment, the message came echoing back to him—merrily, he would have sworn.

For the first time in memory's life he felt curious about his wife. He made a pass at drying himself. He pulled on a Santa-red terry robe and knocked on the connecting door.

"Who's there?" Coyly, he would have sworn.

"Jack Keefe's the name."

"Come."

The door was unlocked, as ever; they were their own best barriers. He opened it. He went from green tile to white tile.

Nora stood by the tub, watching it fill and the steam rise out of it. She was still in her nightgown, dull blue flannel, as if the city were at winter. And a wintry smile for Jack. "To what do I owe?" she asked.

"It's extraordinary, you'll agree. Mrs. Keefe up and about, and the sun barely risen."

"Bad dreams," Nora said. She tested the water. She turned off the faucet. "A tiger was chasing you, and you got away."

"Nora, my love."

"Was it nice last night?" she asked with sudden savagery. "Did your little dicky get all hard? Did she call you Mr. Mayor while you sucked her titties?"

"Nora—" laughing, the famous merry snort—"if I got one-tenth, one-hundredth, the action you give me credit for—"

"No, please, I can't bear it, your cover stories are too awfully boring. You had to go to darkest Brooklyn, I suppose, to see the county leader's grandmother, and one piece of apple pie led to another, and there it was, two in the morning, and not a cab to be had."

"I'm as bad as that? Grandmothers, do I? And here I prided myself on being a liar in the grand tradition." He reached out an awkward hand and squeezed his wife's thin shoulder. "Your water will be cooling. Shall I wash your back for you?"

"I'll manage, thank you."

"Very well, madam. Good day." He bowed. Then, rushing, surprising himself, all mockery gone from his voice and posture, "I don't mean to make you miserable, you know."

Nora looked. She sighed. She checked a smile, as if Jack were a slow child trying hard.

"I know, Jack—" kindly. "And you don't, really. I make myself miserable. You're—how did dear Dr. Howard put it?—you're the instrument of my self-abuse. The willing instrument, but that's a separate issue."

"How very helpful."

"Never mind. You'll have forgotten before breakfast. We can have this conversation again in a few months, and you'll be just as sincere, and it will mean just as little. The light that illuminates nothing. And now, if you don't mind," Nora said, "I'll have my bath."

3.

In the 1960s there existed an art shop, German Expressionist mostly, known as the H. Kahn Gallery. H. was Henry—heterosexual, in love with what paint could do, determined to triumph in the New York art world without ever becoming *of* it. He succeeded well enough to need an assistant who could run the place while he was traveling, buying. He hired Heidi Samuels, a Bennington graduate with flaming hair and a bold-featured face out of a Kokoschka portrait. Six months later there existed a Heidi Kahn and an H. and H. Kahn gallery. The Kahns hired a new assistant, a fortyish woman named Marguerite Koos, with the eggshell eyelids and vaulted forehead of a Memling madonna. Henry was conservative in family matters and wanted Heidi with him when he traveled. Besides, she had an extraordinary eye. A sketchy thing of trees she'd bought at a tag sale in Forest Hills turned out to be, as she'd guessed, an early Schmidt-Rottluff.

When he was just getting his business going, Henry slept—monkishly, illegally—in the office of the gallery. By the time he hired Heidi, he was living on the floor above the gallery, with a real bed and a real shower but no dining table; he didn't want to be able to give dinner parties. Now the Kahns owned the building, a prime cut of Madison Avenue gold coast. The gallery had grown to two floors. The Kahns rented the third floor to an elderly Swiss-Italian, Josef Lucca, who sold rare and fine books. The top three floors of the building were Casa Kahn.

Space abounded. They had a sauna. There was a room—not merely a closet, a room—just for luggage.

Eight-year-old Julie Kahn could have had her own room. She insisted on sleeping with her three-year-old sister, Stephanie. The girls had a suite at the back of the house, overlooking quiet trees: a sleeping room with bunk beds; a pale blue bathroom with fixtures low to the floor; and a playroom-cum-study, with Sonia Delaunay's brilliant alphabet running around the room.

Heidi wondered sometimes, and aloud: Didn't Julie want more privacy? A preteen room with her own telephone? Henry was downright disapproving of the arrangement. But Heidi reminded him, and herself, that Julie alone of her circle lived with both her biological parents, neither of whom had ever been married to anyone else, and had a little sister to boot, warm sometimes damp laughing red-haired floppy dolly who never said no to a cuddle.

They were sisters, roommates, pals against the shadows of the night, the boredom of afternoons.

Seven-thirty, and Stephanie came awake all at once in the bottom bunk bed, happily, the way she always did, eyes homing in on a favorite sunbeam that angled like a flashlight beam through a gap between window and shade. She sat up. She made a fist and put it to her ear. Her other hand dialed air. "Brrrring, brrrring," she said. She looked hopefully at the upper bunk.

Julie didn't answer. Stephanie heard giggles, and she remembered. Julie's best friend, Amanda, had spent the night, was up in Julie's bed.

"Chris Palmer thinks he's such a big shot," Amanda said, and Stephanie heard more giggles.

"I know," Julie said. "He says the *F* curse all the time and yesterday Mrs. Wolfe heard him." The giggles came in torrents now.

"Is he in our club or out?" Amanda said.

"Out," Julie said, and giggled all over again. "Out."

"Brrrrrrrring," Stephanie tried. "Brrrrrrrrrrring."

"The scamp is playing the telephone game," Julie said under her breath. Then, projecting, "Hello?"

"Hi, Julie. It's me, Stephanie."

"Hi, Steph."

"I'm right in your neighborhood, can I pop up?"

The rule was that Stephanie couldn't climb the ladder to

the upper bunk without Julie's permission. The custom was that Julie granted permission.

Amanda said, "Chris still hasn't turned in his map of South America, can you believe that? He says he doesn't care."

"Oh, no," Julie howled.

"We could call our club the Four Friends," Amanda said, and paused before delivering the punch line, "or we could call it the No Chris Club."

Julie spasmed.

"Julie, can I pop up? I'm still in the neighborhood. I'm out doing some shopping," Stephanie said.

Amanda groaned.

Julie said, "I've got to go out in a few minutes, scamp, okay? Why don't you come back after breakfast?" Silence came from below, and Julie felt a sickening stab of guilt. She knew, and Stephanie knew, and Stephanie knew she knew, that Julie and Amanda would be rushing off to school the minute they finished breakfast.

Stephanie lay back down, staring up at Julie's bed, stroking the satin trim on her pink baby blanket, her beloved Banky.

"Hey," Julie said.

"Hey what?" Amanda said.

"That was my leg you kicked."

"I didn't kick anything," Amanda said.

"Amanda, quit it," Julie said a minute later.

"Quit what?"

"Quit shoving me!"

"Boy, you're a case," Amanda said. She flipped back the bedding to make her point: she was a good foot away from her friend. "Hey," she suddenly said.

"Hey what?" Julie mocked.

"Something's tickling my toes. Are there bugs in this stupid bed?"

"You're the bug in the bed," Julie said crossly.

It was Stephanie's turn to giggle. She said from below, "I'm the bug in the stupid bed."

"There are no bugs in my bed." Julie was close to tears.

"Because I can come up without using the ladder and I don't even have to ask you."

"You do too have to ask me. Ow! Something bit me! Amanda! Stop it!"

"If I come up the ladder I won't bite you," Stephanie said.

Amanda sat up. "I'm getting out of here. This is weird city." She scrambled down the ladder. She snatched up her jeans and T-shirt. "I'm getting dressed in the bathroom. I don't want anyone weird to see my body. Where are my ponytail clips?"

"I want to talk about our club," Julie wailed.

"Who needs a club with bedbugs?" Amanda slammed into the bathroom.

"Brrring," Stephanie said.

"Shut up. Steph, I'm not playing."

"You're not supposed to say shut up. Daddy told me. I'm in the neighborhood. Can I pop up for a cup of tea?"

Julie looked over the edge of her bed, her dark hair cascading. "No."

"Then I'll come up the other way." Stephanie's eyeballs rolled back into her head until only the whites were showing.

Julie screamed.

Heidi came running, in purple. "Darling?"

"Mommy!" A shriek. "I don't want to sleep with her anymore. I want my own room, Mommy. Mommy, please may I have my own room? Please, Mommy? Please?"

4.

"And heeere's Nick!"

Bob Geritano's voice, and the delicate scampery barely

there sound of little Nick running across the thick white wall-to-wall bedroom carpet, and Jackie Geritano smiled on the world.

She was home, with her men. How good—how specifically sweet—it was to wake up in her own white bedroom, between her own white-on-white sheets, with her own dark men, her darling darklings, her husband and her son, her life.

Sunday she'd woken up in London. Friday she would go to sleep in London, in a different bed. The pillows always wrong, the smells, and either the terrible loneliness or the presence of men she did not love—

She grabbed Nick as he hoisted himself aboard the bed, tumbled over his parents. She buried her nose in his hair. She sniffed the sweet citrus smell of the baby shampoo she'd bought on her last trip to Rome, and a whiff of salt air left over from their jaunt on the Staten Island ferry, and a muskiness that was the smell of small boys everywhere. When she had a boy Nick's age aboard one of her flights she would sometimes try to sniff his hair while she helped him with his seat belt, but the fuel stink always got in the way.

Friday, London. She would be so far from her Nick, flesh of her flesh—she felt scissored at the thought. And she'd be flying in a DC 10, and all the astronauts on earth doing sobersides TV commercials couldn't make her feel they were safe. But why the bazooly worry? Think of Elaine Cooley, her roommate in stew school. She'd survived not one but two hijackings, then she'd died in a bus crash. Good things, bad things, life was famous for delivering surprises.

Nick said he wanted to do pee-pee. Bob said he did too—such a good daddy, such a good husband—and why didn't Jackie go back to sleep and he and Nick would rustle up some breakfast when they were finished in the bathroom. Her eyelids were great weights pressing her head back on the pillow, but Friday, London. Saturday, Johannesburg. Breakfast alone in her hotel room or, worse, not alone. And Nick batching it with Bob, having to be brave. "Later," she promised her pillow. She got out of bed.

Shower now? Later, she decided. She could hear Nick and Bob in the bathroom, pissing sounds, laughter—lovely intimate music that made her body feel plump with pleasure, and she didn't want to intrude. Her fine men, and not just hers but very much each other's, and that—even more than the money—justified the flying, didn't it? She couldn't imagine Oliver Gray in the bathroom with James; there was a man, if ever there was one, who peed behind a closed door if he peed at all.

She put on bright frothy understuff, and designer jeans, tight, and a red silk shirt she'd bought two of in Paris because Bob liked the way she looked in red. He was right, she decided, facing the full-length mirror on her closet door. Red made her look ripe. She didn't have as much sun blood as Bob, who was Sicilian, but when she wore red her skin looked rich and edible, and her thick crown of curls were the blue-black of fabulous berries. She pulled at her curls to mess them. Bob liked her hair messy. Her grooming supervisor didn't. Perms were okay with the airline, tamed. Saturday, Jo'burg. Sunday, London and home. When you got down to it, Bob liked her to look beddish.

"Breakfast in fifteen minutes," she called out. She smiled as she walked past Nick's room. Looking at the things she'd given him stroked her in a way no museum ever could. Bob moaned and groaned when she brought home something new for Nick. Too much plastic, he said. Too many things, period. Bob had grown up poor, the way she had, but the poverty had etched him differently. She had an endless need to possess. He had never learned a love for things and didn't want to learn it now. It was their one real tension. He thought he was free, and he wanted to free her. She thought he was ducking reality, had to grow up.

Take the question of their apartment. (Hands fisting as she walked down the hallway to the kitchen.) A majority of the tenants in their building had voted to go cooperative, which meant she and Bob had to buy their apartment, for

$70,000, or move. Bob said: So we move. But with the real estate market the way it was, there was no chance they would find another East Side apartment they could afford. East Side, West Side, Bob didn't care, so long as she and Nick were by his side. She cared. She wanted Nick to play with the banker's son, James, and the child of culture, Stephanie, and the beauty born of Yankee coolness, Daisy. No West Side playgroup for Nick, thank you.

Most important, Nick loved the apartment. It was his measuring stick. Yesterday he was tall enough to open the refrigerator, tomorrow he'd be tall enough to see out the bathroom window without kneeling on the radiator. Jackie had lived in four different homes by the time she started school. She wanted Nick to stay on East Sixty-sixth Street.

She opened a cookbook she'd been given as a wedding present, *Beautiful Breakfasts*. She knew she wasn't much of a cook. She was the one person around who just didn't care about food. She didn't understand Elizabeth, who could drop a hundred dollars on a lunch that would end up in the toilet, or Heidi, who was forever quoting magazine articles about the absolutely only place to buy your squid, or Jill, who seemed to think civilization could be saved if everyone ate enough raw carrots. It disturbed her—offended her— that Bob, one of those great lusty cooks who'd learned it all at his grandmother's knee and never opened a cookbook, could sniff a saucepot with the same look of delight she saw when he was sniffing in bed.

She thumbed through *Beautiful Breakfasts*, making faces at the pictures of glossy Eggs Benedict, symmetrically rolled omelets dusted with powdered sugar. Bob said the problem was that the nose was the door to the stomach and hers had been dulled by the flying. *Butter a shallow oval ovenproof dish, sprinkle with coarsely grated Romano cheese, add some heavy cream which you have thinned with a few drops of raspberry vinegar, and put the dish into the oven to warm. Meanwhile, break four eggs into a shallow dish—*

Jackie yawned. Bazooly, she was tired. She loved flying, but it really cost the body. She thought, as she did now and then, about applying for a ground position. The money wouldn't be as good, though. If she bid enough layovers, like the London-Jo'burg-London trip coming up this weekend, she stood to make eight or nine grand over her base pay. And of course a ground position wouldn't have such flexible hours. There was more of a demand for tennis lessons during the week—on weekends the women Bob instructed were off in the Hamptons aiming their top spins at their husbands; so it made sense for her to work weekends, when Bob was free to take care of Nick.

She banged the cookbook shut. She would make scrambled eggs, yet again. Maybe if she put parsley in them the men would look more turned on than they usually did at the sight of her eggs. Bob would be happy to make breakfast; he would happily do all the cooking, nearly all the Nick-tending; he had a perfectly elastic notion of what manhood meant; but she couldn't get away from the feeling that she was supposed to put on an apron when she got home, never mind that she brought in two-thirds of their yearly loaf of bread. She went to the refrigerator.

She found two bunches of parsley, one curly, one flat. Depression weighted her. She wasn't good enough for Bob, for Nick. Lots of women made money and knew their parsley too, and no doubt did in their bedrooms for their husbands what she did for Bob. Heidi accused Jackie of having a supermom complex, easy cruel words from a woman who seemed effortlessly to do it all, the work and the homemade cookies and the elegant looks, though Bob said she didn't excite *him*, he couldn't picture her really letting go. Why shouldn't everything be easy for Heidi? She'd been born to money, had married money, and people who had it made more of it, made more of everything. Jackie's hand hovered. She took out the curly parsley. She rinsed it, shook off the water, rummaged vainly through the drawers for the parsley grater she'd seen Bob wielding over pasta salads, finally plunked the green stuff down on a cutting board, wrested a knife away from the magnetized rack on the wall over the sink, and chopped.

"Nick! Bob! Come and get it!"

Funny to think of Elizabeth as one of those tennis wives. She was generous, sweet, plainly in love with her son, never crabby at the park the way Jackie often was. Well, sure. Elizabeth never had to put six thousand miles between her body and her baby's body. She didn't have to smell the stink of fuel and endure the leers and lunges of idiots to be able to buy things for James. Money, always money. Then again, she didn't get to share her baby and her body with Bob Geritano.

"Nicky! Bobby! Eggs getting cold!"

They pranced in then, almost painfully adorable in the matching LaCoste alligator shirts she'd bought for them in Paris, and matching faded jeans.

Nick said, "One two three! What do I see? Jackie's eggs waiting for me." He climbed into his chair. He looked at his mother, his father, the Bunnykins plate in front of him. He put a fingertip to his nose, the way he sometimes did. He smiled. He said, "I hate green eggs. I want Daddy's eggs."

"Nick!" his parents chorused.

He pushed the Bunnykins plate away. "I want sunshine eggs, the way Daddy makes them. These eggs look yukky."

Bob said, "These are wonderful eggs, and these are the only eggs you're getting today." He took a forkful from his own plate. He did his best to look excited. "Yummy in the tummy. Terrific eggs, Mama."

Jackie forced a smile. Don't cry over spilled eggs, right? Nick was three and a half, and this was what three-and-a-half-year-old kids did, right? James, Stephanie, Daisy—they all had to dig at their mommies now and then, even though their mommies didn't fly, right? Saturday, Johannesburg. The Friday after that, Mexico City.

Nick ate a slice of toasted panettone, conspicuously leaving a burned piece of crust. Nick ate two strawberries. Nick drank a glass of milk. Nick did not eat eggs.

Jackie thought, He's angry because I leave him. He has every right. I shouldn't be doing what I do. I've got to find a way to stop flying.

Bob said, "Who's for 'Sesame Street'?" And to Jackie, "I'll drop him at Elizabeth's, if you like. You really look like you need some sleep, baby."

"Don't say that!" she snapped. Then, contrite hand to his arm, "I'm sorry. I just hate thinking I look as tired as I feel. Bag lady—bags under the eyes."

Nick made a dash for the living room and television set, manifestly relieved to be done with the tensions of breakfast.

"I'll take him," Jackie said. "Then maybe I'll go get a facial."

Bob put his hands in her hair. He kissed her nose. "My bellissima." He kissed her lips. "Keep that face."

They heard Nick clicking the dial, turning on the tube. He came running back into the kitchen. "James is icky and sticky," he announced.

"James on 'Sesame Street'?" Jackie said.

"James James," he said. He made a gagging sound.

Jackie and Bob looked at each other and shrugged their mystification. Bob took Nick's hand.

"I'll watch with you," he said to his son.

Jackie washed the breakfast dishes. She made two cups of cappuccino with the electric espresso machine she'd bought for Bob as a birthday present. She carried coffee into the living room. Nick was sitting on Bob's lap. They were laughing at some bit of silliness on the screen. They looked so complete, so perfect, that she felt jealous, and then, instantly, ashamed. Oliver Gray never watched "Sesame Street" with James, not even on weekends—a certainty. Henry Kahn declined to let Stephanie watch television, period. Daisy Everts had no father, period.

The telephone rang. She went to answer. Elizabeth was calling, to say that James had vomited his breakfast.

Jackie's hands grew cold. She looked over her shoulder at her boy.

"Hello?" Elizabeth said.

"Hi," Jackie said brightly. "I mean, is he okay?" The sound of Nick gagging hung around her head.

Elizabeth said James seemed fine now, she didn't think it was the flu, just one of those freelance pukes kids have from time to time, but she didn't want the rest of the Playgroup to run any risk, so she'd called Jill and Jill was willing to have Nick and Stephanie for the morning, and on Thursday, Jill's day, Elizabeth would take the gang because James was sure to be fine by Thursday.

"Of course," Jackie said numbly. "Whatever. Can I do anything?"

"Oh, no, thanks, we're fine, really. He's not running a fever. We'll probably be at the playground this afternoon."

"I didn't let them eat any of the junk on the ferry. Hot dogs or anything."

"Don't be silly, Jackie."

"Did James—" Jackie looked at Nick again.

"What?"

"Did James, you know, say anything about Nick today? Anything, you know—" Jackie's voice trailed off. "Bob said you're a good tennis player. Terrific, he said, actually."

"He's a terrific teacher. I was going . . . what, honey? I'll read it in a sec. I'm talking to Jackie. Honey, don't put that in your mouth, what's the matter with you? Jackie, would you mind? Saying hi to James?"

"Hi, James," Jackie said. "You feeling okay?"

"Well, I threw up, but I didn't get any on the floor."

"On behalf of mothers everywhere, thank you," Jackie said. The warmth crept back into her hands. "Maybe I'll see you at the playground later, okay?"

"Okay."

"May I speak to your—oh, here's Nick, I think he wants to say hi."

Her son grabbed the telephone. For one giddy moment she thought, But you don't really need the phone, do you? Thirty-odd years of givens blew the thought away. She focused on Bob and Elizabeth, on matters she felt at home with. If Bob and Elizabeth—why not?

5.

A voice yelled from the end of the hall that Mary Girard was wanted on the telephone.

"I hope it's not Mrs. Everts canceling," Mary said to her roommate, as she got up from her desk. She liked babysitting, didn't do it just for the money the way a lot of other nursing students did, and she loved sitting for Daisy Everts. There was always a refrigerator full of good food, though Mrs. Everts sometimes overdid the raw veggies, and there was a big color TV with cable because Mrs. Everts's cousin whose apartment it was worked in television, and Daisy was unfailingly cheerful—happy at the table, happy in the bath, willing enough to pop into bed at the appointed hour.

"Hello?" Mary said into the pay phone.

"Mary? Hello. How are you? This is Oliver Gray."

"Hi, Mr. Gray. How's James?"

"He's fine. Mary, I was wondering, would you like to have dinner sometime?"

"You mean babysit in the evening?" The Grays called on her less than the other Playgroup parents, but once or twice Mary had stayed with James on a Monday when the housekeeper was away and Mrs. Gray had something urgent to do.

"I meant have dinner with me," Oliver Gray said. "Or maybe with me and another man."

Mary observed herself with clinical detachment as her cardiopulmonary system responded to his words.

"Mary?"

"I don't understand, Mr. Gray," she said, though she understood perfectly.

"There must be lots of restaurants you've dreamed about going to. Windows on the World? You look as though you enjoy eating. I bet you enjoy lots of things."

Mary stared at her fun house reflection in the metal of the coin phone. Even in the kindest of department store mirrors her face was round, her body was plain heavy, her hair hung down and didn't do anything. She thought of Mrs. Gray's elegant figure and bouncy blond hair. And nice. "Mr. Gray? Someone told you nursing students were easy?"

"I like you, Mary. I think you deserve a little fun."

"Mr. Gray? Do you know what I think of you? I think you're garbage. You have a nice wife and an adorable son, and if you ever call me again, I will tell Mrs. Gray what you are."

"She's not terribly interested in what I am. Let me give you my office number in case you change your mind."

Mary thought about her special silver whistle. Some men were better put down with words. "Garbage!" she repeated to Mr. Oliver Wendell Gray of Park Avenue. "I'd rather have dinner on the Bowery with some filthy wino. You can take your office number and stuff it." She hung up the phone, went back to her room and rinsed away the conversation with hydrogen peroxide, undiluted.

6.

After Daisy was born, I put my vagina out to pasture. It had done the work I'd primed it and primped it for over a decade; it had delivered me; in turn I would deliver it from the tyranny of desire.

The retired one hadn't sent euphoric postcards but it hadn't protested, either. Now, to my dismay, the protestations were coming. It's boring out here in the grass. Enough with the buttercups already. I miss the streets, broken glass and all. Send me a ticket home.

You could fairly say I'd engineered the griping. Invite a fellow to breakfast, and thoughts are bound to happen. There he was, sitting at the small pale round oak table with Daisy and me, all khaki hair and jokes for the kid and coffee cooling in the cup and the crumbs of toasted Vermont sweet bread everywhere. How not to feel that bed had already happened for us? I was convinced that my pillow remembered the bones of his face, that my sheets had his body smells trapped in their devious folds. Ken Huysman and I hadn't kissed, we hadn't so much as exchanged lubricious looks, he had been every inch the solicitous neighbor playing to my anxious mama; but this breakfast scene, these intimate crumbs, banged at my attention and put the lie to mere sequence. Our first time would be our second time.

I'd thought about men over the last three years, God knows. I'd thought about them intensely over the last two months, since our move back to New York. I'd taken Daisy to the Museum of Natural History on rainy Saturday mornings, I'd smiled at the divorced daddies grappling with the hoods on the jackets of small boys, I'd sailed out a joke or two over the head of tyrannosaurus rex. I owed Daisy the search. I'd snared the best DNA for her making, but three-year-olds don't give a fig for genes, they want to walk down the street hand in hand in hand. If she had three Brussels sprouts on her plate, she named them Mama, Baby, and Papa. Basic is basic.

I had a basic too. I might have been heavily invested in styling myself extraordinary, but I didn't altogether place myself outside the herd. I needed coffee to get going in the morning, and Christmas carols made me cry, and I wanted to see another adult-size toothbrush in my bathroom. I sized up the way the daddies handled hoods and I thought about them handling me.

Thoughts are one thing and juices are another, though, and this morning, this innocent breakfast, was the first time in three years that my juices had run. Ken Huysman was too boyish for me, was maybe the enemy, but he was a man whose work it was to nurture children, and what bigger turn-on was there for me? He could open his heart absolutely to a Daisy not of his loins; he would want me the more for being her mother. I imagined a bed with the three of us in it, Daisy asleep against my breast, Ken's gentle breath on the back of my neck, the room rocking with tenderness. All the kinks of the world had claimed me in turn. Now I wanted one, and one alone, the most insidious by far, the ultimate, the killer, the owner: I wanted the love of a man who loved my child, I wanted sex at home.

Daisy could sense my lusts. I could tell. She shot me looks of complicity and some plain old edgy glances. I came back to the hard and now. I reached for the coffee.

Ken drained his dregs before I could offer to dump them, made the appropriate face, held out his cup. I filled it. Daisy held out her pretend cup. I pretended to fill it. We said cheers all around.

Ken gave Daisy a preppy smile, a golly gosh gee whiz aren't we both terrific smile. "You make sensational coffee, Daisy," he said. "You can have me for breakfast anytime."

Daisy had gone to a few proms herself. She flung her shoulders about, she cocked her gorgeous head, her mouth and eyes were astonished *O*'s. "I didn't make the coffee, Ken." She looked exceedingly pleased at the feel of his name in her mouth. "Only grown-ups make coffee, didn't you know that? My mom made the coffee." Her right arm described an elegant arc. She pointed my way.

"Your mom? Made the coffee? That nice woman over there?" Her straight man mugged astonishment of his own. "Hooray for your mom, I say. You can still have me for breakfast, Ms. Daisy, anytime you want."

"I'm having you for breakfast." Daisy gobbled at a Huysman arm, his blue Oxford cloth sleeve rolled up two notches, pale hair on the forearm, serious tendons at the wrist—I must have been right about the squash games, I thought. Daisy gobbled; she cracked up at her own cleverness. The grown-ups smiled.

Our eyes met over the smiles, and all at once the lubricity was flagrantly there. My stomach quaked, my lips sprang apart, my tongue jammed against my teeth. I had to look away, run away. "More coffee?" I asked stupidly. Ken's cup was still brimming. "Yes, please," I unfunnily answered myself. I topped up my cup with a brew I had no use for.

But sexual encounter between Ken Huysman and me was happenstance, a coefficient of the time and place we lived in, of our looks and brains and age and unfetteredness. Desire might own the moment; it was quite beside the point. I'd called Ken Huysman because fear had called me, and he was a wall against the fear. I'd called him because he was more dangerous than the danger he was making me feel safe from, and I had to meet that danger and know it perfectly well and get us beyond it to the only real safety there was.

He'd come minutes after I called him. He'd done a brisk security check—the dead bolt and the thick chain at the front door, the structural steel gate at the window in Daisy's room which led to the fire escape. First rate, he'd declared. Safe as houses. Daisy had woken up, and the next thing I knew, he was reading *Tom Kitten* to a snuggly little girl, and I was in the kitchen bending my wrist to a pot of scrambled eggs.

Now what? I'd not only let him get a foot in the doorway, I'd invited him to come on in and have his shoes shined. Would he take the invitation to mean he was free to pursue his ambition to dissect the heart of the Playgroup? I knew he wanted nothing less. The only issue was how he would proceed. Maybe he'd offer a little dinner in return for the curdy eggs, then pop the big *Q* when he had me wined up and wound down.

Hey, Mrs. Mozart, you want to do right by your kid?

And Iceman has a penis, just like Daddy.

Daisy knew about the clams. She KNEW about the

clams. She KNEW about Stephanie and Nick, and James is coming later. And their eyes, and the toys they shared, and the rhymes, and the castles they sculpted together—

You want them to be different, said Heidi. And Jack—I could hear him so clearly, I could almost smell his spice—Jack would laugh and shake the silvery head and say, Must you go to bed with every magician who wants to saw you in half?

She KNEW.

Thomas wandered into the room, made familiar with Ken's moccasins, wandered off again.

Ken said reluctantly, "I suppose I better clear out before your gang arrives."

I'd volunteered to take Stephanie and Nick for Elizabeth, whose James was sick; Ken had heard my side of the conversation.

"You have to go? Maybe you can meet the kids another time." I was deliberately thick, happily cruel. I got up from the table, ever the gracious hostess. "Thanks for coming over the way you did. You were very sweet. I can't believe I made such a fuss about a phone call." He made no move. I briskly collected plates and carted them into the kitchen.

Now he got up and followed, with a crockery tub of butter and a squeezable plastic bear full of honey. "I don't have to go," he said mildly. "I don't have any appointments until this afternoon. May I stay? I'd like to play with the Playgroup."

My shoulders tightened so, I could almost hear the twang. My temples pulled their usual number. If I said yes? If I said no? "What are these kids?" I bleated. "Do you know?"

Ken leaned back against the shelf that ran the width of the window. Light bounced through the rumpled hair, weaving golden threads among the khaki. "We know a Playgroup syndrome exists—clusters of children who bond very deeply and have a kind of aggregate strength we don't see elsewhere. We don't know why it occurs among some groups and doesn't occur among others. We're examining every conceivable factor. Race, religion, age of parents, proximity to microwaves, the cereals the kids eat. There may be a sexual link—a mother's partners prior to conceiving a child."

"Come on. Daisy may be what she is because of what I did one spring afternoon my freshman year in college?"

"It's just one theory," Ken said.

I couldn't let go of it. "That's flat earth theory. The sun revolves around the earth. Madness."

"Darwin believed any of a mother's mates might affect a subsequent offspring. What did you do that afternoon in college? Want to show me?"

"I'm going to run away. I'm going to take Daisy away."

"Jill. Jill. Listen to me. Don't you realize? Daisy is what a child ought to be. It's the scared, closed-up, dead-end child who's the perversion. It's the parents of those kids who ought to be tearing their hair and wondering where it all went wrong."

"Charles Darwin believed that? The real Charles Darwin?"

"None other," Ken said.

"Well, so much for Charles Darwin," I tried. But I was as reluctant to dismiss new ideas as I was slow to accept them. I'd heard a dozen charlatans grandly proclaim that the magic of one era was the science of the next—and it happened to be a truth. Primitive healers putting mold to wounds anticipated Fleming's work with penicillin. Twenty years from now, someone might get a Nobel Prize for undoing the work about DNA that had won Crick and Watson their Nobel. I folded my arms across my chest. "Do I get the footnotes? Lay it on me, doctor. Spare me nothing."

"I like what we call the infection hypothesis," Ken said. "We know sperm dies within a few days after ejaculation—loses its power to fertilize—but some part of its disintegrated substance might linger on, with a very long latency period, like certain germs."

"Nice. Like all the brave new venereal diseases."

"Exactly. Only instead of affecting a mother directly, this germ affects her future children. A woman has all her ova when she's born, so in a sense anything that happens to her from day one happens to her ova."

I strained to hear a summons from Daisy, a summons from anywhere else. I tried to think Ken away, but mine was an ordinary mind and he stayed where he was, with the light in his hair and a kind little smile on his face. Damn the kindness. I wasn't collapsing without a fight.

"Okay," I said. "Given—just for the moment—that your ludicrous hypothesis may have merit, how on earth does it explain the Playgroup? We're hardly an incestuous bunch of old friends. Elizabeth Gray was a virgin when she married, and she's not about to take a lover, no matter how horrible her husband is. Jackie fools around when she's away from home, and I guess Heidi had a couple of lovers in college, but you're not going to tell me there's some wondrous man who's figured in all our lives. Anyway," I sailed on triumphantly, "what about Stephanie's older sister?" I was sure I had him now. "She's a normal precocious New York eight-year-old. If Heidi had a lover in college who affected Stephanie, why didn't he get to Julie?"

He shrugged. "Suppose this germ can survive several generations of transference. Then you and Heidi and Elizabeth and Jackie needn't have a lover in common. Enough that if you all trace your lovers' lovers' lovers, you eventually get back to a common source. Is Elizabeth's horrible husband promiscuous? There you are."

"But it seems so improbable that we'd link up." I opened the refrigerator door, I looked inside. Wanting cold comfort? "There are seven million stories in the naked city." I slammed the door shut.

"In fact, the improbability is that you wouldn't link up. I have some calculations that will make your eyes pop. I'll show you tonight."

"Tonight?"

"You'll have dinner with me, won't you? As that nice old witch said to Hansel, you could use some fattening up. I know a place that makes sensational tortellini. We could have a bottle of Brunello, and an arugula salad—"

My tongue leaped at the thought of the tangy arugula sneaking up behind the creamy tortellini. I was sure they were cooked with cream in Ken's restaurant. Here was a man who liked his rough and smooth together. We would have recognitions in bed. Too many? "Thanks," I said, "but I don't think so. I'm busy tonight, actually," I tacked on, truthfully but feebly. "Anyway, what about Julie? I'd bet anything Heidi and Henry have been monogamous since they met. They're fetishists about the sanctity of marriage. How did the Julie ovum escape this invasive pervasive latent potent germ of yours?" I felt something maidenly happen to my cheeks. "Germ of someone's, I mean."

"If I give you the right answer, will you have dinner with me?"

"A true answer?"

"All too true, Mama. The truest, saddest thing I know. One of life's mean tricks. I shouldn't tell it to you. You'll use it as an escape hatch." The brown eyes reproached me in advance.

"Tell me."

"Okay." Arms crossed, ankles crossed. A well-defended igloo, my Iceman. "Julie probably did have the special something. Nearly all three-year-olds have it to some degree, maybe only to a tiny degree, but it's there, a magical openness that sets them apart from other human beings. You've read the literature. Even the most conservative of the early childhood experts waxes rhapsodic about three. And the magic goes. I've met five-year-olds who were geniuses, but I never met a magical five-year-old. They close down. Parents' fears, the schools, maybe some internal chemical changes—the magic just goes. If Julie had met other kids like herself, if the right grown-up had helped, she might be something today that would make the planet take notice. Instead she's normal. What a joke. Normal!" His arms flew apart. "We're deaf men telling Mozart that silence is normal. If no one intervenes, Daisy's magic will dissipate just the way the smaller magic disappears from all kids by a certain age. She'll be one more bright nice little girl the day she starts kindergarten. Congratulations."

"Oh," I said. I thought about clams. I thought about many things. "Oh."

"Maybe she'll have some undefined regret all her life," Ken said, "some feeling of being cheated, but who doesn't? She won't even remember what she was, her mind will be so different, so many doors will be closed. Normal. Jill, don't you see? If we can teach the kids with the big magic to hold onto it, to use it, they might pave the way for all kids to hold onto their magic. Was the planet ever more in need of magicians? Look where normal has taken us. If that's what you want for Daisy, for civilization—well, you've got it. Guaranteed. All you have to do is do nothing. You'll have a normal five-year-old. I tell you that as confidently as I tell the mother of a newborn that her baby will smile a social smile around three months and sit up around six months and walk and talk around twelve months." He wiped sweat off his forehead. "Let's have that bottle of Brunello so you can toast the inevitable erosion of what's most special in your daughter and I can drown my sorrows."

"You are the unfair beast of the western world," I said. "When I was pregnant I was full of thoughts about how the world would be different because of my child. Like every other romantic mother. You know that. You're keying into it." I was whining like the least magical of children, but I couldn't stop, didn't want to stop. "Isn't it enough that I'm bringing up a kid on my own? A truly great kid? Whole and happy? Now you want me to be the mother of the whole goddamn future. Who do you think you are?"

"Just another piano teacher. Who wants to have dinner

with you. Let me show you those probability calculations." He got out the boyish grin. "Let me show you a good time, lady."

"You—" I shook my fists at him.

"I know." He gave me one of those blasted understanding nods. "Mixed metaphors are a bitch. I do like you for yourself alone and not your silver-haired girl. Believe me, I almost wish I didn't. I could use a little professional distance at the moment. I know I'm asking a lot of you, but I'm also taking a lot on myself."

"I don't want to hear your troubles, doctor."

"And you won't. It'll be jokes from dusk to dawn. You could do a lot worse. I'm cute, don't smoke, have decent manners without being stuffy, I'm safe—"

"Safe!" I walked back out to the living-cum-dining room to collect the salt and pepper mill, to collect myself. If only Kenneth William Huysman were some Siggy sort of patriarchal shrink, with musty breath and hushed gonads and an absence of apocalyptic visions and ambitions. And how nice if there were a second Ken Huysman, your average decent divorced lawyer who would be properly awed that I was Jack Keefe's ex-mistress, who would bring Daisy stuffed thingies and not see beyond her clownish beauty. I could heap my anxieties and hopes at the feet of the first, drink cream from the hands of the second.

Daisy was still at the table, searching under forks, placemats, glasses, for something. She crooned, "One bacon, two bacons, three bacons, four bacons, this girl wants some more bacons." She liked her poem so much, she let us hear it again. Then, "Five bacons are alive bacons."

I said, "I like to fix bacon. But nix on six pieces of bacon. Your stomach will be achin'."

Ken was right there. "Surrounded by daft women."

"What was that?" I cupped hand to ear. "I didn't hear you. I'm a little daft." I fled to the kitchen, suddenly overcome. That perfectly ordinary passage was more exotic than peacocks to me. This was the first time, you see. Daisy and her mama and a fellow makes three. The cornerstone of civilization, the fundamental configuration, but so new to jaded me that my mind was making the most improbable jumps. He did like us, by God. He wasn't here because he liked us, but he did like us. I was blown away.

He came up behind me.

"Oh, no," I said.

"Oh, yes."

I felt his breath in my hair. The skies were crowded with kisses awaiting permission to land.

I moved out of range. "I'm not ready."

"Aren't you? Whenever." He was so casual I wondered if we were talking about the same thing. Of course we were. We might not agree on much, but we were always talking about the same thing. Had I felt that before, even with Jack?

"Should I cover the butter with tinfoil?" Ken asked. "Or just put it in the refrigerator?"

"There's a lid for the pot. In the butter compartment in the refrigerator door." My heart was speeding. The sexy talk.

"Such order," he said. "Admirable. Frightening."

"Don't worry, it's pure chaos, starting half an inch down. You have to submit to chaos, don't you think, when you have a child? Otherwise you go crazy?"

"And the kids go crazy. You're very brave."

"Me? The woman who was scared by a stupid phone call?"

He waved away the phone call. His fine hands made me want to sit on my own, with their kitchen cuts and worried-at cuticles. "I meant the chaos," he said. "That's hardly your environment of choice, is it?"

I groaned, though I was more relieved than upset to catch him being foreign. "You dress New England, doctor," I said, "but I have a feeling you're about to start talking California. Yes, I'm very controlled. Overcontrolled, if you like. I have no interest in changing. Want to know an ambition of mine? I'd like to be one of those yogis who stay conscious even in sleep."

"But you've brought up Daisy to be different," he said. "That child is fearless."

"Nobody's perfect."

"Come on. You wanted that for her, and you deserve a dozen medals for making it happen. It's the flaws, you know, not the virtues, that parents are usually most eager to perpetuate in their children. For confirmation of company or just to reduce the chance of conflict. But you went the other way. Bravo, Jill."

"You're a condescending creep, did you know that?" But I said it unrancorously. "Anyway, I'm not at all sure I agree that being controlled is a flaw." He didn't answer, and I didn't press the point. I said, "I just want her to be able to go to Paris someday and be in love and eat croissants."

"And so she will."

"Even if you take her to stranger places?" I retreated one last time. "Who sent you, dammit?"

"Who sent *for* me? Tortellini tomorrow night? They do them with cream and peas and prosciutto."

"Look, maybe I can work it out for tonight. There's an opening at Heidi Kahn's gallery. I suppose I could bring you. Want another coffee?"

"Do I know you well enough to say I like it very hot?"

I turned a flame on under the Chemex. Daisy came running into the kitchen waving her dearest doll.

"Grouch has to make a pit stop," she announced.

"Okay, darling. We'll be right back, Ken."

"We'll be right back, Ken," Daisy echoed. She put her hand into my hand as we hurried toward the bathroom. Most often she went on her own, sometimes she wanted my company or help. I liked the balance of independence and need. I liked so much about her. "I think," she said confidingly, "that Grouch's panties are a little damp. Because overalls are hard for a dolly sometimes."

"Aren't they just?" Grouch wore a dress, but who was

counting? "Never mind. That's why washing machines exist. I love you, girlfriend."

"I love you, Mom. And I love Grouch, and Iceman, and my mice, and Stephanie, and Nick, and James—and Ken," she added proudly.

My heart thudded. "Do you? That's grand. It's nice to love. Uh-oh," playing the game, pretending to be surprised, "It looks as though Grouch isn't the only damp one. Let's get these off. Do you want privacy? Or shall I stay? Put them in the hamper, honey. Please."

"Stay."

I perched on the rim of the bathtub. The lobby buzzer sounded. Heidi or Jackie? It was too early—just past ten, And—damn, no, don't be an idiot, only coincidence—Daisy wasn't shouting "Kids!" the way she usually did when Playgroup people were arriving. I ran to the kitchen. The ugly phone call lived again in my head. Where had Ken gone? I asked the intercom who was there. I tensed for viciousness.

"Everts?" came back through the perforated metal. The voice was a man's, rough, unfamiliar, not the voice that had poisoned the dawn. "Florist."

"What?"

"Green Witch Florist," through the static. "Flowers for Everts."

Green Witch Florist! Shades of my Greenwich Village days, my blossom days, my perfect little apartment days. Who—? "Six E," I shouted into the intercom, and buzzed.

I was assaulted by a sizzle and a burning smell. The Chemex was boiling. I turned off the flame. Who—? Daisy called to me from the bathroom. Submit, submit. Where had Ken gone? He hadn't flown, had he, put off by my ungracious invitation to Heidi's opening? I looked into the living room. There he was, reading the spines of the books.

"Do you mind?"

I minded. "My underwear is in the middle bureau drawer in the big bedroom," I growled.

"Mama! I need you!" came from the bathroom, simultaneously with a rapping at the front door of the apartment—the flowers.

"Coming!" I called out. "Please come to that opening with me," I said to Ken, surprising us both with my warmth. I ran off in two directions at once.

I did what needed doing for Daisy, pointed her toward dry panties and jeans, signed for the flowers, and dug out a dollar for the delivery man because he looked eighty-eight years old and had probably taken the subway. What had happened to Slow Steve the delivery boy? I took the long shiny green box into the kitchen. I stopped.

The delivery tag didn't say "Jill Everts," it said "Daisy Everts."

"Can I open the box, Mom?"

"This one's mine, baby," I said, interposing my body between Daisy and the box. I flipped the tag over so she wouldn't see her name. I flashed her a gay old smile, hating myself for a coward, a censor. In fifteen years would I open her mail if an envelope smelled funny to me, if the angle of the stamp looked wrong? Maybe I was just jealous because they weren't, after all, my flowers. I left the green box in the sink and carted Daisy out to the living room and Ken.

"Would you read to Daisy for five minutes?" I said.

Ken said he would. Daisy considered objecting, then went to get a book.

A bomb, I thought, mocking myself but completely serious. Tarantulas. Or maybe, silliest of persons, flowers? I took a deep breath. I opened the box.

Flowers.

They were big splashy Gerber daisies in poster-paint reds and yellows and oranges, no two quite the same tint, eleven of them. Who—? I worked the card out of the small white envelope tucked into the frondy ferns. The card said, "One more Daisy makes a dozen. Love and kisses too from a Daddy who misses you."

I backed away from the box. My hands sought the sanity

of the rim of the kitchen sink. Breathing hurt. I held onto the sink but I didn't want to hold on, I wanted to fall, give up, go under, because the cruelty of it, the hate in it, someone hating so much—

"Mommy?"

I surfaced. "Honey?"

"Hello," Ken said. "I've just been introduced to Grouch. I think that means I'm in. Jill?"

"Curfew, I think. Kids'll be here any minute. And I just can't—not today. Would you take these flowers?" I thrust the green box into his arms. "And give them to someone? Anyone? There's Leroy Hospital down on Sixty-first Street . . . anywhere."

"You're an interesting woman," Ken said.

Daisy said, "Mom, Grouch has to make another pit stop."

"You didn't send them, did you?"

"A really big pit stop, Mom—" tugging.

"No, I didn't. I wish I had. Oh. I take it back. I'm glad I didn't." He relieved me of the box.

"Mom—"

"Okay, baby. Sorry. Let's go."

7.

Nora Keefe quit her corner now and then to take a solitary walk. She addressed no one, let her eyes rub up against no other eyes. Her neighbors knew about her need to stay cocooned. Strangers seemed to understand. No tourist had ever asked her the way to MacDougal Street. No mugger had ever made moves toward her alligator shoulder bag.

Usually she walked west to the Hudson River, or south to the Italian neighborhood, or east to the rough vividness of Old World poverty, but today was nothing like a usual day. She walked north, up Fifth Avenue, past the linen wholesalers and foreign bookshops, up through the densely populated sidewalks of midtown, up into the heart of expensive commerce and out of it into the quiet Sixties. She steeled herself to her purpose. Head down. Eyes on the sidewalk. Shoulders hunched. Breathing shallow breaths so she didn't have to share oxygen. Daisy. Daisy.

She thought about Jack referring to her "ways." She thought about Dr. Howard and how proud he would be of her for venturing to foreign shores—never mind the shallow breaths. Too bad she would never tell him. She'd asked him once if her affliction had a name. Was she xenophobic? She thought that had a certain ring—she imagined a garden abloom with xenophobias, in various shades of blood. He'd said yes, and no, there was no simple name for her, and she'd said, "How about misanthropic little bitch?" and he'd laughed, and she'd liked him for laughing—she'd wanted to suck his cock, to let him spank her with a file folder. She'd wanted to be like other people and have lunch with him at the Plaza Oyster Bar.

Here it was. Sexty-sex Street. Jillville.

She went to the playground first, striking attitudes—nature lover, grandmother. No Daisy, she knew at once. The children here were all ordinary. But she recognized the swings from Mr. Kojak's photographs, and the sight of them was a hundred kinds of torture to tender places. She dwelled. She turned. She watched another watcher, a tall fair man in a trenchcoat. She verged on giggles. What if it were Mr. Kojak? And what if he reported, during their next conversation, that he'd seen some musty old scumbag of a woman hanging around their darling Daisy's playground? It would be very much like Mr. Kojak to wear a trenchcoat on a piping warm June day. But Mr. Kojak was short, she was sure of it. The man in the trenchcoat was nearly as tall as Jack—too tall to be happy in phone booths.

A small boy whizzed past her, stirring her air. She started. She let out a shriek. The man in the trenchcoat emanated concern. He took a step in her direction—Nora had forgotten to maintain her invisible shield. She erected it now, painting the air with witchy hands. The man withdrew his attention and turned the other way.

But if Daisy—

Different. Her own. Her clone. Daisy could look at her, talk to her, walk to her, hug her knees. Hunt for milk at her breasts. Retrace the route of your birth, I baked you in my hearth, darling flower. Daisy, Daisy, give me your answer, do. I'm half crazy, all for the love of you—

She left the playground and the park. She crossed Fifth Avenue. She went east on Sixty-sixth Street. And there it was, across from the Armory, number 114, as eerily real as something come true from a dream. She counted eight stories. She studied the facing on the bricks, the shamrock pattern wrought-iron grillwork that covered the front door, the tattered green canopy out to the curb. The potted dwarf Japanese yews on both sides of the entrance needed water. No doorman, dear Jill. How disappointing for you. You made it to the Upper East Side, and no doorman. But it's better that way, isn't it? No one to report on your comings and goings and goings and comings and comings. Whore. The Village stinks better without you. Did he bring you violets from my greenhouse? He brought you violets for your fur. Fuck me, Mr. Mayor, say it with flowers, fuck me with flowers, Daisy.

She set aside her misanthropy long enough to go to the Parkview Realty Corporation, which she had decided to favor out of the real estate agencies listed in the Yellow Pages, and to say, with a civility which would have thrilled Dr. Howard, that she was Mrs. Nora Mayor from Greenwich, Connecticut, and she wanted a summer sublet immediately if not sooner—someplace very, very nice, money no object, preferably near the park, with a child's room if at all possible because she hoped to have as her occasional overnight guest her darling granddaughter, her reason for coming to New York, you see, because her daughter was ill and might have to undergo surgery, and her son-in-law would have his hands full with the boys, she did love the boys awfully much but not as much as her daughter's little girl, her dearest Lily.

8.

"Mark? Hi. It's Heidi Samuels. Remember?"

"Holy speculum, it really is you! How are you, dear old thing? I couldn't believe it when my nurse told me. Where are you?"

"About ten blocks away. Where I've been for the last fifteen years."

"You're well? Successful? Married? A ma? The Samuels is just your Ms. nomer, I assume."

"Just so you would recognize the name. I'm married to Henry Kahn. The art dealer? We have a gallery on Madison and Sixty-sixth, German Expressionist mostly. He's the most difficult man in New York and I'm madly in love with him. We have two darling girls. You?"

"Married, divorced, married again. She's a surgeon—extraordinary woman. No kids, but we're keeping the tubes open. I'm, I don't know, the third or fourth best ENT man in New York, and every time I go to the theater, I wish I were a playwright. But you didn't call to hear that."

"No. Mark. Do you remember—? Oh, this is silliness. I shouldn't—"

"Remember what? I probably remember things you wish I'd forgotten. You still like having whipped cream licked off your thighs?"

"Oh, Mark, did we really?"

"Did we! And what about the time—"

"All right, all right. Do you remember, the day you got your acceptance letter from med school, and you said when you were a doctor you'd get me anything I wanted, and I said—I bet you don't remember this, do you? You probably think I'm cracked—and I said when you were a doctor you'd feel differently about it? Do you remember? Oh, Mark. I'm sorry. I shouldn't have called."

"What's up, Heidi? Abortions are legal now."

"Thanks, Mark, I think I know that. No, I was wondering—well, I'm getting terribly fat, you see. Diet pills."

"I don't believe it. You had the metabolism of a Porsche. Do you remember the time we went to what's that place in Little Italy and you had three different kinds of pasta? I used to think you took secret enemas. What do you weigh?"

"A hundred-twenty."

"And you're—five feet, eight? Nine? Bones."

"Mark, I weighed one hundred-twelve when you knew me, and it's what I ought to weigh now. I just can't shake those eight pounds. Look, the truth is, I'm becoming a compulsive eater. I eat while I'm cooking, I eat while I'm cleaning up, I eat the leftovers on the kids' plates. This morning Julie didn't touch her breakfast, and I ate it—Familia. Strawberries. Whole milk. After eating my own Familia and strawberries and whole milk."

"Maybe what's wrong, old thing, is that Julie didn't eat breakfast."

"So when did you get your degree in psychiatry? I'm sorry I—"

"How old is Julie?"

"Eight. The other one is three. Nearly three and a half."

"Well. There you are. Eight is one of the toughest times, did you know that? That's when they realize they're mortal, poor buggers. And three and a half—no wonder you want a boost in the energy department."

"Mark, they're fabulous kids. With all due respect, I just want to lose eight pounds. Two of them by tonight. We've got an opening, and at this rate I'm going to have to wear one of Henry's old shirts. If you'd like to come, and your wife, it should be very splashy. The mayor is coming, some Metropolitan Opera people, Josh Baskin—"

"Who?"

"The new Yankee shortstop. Don't you live in this

world? Not to mention the show itself—but nobody ever does mention the show itself. It's called '1935.' Paintings done all around the globe that year. A slice of time. A beautiful round slice. Nobody's done anything quite like it. We're very excited. Oh, Mark, I can't bear being fat."

"Amphetamines are controlled substances, I don't suppose I have to tell you. I can't just call your friendly neighborhood pharmacist and have them send over thirty Dexies. Anyway, I wouldn't. A promise is a promise, but I have to answer to my conscience, not to mention various government agencies. This isn't a plot to get my license, is it? You'll have to come see me and let me play doctor, and then we'll discuss it. Why didn't you call your physician, by the by? Don't tell me. He's a friend of the family, right? And the most difficult husband in New York wouldn't approve?"

"Can I come now, Mark? Julie's at school, Stephanie's with her Playgroup, the gallery can spare me for an hour. Can I come right now?"

9.

For the first time in nearly a year, Master James Gray, a famous nonsleeper, was napping of a morning.

Elizabeth stood over his bed looking down at the delicate face, loving the echoes of her own face, loving the absence of her husband in the finely honed small features, feeling guilty about loving the absence of her husband, chasing away the guilt by wondering if she shouldn't worry about a boy who only an hour ago had been engaged in a raucous puke. Better check him out.

She laid tender maternal fingers on his forehead—temperature normal. She eyed the nuances of his color—slightly flushed about the cheeks, but the sun and wind on the Staten Island ferry crossing were more probably to blame than illness. She weighed the quality of his sleep—

undreamy at the moment, peaceful. This was not a boy about whom to be anxious. He'd vomited, he was napping, he would wake up whole and hungry, ready for Central Park. She kissed his blond hair, the hair she snipped locks from and bore in secret envelopes to the woman in charge of the color of Elizabeth's own long hair. She perfected the drift of his top sheet and summerweight blanket. She edged toward the doorway—and didn't go through it.

James looked *edible* lying there, like a petit four on a flowered plate, delicately crumbed, sweetly frosted, waiting for the fingers that would carry it to the mouth that would crush it and swallow it to death. "I could eat you to pieces," Mrs. DuPont, their housekeeper, sometimes said, stroking his vanilla skin. Lots of people said it. Strangers on the street—he was that kind of child. Because his cheeks—

"Elizabeth?"

"Oliver?" Her husband's voice got her out of her son's room and down the spiral staircase that linked the two floors of the apartment. Oliver home at ten-thirty of a Tuesday morning? Had the bank collapsed, the president been shot? She pushed her hair back off her face. She repented of her green Indian gauze cotton shirt and pants, grabbed from the closet after the hasty shower that had followed James's bout. Oliver always said the outfit reminded him of a surgeon's scrub suit.

"Where is he?" Oliver Gray, small boy petulant in seersucker, stood there, legs slightly apart, posture accentuating the beefy shoulders and low center of gravity, right hand gripping the blue-and-white leather tennis togs bag Elizabeth had given him one Christmas. "Where's the kid? You have them today, don't you? Where is he?"

"Oliver? Is something wrong? What is it?"

Oliver thrust his tennis bag at her. "Open it." His cheeks were puffy with temper. His gray eyes had taken on a scary yellow cast.

Elizabeth unzipped the bag. Her senses recoiled. The bag was heaped high with garbage, a pig's feast—sucked-out orange skins, coffee grounds nesting moistly in paper filters, mucousy eggshells, carrot peel, spinach shards, a leavening of tea leaves. Beneath the stinking muck peeped the cuff of once creamy flannel shorts, only recently perfected by Mrs. DuPont's iron.

"Where is he, Elizabeth?"

"Oliver?"

"In his room?"

"You think James did this?" Elizabeth could not take her eyes or nose from the awful bag. Then she thought she saw something crawling among the crud, and she gave a little shriek and dropped the bag, right onto the blue-and-ivory Peking rug.

"Who else?" Oliver looked a stranger as he issued the words—not the man who had made a child with her, not even an irate neighbor whose window had been broken by a baseball. He was the person placed by fate on the highway at the moment when you needed to drive too fast and impose your existence on others.

"Madness," Elizabeth said. "Why would he? How could you?"

"Who else?" Oliver repeated. "You? Mrs. DuPont? The Shadow? Come on."

"But—" Elizabeth forced herself to look down at the bag. She was looking for something without knowing what it was. She found it. "There! You see? The coffee filters. We use a Melitta. Flat bottom filters. These are Chemex. Pointed. You see?"

Oliver looked at the bag. He looked at his wife. He jerked loose his red-and-gold striped tie. "Then who?" His voice still accused.

"I don't know. Someone at the bank?"

"At the bank?" As though she'd suggested God had personally staged the insult.

Elizabeth sat down on the spiral staircase. She studied the man she'd been married to with the full array of hopes

When she'd first met him, she'd been enchanted by his self-possession, his indifference to fashion and the opinions of others. He could wait a week, a year, forever to try the quenelles at the new four-star restaurant the world was flocking to, to see the film that was generating lines from here to there. He could spend February on this year's in Out Island, or last year's, or he could stay at home. Slowly Elizabeth had learned the indifference was all-inclusive. Oliver would have been as happy, or unhappy, with another wife, another child, or possibly with no wife and child at all.

Elizabeth said, "Maybe somebody wanted to see the expression on your face change."

"Jesus." He pushed stubby fingers through his hair.

"What I don't understand," Elizabeth said, "what really upsets me, is why you thought of James. Thought of him first. He loves jokes, but this isn't like putting Legos in your shoes. He loves you. You know that, don't you? To tell you the honest-to-gosh, sometimes I wonder why he does, but he does."

Mrs. DuPont sailed into the room, bearing lemon oil. "Good morning again, Mr. Gray. You're here to see the little fellow? Don't worry, I guard him, he is fine."

Oliver looked puzzled.

"He's upstairs asleep," Elizabeth said. "He vomited just after you left. I got Jill to take the Playgroup."

"You didn't call me," Oliver said defensively, as though she were attacking him for not knowing about their son's condition.

"If I had?"

He shrugged. He grinned weakly. "I wouldn't have done a damn thing."

"Oh, Ollie." Elizabeth sighed, but her voice was warmer. There was this much to be said for Oliver Wendell Gray, little banker: at his best he had the decency to concede what he was like at his worst.

"He's a wonderful boy," she said.

"Does he have a virus?" Oliver asked politely.

"It's nothing. He'll probably go to the park this afternoon. He does love you."

"Do you? Love me?"

Elizabeth blinked. She couldn't remember the last time her husband had popped the question. They exchanged expressions of tender appreciation during intercourse, but outside of bed they asked for nothing more affirming than compliments on new clothes.

"You see?" Oliver jumped into her silence. "He gets it all. Everyone knows I'm the insensitive clod of the Western Hemisphere, but don't you think I mind that a little?"

"He lets me love him."

"I don't?"

Elizabeth put her face in her hands, rubbed at her cheekbones. "Oh, heaven, you don't really, do you? If I ask Mrs. DuPont to cook something special for you, or I take a tennis lesson so I'll be a good partner for you, it doesn't really please you. If I do wonderful things in bed, you're pleasured, but you're not pleased. I don't think it pleases you that I'm faithful to you."

"It doesn't displease me." Oliver tried a grin.

"Thanks."

"And pleasing and loving are synonymous? You're faithful to me because you're sexually obsessed with me, wildly devoted to me? Or because you think you're supposed to be faithful?"

"It's the way I want to be," Elizabeth said. "It feels right. I don't really want anyone else. Unlike you."

"You do want someone else."

"I do?"

"James," Oliver said.

"Want him sexually? That's revolting." Elizabeth started to rise, then sank back down onto her step. "I hope you realize that your jealousy of your son is on the verge of being pathological. Over the verge, probably."

"I'm not saying you want to perform unnatural acts with him."

"Thank heaven for small favors," Elizabeth said.

"But there's an intensity of interest in him—"

"Listen, Oliver. I was a virgin when I met you, I've been faithful ever since. I've never even come close to making love with another man. I don't think you can bear that. You think it's some kind of reproach. What did you do, just start a new affair? Or end one? Maybe you dumped some poor teller, and that's why you got garbage dumped in your tennis bag? The tennis bag which I gave you—and now it's got to be thrown out." She gave a satisfied little smile. For once she seemed to have her husband's full attention. Her next words rushed out before she even knew they were forming. "Did you have an affair with Kelly? Is that why she went away?"

"No, I didn't have an affair with Kelly." He looked at a beam of light playing over the roses on the rug. "Absolutely no."

"No? Or absolutely no? The whole world lies between for you, doesn't it, darling?"

"I've got to get down to the bank," Oliver said. He kicked the fouled tennis bag. "I'll put this in the back hallway. Mrs. DuPont can deal with it. May be something salvageable in there. Good thing I keep my rackets at the club."

"Oh, that's a *very* good thing," Elizabeth said. "One of the marvels of the ages. You either throw that bag out, Ollie, or deal with it yourself. You're not asking Mrs. Du-Pont to clean up your messes. Sorry."

"Out it goes then. I'll go upstairs and get some fresh gear. Don't worry," as she moved to let him by, "I won't wake up your angel."

"You haven't forgotten about tonight, have you?" Elizabeth asked.

"What's tonight?"

"The opening at Heidi's gallery."

"Did I say I'd go? You know I hate those things."

"Oliver, I don't believe you. You said you'd sit with James."

"Oh, Christ, did I? I just rescheduled my tennis game for six. Damn lucky to be able to get a court. I'll be home by nine. That cover you?"

"The opening's from five to eight. You promised, dammit. James had it all planned. You'd watch 'Electric Company' together—"

"What's wrong with Mrs. DuPont?"

"She's not his parent, that's what's wrong." Elizabeth started to cry. "You know how I feel about that. You know. Why do you have to act as though we met five minutes ago? What the hell kind of marriage is this? Cancel your damn tennis game. Cancel it."

"I can't cancel it. I'm sorry. Not after what happened this morning. He was right there in the locker room when I opened my bag. Jim Lauterman, from the Federal Reserve. Do you know how humiliated I was? It's not as if I were leaving you in the lurch. Talk about pathology, Elizabeth. You've got to let go of him a little. You'll suffocate him. I think it's a good thing for him to stay with Mrs. DuPont. There ought to be more sitters, more strangers. I should have put my foot down about school this fall instead of that mother-ridden Playgroup. Kids need room to grow."

"We had all the room we needed, and look how we turned out." Elizabeth ran off to the book room and closed the door behind her.

10.

I wanted to work again, for the first time since Daisy's birth.

The desire was as sweet and as focused as my lust for Ken Huysman, and absolutely connected. A certain sort of man had always had the power to make me want to spend my life commuting between bed and kitchen (and now baby). Spring might have come a little late that year but oh how it had come.

I was a cookbook writer, and a good one. I taught people not merely how to cook but how to be cooks, how to get inside the minds, the wrists, of cooks all over the world and thereby how to find all the cooks within themselves. When people read me right, they could throw out all the books, including mine; they could measure without spoons and cups, smell the doneness of pasta, marry rabbit and chocolate, find the nourishment in light. Four of my six books had gone into multiple printings. One—on New England cooking—was a genuine best seller. My only failure was *How to Cook for Your Mother*, which failure I blamed on the cover.

I'd been unhappy about Ken Huysman nosing around the bookshelves because I didn't want him sniffing out my profession. I worked pseudonymously. My parents had persuaded me that a measure of power lay in living part of one's life under a separate name. Would my *nom de cuisine* fool Ken? Not for a minute. I could just hear him saying coyly, "I see you've got some cookbooks by J. Everstill. What nationality is that name, do you think?"

I wanted to tell Daisy about my hunger to work. She might not know exactly what I meant, but she would respond to the intensity of feeling. I didn't want to share the news with Stephanie and Nick, though, and my girl was snug inside some game with them, there were blocks and Lego people and old scarves of mine and poems everywhere.

How to Cook for Your Daughter. Did I dare? For the sisterhood of the bud? Darling little heart of the flower—

But who—?

My mind came to. I went to the telephone. I called the Green Witch Florist and said my name was Jill Everts and please was Nelson there. Nelson had been gone for a year, I was told—moved to Florida to raise avocados. Then maybe somebody else could help? My daughter had received a bunch of Gerber daisies, ever so lovely, but the card didn't have a name, and I didn't recognize the writing, so could they check their records? The man at the other end of the wire told me, none too graciously, that he'd talk with Chick and call me back. I gave him my number.

The kids were laughing. The sound bounced off the Delius in the air, then blended with it, then took over the room. I was desperate to know the joke, but would I get it even if they told me? Childhood was a fortress, not to be stormed, not to be sidled into, no matter how much one had the children's trust and love. All parents were outsiders, weren't they? Not just the parents of these kids like no others? I thought about my own mother and father. Come back, come back, I'll let you in.

The telephone rang. Good—that would be one question answered, a mere million to go. It wasn't the Green Witch Florist, it was Ken Huysman. He felt like a complete ass, he said, but he'd somehow managed to lose his keys, he was locked out of his apartment. Had they maybe dropped out of his pocket when he was roughing around with Daisy in her room? I told him I would look. Near Daisy's bed, he said. I looked, and there were the keys, sheltered by the skirt of Daisy's bedspread. How neat. I went back to the phone and told Ken to come over.

I was hurt, I felt dopey, I was just plain mad. Ken was no key dropper, never mind if he'd stood on his head with my girl. He'd left the keys on purpose so he could come back when Stephanie and Nick were there, I was sure of it.

Well, he was in for a surprise. He'd made the wrong move. I would hand him the keys through a chained-up crack of air; I would hand him his hat. He could stuff some other mother with tortellini. He could dissect little psyches in another part of town.

Relief settled around me. I would confess to Heidi how I'd almost gotten sucked in. I would give her the satisfaction of hearing that she was right. I did want Daisy to be different—had wanted it, anyway. Had seen the error of my wanting. Would wage silliness no longer.

Stephanie asked for apple juice, and the others chimed in, and I served it, and got three thank-you's, and no one spilled a drop. Super terrific kids, they were. No more, no less.

I went over to the bookshelves and took down my collected works. I caressed bindings, dared myself to look at dedications, smiled at my favorite picture—a clear glass tureen of wild mushroom soup, photographed atop a tree stump in deep summer woods near my parents' house. The secret is to chop up some fennel and leek and sauté them in butter for twenty minutes before you throw in the mushrooms. The secret is to know that if you don't have fennel and leek you can still make an exquisite soup.

I heard Stephanie, at the window, call out, "One two three. What do I see?"

Daisy, yards away, facing the dining table, called back, "The umbrella man is watching me."

Nonsense or—

—ultimate sense? Sense beyond sense?

I sauntered to the window, casual as your average elephant. Mrs. Mozart would have done the same. I saw a cop car going by. I saw a stocky mustached man who looked like our local pretzel vendor walking toward the park. I saw a blonde with two Dalmations. I saw a man in a veddy, veddy British trenchcoat shading his eyes as he looked up at our window. He was carrying a furled umbrella.

When Ken got to the door, I invited him right in.

11.

The astonishing thing, to Nora's mind, wasn't the ability of Ms. G. Arthur of the Parkview Realty Corporation to conjure an apartment that sounded made to order for Nora; it was Nora's ability to share an elevator to the apartment with Ms. G. Arthur. It was a six-passenger elevator, tarted from here to there with highly polished chrome which reflected a thousand Ms. Arthurs, distorted. Horrible height, electrocuted hair, blowfish face, arms that did not end in hands, breasts that threatened the borders of the mind. Ms. Arthur was apparently menstruating—she had wanly referred to "cramps." Nora hunkered into a corner of their upwardly mobile gilded cage. She staved off pain with an analgesic that went back to the broken bones of her horsy childhood. One, two, button my shoe. Three, four, close the door. Five, six, pick up sticks. Seven, eight, lay them straight. Nine, ten—

"And here we are," Ms. Arthur said brightly, as the elevator stopped and the doors opened, just in time. Ms. Arthur looked to be about Jill's age, but oh so different. She was a plodder, plump, with frizzy hair and violet-tinted glasses. She wore a seersucker suit, plain stockings, patent leather sandals with chunky heels—dreary career gal stuff. Sluttish in her own way, they all were these days, but at least she didn't sell it on the street. Ms. Arthur fumbled with unfamiliar keys, then got the door unlocked. She held the door with the bulk of her body; Nora had to brush right by her. Nine, ten, a big fat hen.

Into the living room, and for an instant Nora's life swallowed itself and she was home. Home, where people read, and it mattered if the pillows on the sofa got dirty because they'd been bought lovingly, but it didn't matter too much because love was all over the joint. The room yelled Mexico, softly. White woven rugs and baskets and leather and flowers and gods. Old money having fun in the fourth generation.

They were right across the street from the park, from the Sixty-sixth Street playground. Nora couldn't believe her luck. But Mrs. Nora Mayor of Greenwich, Connecticut, was used to having luck on her side.

"How pleasant," she said, merely polite.

"Very different, isn't it?" Ms. Arthur said. "Not to everyone's taste, of course, but for the right person—I always say there's more to life than Louis Quinze. Not that I don't like Louis Quinze—"

"Exactly," Nora said. She perched at the window. She stared at the playground, four stories below. Colors rose and fell. A solo "Mama!," sweet soprano, came piping through the hum and drum of traffic. Nora could have perched there forever, as lost to time as the shirtmaker dress she wore. Her purpose dropped away from her. She was eighteen years old, a debutante, a beginner, a believer, not beleaguered, angled hopefully at Fifth Avenue windows. In her mind she heard Meyer Davis making music. Snowflakes trickled through the fostering light of streetlamps. Perfume owned the air. Any moment she would meet young Jack Keefe, and life would happen.

"If you'd like to see the bedrooms," Ms. G. Arthur said.

"The bedrooms." Nora came back. "We must have bedrooms."

"There's central air conditioning, of course, if you'd like me to—"

"Oh dear, my goodness, no." Nora drew her arms across the frugal plains of her chest. "Sooner a fire in the fireplace."

They walked down a hallway together. Eleven, twelve, dig and delve. Thirteen, fourteen, maids a-courting.

"Here's the master." Big vulgar playground of a bed. "That's a lovely old armoire, isn't it? Plenty of space for your things." Ms. Arthur yanked open a drawer to display the void within.

"Perfectly satisfactory. And the child's room?"

"Oh, you have to see the master bath."

"There's indoor plumbing? What a nice surprise. I'm sure it's fine."

Ms. Arthur produced a titter but didn't relent. The master bath had to be seen. Nora understood when she saw the bidet. Poor dumb seersucker cunt looked quite beside herself. Her first bidet, probably; and probably her last. She would not take a wedding trip to Paris and Rome, as Nora had. Sluicing her juice at the Georges Cinq, at the Excelsior, married, holy, wholly happy.

"It's fine," she said, deliberately disappointing. "May I see the child's room?"

It was a body blow. Bunk beds, made up with Mickey Mouse linens, outrageous reds and blues; shelves stacked with books and games, ten Christmases' worth; a perfect fake log cabin built for one; teddy bears and trucks; the works.

"He's a little older than your granddaughter," Ms. Arthur said, "but if you move some of the games up out of her reach, I think it will work out well. Does she sleep in a crib or a bed?"

For a moment Nora panicked. "A bed. No, a crib. A bed actually, some of the time—"

"In transition," Ms. Arthur said wisely.

"Exactly. When she comes to visit me in Greenwich she sleeps in a bed, so she'll be fine in one here." Did that make sense? It would have to. "In transition. Goodness, I hope the little boy doesn't miss his toys. Such nice things. My— one of my grandsons has a log cabin just like that one." She could almost see him: the silvery blond hair, the rosebud mouth. Jack Junior. No, Jack the third. Except—Jesus— she was married to Mr. Mayor, whose first name was— Norman. N my name is Nora, and my husband's name is Norman, we live in New England, and we sell nuts. "Little Norman," she said.

"Well, the kid who lives here won't have any trouble finding new toys in Japan. That's where all these things are made—the computer toys, anyway." Ms. G. Arthur sighed hugely. "Japan."

Nora had been waiting for that sigh, that sign. She said, "You like to travel?"

"Well, let's put it this way. I *want* to travel. Frankly, I wish I'd become a travel agent, but I heard about this job when I needed a job—" A shrug of her pillowy shoulders finished the tale.

Mrs. Nora Mayor of Greenwich, Connecticut, said, "I'm satisfied with the apartment. The location is ideal. The rent is acceptable. I'm sure you won't object if I pay you for the entire three months in advance? In cash. My late husband and I nurtured each other's abhorrence of paperwork. I can give you whatever references you require, of course; but, as my husband liked to put it, I like to think I'm my own best reference." Dear Norman. What a wise old codger. Be with me now, and in my hour of need. "As for your commission—"

"Not on sublets," Ms. Arthur said. "On sublets we collect from the tenant proper."

"As for your commission, if you would be so good as to spare me the tedium of paperwork, I think that three thousand dollars would be fair, don't you? In cash. Today. Right here. But if you have any anxiety about me, if you prefer to be ordinary, we can go back to your office and waste each other's time with your blessed forms and you can call my attorney and waste his time learning what you already know about me: I will not throw noisy parties, I will not steal the stemware." Nora gave a tender little pat to the chignon into which she had marshaled every last gray hair. She swung the alligator bag which had cost $200 in 1959.

The Arthur mouth simply hung open. Nora smiled. She was having quite a nice time now. Pity that dear Norman, bless his soul, could not be there to share the fun.

12.

But—bazooly and double bazooly!—the news was too delicious to be contained.

Jackie Geritano turned off the kitchen radio and hurried into the living room. "Bobby?"

Her husband looked up from the June issue of *Tennis*

International. His face reflected a shy eagerness that never failed to stir her—as though, after six years of marriage, and the birth of a child, and bathroom intimacy, and a fancy bed life, he still saw her as freshly dug-up treasure, not quite yet believable, much to be gazed upon and wondered at.

"Bobby? Do you remember? The time in Dublin I told you about? With Ingrid and the hotshot lawyer?" She crossed to the beige sofa, she put her hands into her husband's dark hair. "The one who poured champagne over Ingrid and me?"

"And fell asleep after Ingrid and never got to you. At least that's the way you told it." Bob zigged and zagged a finger over one of Jackie's red silk sleeves, let his finger stray to bare wrist, made it a sultry zone.

"That's the way it was," Jackie said. She didn't add—she prided herself on having a highly developed sense of what little details not to heap on her husband—that a young roadworker they'd acquired at a pub had also been present, had seen to the needs of the ladies when the lawyer bit the pillow. "Guess what?"

"What?"

"He's running for mayor. I just heard it on the news."

"Jack something?"

Jackie shook her head for amazement. Bob had a startling memory when it came to her bed friends. The night of the thousand bubbles had to have been five, six years ago. "Right you are," she said. "Jack Keefe. I heard an excerpt from some speech. All about how he's not going to lie back and watch the heart's blood drain out of New York."

"Great." Bob threw the tennis magazine onto the coffee table. The curly-haired boy scowling through his racket on the cover was worth several million dollars at age sixteen and was just beginning. "What difference is it going to make to us, anyway? No one can run this city now."

"I wonder if he remembers me."

"Doesn't Lindsay seem a century ago?" Bob said. "When

there were things like inner city tennis programs. You could make a buck and still like yourself."

"I hope he remembers me," Jackie said. She tugged gently at Bob's hair. "I like to think, I don't know, that I'll make it to Gracie Mansion, at least in the corner of his mind. If he gets the nomination and wins. Wait till Ingrid hears." She undid a button of her shirt. "I wish we had champagne in the house. You could pour it over my tits and lick it off. I remember the way the bubbles tickled."

"We have club soda," Bob said.

"Oh, you—" Jackie slid off her perch on the back of the sofa, draped herself around him. "Do you want to hear about the man I met in London last weekend?" She sent her hand meandering up Bob's thigh. "He liked making me hold my legs wide apart—" Her hand found home, then fell away, disappointed. She tried lowering her eyes, letting her lips plump out. "You're not going to punish me, are you?"

"There has to be a punishment, you know that."

Bob had said the ritual words, but the resonance was missing from his voice. Jackie pulled back out of the game. "Bobby? Something on your mind?"

He kissed her tenderly. "You're on my mind."

"No, really. Tell me."

"I love you, Jackie."

"I know—" almost impatiently. "I love you. What is it?"

"You're going to say no. I know it."

She shook her head. She had no idea. A woman? Whom he wanted to bring home? She didn't say no to those things. But—bazooly! "You want Elizabeth?"

"She's cute—no." He put his hands on either side of her face. "I want us to have another baby."

"Oh, Bobby." She crumpled across his legs. She thought, We need new covers on the sofa. Only Nick hated change. "I'm not ready. I can't, you know, bend my mind to it. I love you and Nick so much, and I—"

"What?"

"And we can't afford it. If they coop this building—"

"If they coop this building—" firmly—"we move."

"We can't move," she insisted. "The Playgroup, and—" She shivered. In her mind she heard, James is icky and sticky. She said, "I'd have to stop work. Or get a ground position. I hate being so far away, you can't imagine, I've been dreaming about quitting, but—"

"Look, so we'd have to watch pennies for a while. But which would mean more to Nick in the long run, another stuffed giraffe or a brother or sister? You liked growing up in a big family, didn't you?"

"He's got a brother." Icky and sticky. "And two sisters."

"Not blood," Bob said. "Another year, and James will be in private school, and the girls, I bet."

"And Nick too," Jackie said stubbornly. "We'll find a way."

"I've been offered a job," Bob said.

"You have?"

"Not much, but it would be worth it. For another kid. Assistant pro at the Hudson River Racquet Club. I'd still have time to help with the baby. You're so beautiful, Jackie. I want more of you. More of us. If we wait too long, who knows what will happen?"

"How much not much?" Jackie said.

"Twelve-five a year. And I can give lessons on my own there after hours, charge what the traffic will bear."

Jackie stretched out on the sofa, her body tight against Bob's, looking at the chair with the cigarette burn on the arm, at the standing lamp with the cracked fake Tiffany shade. "That's insane. It's hardly more than you make now, and you'd be at their mercy. It's half what I make, and that's not even counting my overtime, and the health benefits, the pension—"

"But, baby, you're always so wiped out."

"And I wouldn't be with two kids? And the laundry to do? God, Bobby, I'd be useless in bed—a rag. Oh, it's all so complicated. Earlier I was thinking I'd do anything to give up flying, to spend more time with you two. But when

I think of you having some grotty job, and me never getting out at all, and not being able to buy things—I could blackmail Jack Keefe."

"Sure."

"If you had an affair with Elizabeth—"

"She'd give me a graphite racket? I don't want her. I want you. With your IUD out. It's the right time, isn't it?"

"You're supposed to wait a month. After you have it taken out. Anyway, I can't get an appointment with my doctor just like that."

"Are you kidding?" Bob said. "If he thought he was going to have another thousand-dollar delivery? He'd probably make a house call."

"But Nick—"

"Nick what?" Bob said.

"I don't know, but this morning—" Jackie shivered, then ran from the strangeness of icky and sticky, ran from everything. Jet lag, thy name is Jackie.

"Okay, he upset you with the eggs," Bob said, "but he's crazy about you, you know that. Are you afraid he'll feel betrayed if we have another?"

"He would feel that way. Kids do. Elizabeth is desperate to have another, but she wants to wait until James is older."

"Or Oliver is younger," Bob said.

"I know," Jackie giggled. It was one of their great jokes—Oliver the geriatric preppy. She laid her hand flat on Bob's hard belly. "You and Elizabeth should have a baby."

Bob pulled away from her, sat up. "Jackie, stop. We'll talk about babies another time. I think I'll go up to the Hudson River, hustle a couple of lessons."

"I hate that place."

"It's a good place. You don't have to own a hundred shares of IBM to be able to play there. One kid I work with, black, he has eighty-seven posters of Arthur Ashe in his bedroom—he gets up at five and puts out the garbage for the supers on his block so he'll have the money to play an hour after school."

"What do you charge him for a lesson?" Jackie asked.

"What difference does it make?"

"What do you charge him?"

"Well, I don't. He's paying twelve bucks to have the court for an hour."

"Oh, Bobby—" Jackie edged over into his space. "You're so good. And I'm so bad."

"I'm not so good. I don't make us enough money. And you're not bad. You work hard. You're a wonderful mother, a wonderful wife."

"Even though I don't want—"

"We've dropped the subject," Bob said. "We'll discuss it again in the fall."

"On Labor Day."

Bob put an arm around her. "You're a character. My bellissima." He kissed her. "I want you. Now."

"IUD and all?"

"Any way. Every way. I love you."

"I love you, Bobby. Do I make you happy?"

"You know you do."

"And Nick?"

"You know how much I love him."

"No matter what?" Jackie asked.

"Hey, what is this? No matter what. You okay, honey? If you're not in the mood, I can wait. At least five minutes."

"No, I want to."

"Let's go." Bob started to get up.

"Right here. Let's do it here."

"It's so funny," Bob said. "When I was a kid on couches I just wanted to be grown-up and get to do it in bed."

"We'll be grown-ups someday," Jackie said. "In about a hundred years. Does that feel nice?"

"Oh, baby."

"Shhh. My parents are light sleepers. If they catch us it'll be hell."

"Never mind," Bob said. "I plan to marry you anyway."

"You mean it? And take me to New York?"

"Wherever you want to go. What shall we call our first kid?"

"Nick if it's a boy," Jackie said.

"That feels fantastic, baby. Are you sure you've never done this before?"

"Cross my heart," Jackie said.

13.

"Mrs. Everts? Hi. This is Chick at the Green Witch Florist. I took that order for your daughter. Gray-haired woman, sixties I'd say, thin, that ring a bell? Picked the flowers out one by one, very particular. Let me look at my slip here. The way people write, I don't believe this. You got a pencil? The name is Major. That sound right? Mrs. N. Major. Phone number, 929-9423. No address, she paid cash. Hope that solves the mystery. Nice blooms, aren't they? Don't give them too much water, they're lushes, those Gerbers, they'll keel right over."

14.

John Francis Xavier Keefe and Olivia Alma Martinez had been partners at law for ten good years, which pleasant condition derived from two facts. The first was that they had never been bed partners and had agreed never to be, though her beauty stirred him and his womanizing roused the competitive beast in her. The second fact was the disparity in their professional inclinations. Jack did social work for the rich. Olivia's typical client was under indictment for welfare fraud. Jack's work had helped buy Olivia an apartment in River House; Olivia's work had helped keep Jack's conscience solvent. He had considered no one else to manage his run for mayor, and she would have been furious if he had, though she managed mostly by insult.

"Well?" he asked, after the press conference.

"Thank heaven the reporters were too amused to ask any tough questions."

"Olivia, light of my life, you always make it sound as though you think I don't have politics."

"Jack, if you had politics, I'd be working against you, guaranteed."

"By God—"

"Oh, now don't go getting offended, big man, we're well past that. You're the one who's always ranting about the folly—" her voice going stage Irish—"of replacing one mad scheme with another." She tugged at the jacket of her peach linen suit. She was a great jacket tugger. "Look. You left the church when you were fourteen. You're not a true believer. In anything. And that may be all that will save the city—a mayor who doesn't believe he has the answer to saving the city."

"You're sure, are you now, that you're not in the camp of our exalted present mayor?"

She linked her arm through his. They stood in the deserted conference room, silent, looking at the tangible signs of their success—the impeccably restored walnut paneling, the French glass wall sconces that gave the room its polished amber hue, the bookshelves—open, because Jack hated books under glass—that boasted signed firsts of Oliver Wendell Holmes Junior's *Common Law* and Fred Rodell's *Nine Men*. Amid the Victorian splendor lay a ruin of paper cups and half-eaten Danish, the eternal detritus of the early morning press conference.

Olivia tenderly blew ashes off the rectangular walnut conference table. "You really want this?" she asked.

"The city needs me, Olivia." Earnestly.

She laughed. "You'll be saying it in your sleep. You're a good hooker. The best. A thousand-dollar-a-night pro. Maybe you'll pull it off."

"With a madman like you behind me, why not?" He went

over to the conference table and poked around for the makings of tea. "What's on for today?"

"There's the fund-raiser for Teddy at '21' at noon," she said. "He'll be pissed at the attention you'll get."

"Let him." Jack found a teabag, read the label, threw it down. "Marv Mooney's producer called. They want me on the air between three and four. Telephone hookup and call-ins."

"Tell them no. I hear the management of WYOR is out to get you."

"Next time tell the caterer we want McGrath's Irish tea, or Ceylon from Schapira's in the Village. The press may have to swallow a lot of bullshit from me, but they don't have to wash it down with Lipton's. I can't say no to Mooney, you're crazy. He loves me so much, it's an embarrassment."

"His contract is up for renewal," Olivia said.

"All right, I'll tell him no. Sonofabitch, that's why he didn't want me in the studio. Couldn't face me. Come into my office. I'm desperate for a real cuppa."

"Drink the Lipton's, Jack. You've got to get in shape for the campaign trail. Unless you've got some groupie who'd like to spend the summer following you around with your private stash."

"Don't think I couldn't find one. Where else today?"

"It's Tuesday," Olivia said. "All the gallery openings. Lots of money and power on the avenue of President Madison tonight. You going to keep harping on the mayor and the music in the subways, you want to show you're not a philistine."

"Maybe if we hung paintings in the subway, that would end the graffiti." He broke up.

"And I want you to go alone, Jack."

"They'll never believe it."

"Fifteen minutes here, fifteen minutes there, and if you buy something, I'll get an item in one of the columns, guaranteed. In fact—what a genius I am, Jack—buy a painting for Nora. Flowers. Lovely. I can see it in Liz Smith. 'Everybody's favorite lawyer, dashing Jack Keefe, said it with flowers, and I mean wow. Jack popped into the XYZ Gallery last night and bought one of blah-blah's smashing watercolors of roses as a present for his invalid wife, Nora, who's famous for her green thumb,' dot dot dot. That'll help take the sting out next time you're seen groping some bit of fluff at the Carlyle."

"You're a terrible woman," Jack said. "The trouble with you is, you have a happy marriage. It's perverted you. You're out of touch with reality. The rest of the world— they think I'm a saint, they do, married twenty-eight years to an invalid and never a move to divorce. It brings a tear of relief to their eyes when I take off the halo." He nodded. He issued one of his famous merry snorts. "You should have been a mother superior. Or a dominatrix."

"What's a dominatrix?"

"Oh, sure. What galleries do I grace with my presence tonight? Or do I just wander Madison Avenue, howling?" He took a sip of tepid tea. He put the cup down. "Holy Mother of God, it shouldn't be allowed."

"You go to the biggest and the best, of course," Olivia said. "Gimpel. Fox. Knoedler. Kahn."

15.

"1935," the show set to open that evening at the Kahn Gallery, had been Heidi's idea—a slice of time, as she kept putting it to people, cultural history without tears. Henry had balked at first, such a departure for the gallery, but their assistant, Marguerite Koos, had loved the idea from the start, and the women had won Henry round. They'd debated the merits of various years, as if they were talking wine. In the end, done with reason, they'd gone for sentiment: 1935 was the year of the birth of Henry Kahn. At the opening

Heidi would leak that bit of information to friendly ears—
The New York Times maybe, or maybe *Art News*.

Eleven-fifteen in the morning, and the gallery was a madness. Extension ladders, packing material everywhere; an electrician at work on the lights; a young man named Eric Sloan, an art history doctoral candidate at Columbia, doing the actual physical installation under Henry's shouted instructions (Henry did not climb ladders himself); Marguerite on the phone with their catering service, Daily Bread, upset because Sam Jones, their usual bartender, had woken up feverish with flu and wouldn't be able to be there that night.

"Marguerite, I'll bartend," Eric called out, as Heidi walked in, back from foraging for diet pills.

"Are you sure he's really ill?" Marguerite was saying into the phone for the third time.

"Sam has the flu," Eric explained to Heidi.

"Marguerite, for chrissake, we don't want him contaminating everyone," Henry said. "Let it go."

"I know just how what's-his-name from *Art in Review* likes his martinis," Eric said.

"I bet you do." Henry looked at the painting Eric had suspended from the molding, an Arthur Dove called *August, 1935*—cresting electric green that might have been wave or leaf or Leviathan or breaking plane of light. "I don't like it there. Try it where the O'Keeffe is. Put the Münter there."

"Oh, Henry, don't move the Münter," Heidi said.

Henry snapped around. "Where the hell have you been?"

"I had to go out. Emergency. I'll tell you later," though she wouldn't. Henry abhorred drugs. She had to sneak cigarettes. She felt a pleasant warmth in her belly as the Dexamyl started to hit. She pictured the hundreds of tiny green and white beads breaking free of their gelatin prison and swimming to their various destinations. Mark, the old softie, had given her the Dexies, thirty of them, rather than writing out a prescription—too much scrutiny of pharmacy records these days, he said. And, she thought, he wanted her to feel the favor in what he was doing. He hadn't made a move out of line, but he'd let her know he remembered her body.

She heard the doors to appetite closing as she stood there smiling at unsmiling Henry. Other doors seemed to open. "Hi, high Heidi," she said to herself. Mark had told her the pills would make her high; he was sure that was why she wanted them. No, she'd said, she wasn't high material, she'd lost the knack, the inclination, hadn't so much as smoked a joint since she'd met Henry, rarely drank more than a glass of white wine. She was too motherish, she'd told Mark, to get high. Just make me unhungry, please.

She waltzed over to her husband. She planted a kiss on the bald spot on top of his head. "Hi, 1935," she said gaily.

"We have an opening tonight, did you know?"

"No!" she mocked, refusing to be chastened. She rubbed his cashmere shoulders. "Tight, my darling. What we need is Julie with some elephant jokes."

"Hey, Heidi," Eric called from his perch. "Did you hear about the elephant who told people jokes? What's red and white and flesh-color all over?"

"Campbell's Cream of People soup," she shot back. They found themselves funny, and Eric's aluminum ladder wobbled, under his laughter, and Heidi ran to steady it. Eric was skinny unto frailness (the lucky). Heidi was forever expecting him to do something annihilative like fall off a ladder. "Don't you have a mother?" she said.

"God! Do I! I mean!"

Henry marched off to the office, looking offended.

"What about the Dove?" Eric asked Heidi.

"Leave it. You know how he is. Poor baby," not making clear who the poor baby was. "What about the Japanese stuff?"

Marguerite came away from the telephone. Her eggshell eyelids were fluttery with tension. "They want to send a woman bartender," she lamented.

"So?" Heidi shook her head. "Don't you know there's a lib on?"

"I think," Eric said, "that I should bartend. Really."

"You'll think different by five o'clock," Heidi said. "Lots of work still ahead. By five you'll be happy just to be boozing and cruising."

"Hula hula." Eric blew Heidi a kiss.

"Hula hula." She pirouetted away.

The telephone rang. Marguerite answered. "For you, Heidi. It's Julie. She says," as Heidi paled and hastened toward the phone, "it's not an emergency. Don't be such a Jewish mama."

Heidi hastened nonetheless. Calls from school seldom boded well. Julie had been so tense that morning. "Sweetie?"

"Hi, Mom. I'm not sick or anything, don't worry."

"What's up?"

"I was just wondering, if it's okay with her mom, could I stay at Amanda's tonight?"

"Julie—" a wail. "You begged me—you *begged* me—to let you babysit Stephanie tonight. How am I going to get a sitter now? I have a thousand things to do."

"Can't Marguerite watch her?"

"Julie, don't be silly. We've got a very big opening tonight. We need Marguerite here."

"What about Mary Girard?" Julie's voice was getting shrill. "I'll pay for her out of my allowance."

"Mary's sitting for Daisy. Julie, this isn't like you. Can't you stay at Amanda's tomorrow night? I need you, honey."

Julie started sobbing wildly. Heidi heard soothing adult voices in the background—Julie was calling from the headmistress's office. Heidi's heart went into a rush. She gulped for air. The damn Dexie. She tried to push the drug away, to swim through it.

"I hate her," Julie sobbed. "I don't want to be her sister anymore."

The sharks got Heidi. Her temper snapped. "What the

hell are you trying to pull?" she shouted. Then, appalled at her words, at the wilder sobs that greeted them, she clutched the phone, she tried to reach down through the wires, put her arms around her daughter, hold her to her breast. "Sweetie, I'm sorry, I'm sorry. You know how it is when there's an opening. I'm sorry. And you're always so dependable. You see," trying to make light, "what happens when you're a wonderful person? People expect too much of you. Did you hear about the elephant who told people jokes? What's red and white and gray all over? Whoops." Her mind clawed at her mind. "What's red and white and flesh-color all over?"

"You love her more than me," Julie sobbed. "She's bad, and you love her more than me."

"Julie, Julie, my dearest Julie, I love you both as much as it's possible to love, I love you both to infinity." Across the gallery she heard Henry shout at Eric to put the O'Keeffe where the Dove was, and the Münter where the O'Keeffe was. "You're my wonderful girl, and so is Stephanie. I know you had a fight this morning, but you've had fights before, you'll get over it. And if you want your own room, you'll have it. You can start thinking about colors."

"Mommy, please, please let me stay at Amanda's until my room is ready."

"Julie, for God's sake—what's going on? What happened this morning?"

"I can't tell you, please, only let me stay at Amanda's, I'm going to die, I'm going to DIE."

"Julie. I'll tell you what. I'll make you a deal. You can stay at Amanda's tonight—assuming her mother is willing—on one condition. Tomorrow we're going to have a talk and you're going to tell me what this is all about."

"Oh, you're the best mommy in the whole world."

"Do we have a deal, Ju?"

"Okay."

"For real?" Heidi pushed.

"Cross my heart, hope to die, stick a needle in my eye."

Then she said, the old Julie, the responsible one, the devoted one, "What are you going to do with Stephanie tonight?"

"I think what I'll do is ask Jill if I can park Stephanie over there. Mary can take care of two as well as one, right?"

"Right."

"I'll call Amanda's mother myself," Heidi said, "and if everything is okay with her, I'll drop a bag off at her house. What do you want to wear tomorrow?"

"You don't have to bother, Mom, with the opening and everything."

"Thanks for being so thoughtful," Heidi said tartly. "How could I enjoy the opening thinking about you wearing dirty underwear tomorrow? Yuk."

"Yuk," Julie giggled.

"Want your red sundress? It's supposed to get hot."

"Okay."

"Feel better, sweetie?"

"I feel much, much, much better."

"That's my Julie." Heidi hung up. She skittered across the glossy parquet floor. Her frightened sandals echoed off the high white walls. "Henry! Henry!"

He turned to show a testy face, then saw what was in her face, and instantly offered sheltering arms. "The girls?" he asked, all concern, all connection.

"Henry, I'm just undone. I think something's really wrong with Julie. She's so tense. So hostile to Stephanie. What can it be?"

Henry held her closer, let her feel his height, his solidness. "Poor Mama," he murmured tenderly. "This isn't the moment," as the electrician shouted and the telephone rang again, "is it? We've got to talk. Definitely. But I think you're worrying about the wrong girl."

16.

I wanted to freeze the moment.

There stood Daisy, grubby and shiny in her inked-up pink boxer shorts and silly kangaroo T-shirt, arms locked around one of Ken's khaki legs in a clowning parody of ownership too broadly played to be anything but a take from the deepest dreams. There stood Nick, with his watching and waiting air, one finger alongside his nose, St. Nick the night before, about to deliver. There on her coppery head stood the smallest, Stephanie—the sibling, honed to compete. I see London. I see France. I see Stephanie's underpants.

The moment was perfectly ordinary, and extraordinary, too, because what was more unusual, more arresting, than people being themselves? Not that the kids weren't posturing; they were. This was their own real fakery, brand for brand. Therein lay the beauty of the moment.

The light was right, too—a big morning light, showing off the high-ceilinged splendor of the apartment, showing up the grubby woodwork, the fingerprinted walls so nicely at odds with the splendor.

I did love those kids. Daisy wildly, and the others more than I ever thought I could love kids not my own. I loved them because I knew them. I loved Daisy the best because I knew her the best, and I cared more about the others than I cared about the screaming horde at the playground because I knew these kids better.

A poem came to mind—"The Lost Children," by Randall Jarrell.

> *It is strange*
> *To carry inside you someone else's body;*
> *To know it before it's born;*
> *To see at last that it's a boy or girl, and perfect;*
> *To bathe it and dress it; to watch it*
> *Nurse at your breast, till you almost know it*

*Better than you know yourself—better than it
   knows itself.
You own it as you made it.
You are the authority on it.*

And in an instant that perfect connection could change. It would change. These children would become those other children, not really known, not really knowable, ever. Even Daisy would become a stranger, more different from me who had made her than a daughter adopted from far-out foreign soil.

I would still love her, but the intimacy would go, the feeling of being bonded cell to cell. A part of her would be off limits to me, as if I were a single woman and she were a married man. I knew the cost of such connections.

All mothers lose their children; yes. The end of nursing had meant loss. Each inch of growth meant loss.

*But as the child learns
To take care of herself, you know her less.
Her accidents, her adventures are her own.
You lose track of them. Still, you know more
About her than anyone except her.*

Only: Ken Iceman was there, and the normal equation was unbalanced. He might know Daisy, have Daisy, in ways I never would. Freeze the moment, not just to have it for the scrapbook but to stop time. Freeze the watershed moment.

Jack had laughed. Jill and her moments. I did not argue. He knew me. He was the authority on me. I would buy a new shade of lip gloss, Summerberrywine or some such, the right licks of plum and brown, the one I'd been searching for, the one I didn't dare hope existed, and I would think my life would be forever different, the world forever different—I would never again be a man's fool or forget to pick up the towels before the laundry closed, and war would be no more. Moments, events, turning points. Kid Epiphany, Jack had called me. A believer. Connecting to the All at the cosmetic counter.

Jack had envied me, though. My hopes. We'd smashed idols together, we'd shared the dry bread of facts, but he'd seen in me (and scorned, and envied) those funny little puffs of faith. Not that he was free of belief. Look at his marriage-unto-death to Nora, who only tormented him. No explanation existed for that unending union except that the church owned him way deep down. Maybe. Jack always said it wasn't so simple. "Someday you'll understand." My parents had used those words now and then. All grown-ups used them. Someday. Someday. My parents had told me— teasingly, not heavily—that someday I would understand what it was like to be a parent, and I would call them up and tell them I understood. I wanted to be able to make that call now. But I couldn't, any more than Daisy could call her daddy on her yellow plastic phone.

Ken said, "Daisy. Stephanie. Nick. Someone's missing."

"James," declared a young chorus.

"Ah. James. Is James late?" Though he knew the truth.

"Icky sticky sick," Nick said. "He got throw-up in his mouth and then it went into the toilet."

Daisy made retching noises. She tumbled across the floor in a spit of laughter. Stephanie made louder retching noises. My little red-haired friend was in some kind of mood today.

"Aren't you glad you asked?" I said to Ken.

He gave me a look. The message was more warning than warming. This isn't the moment for complicity between us, he seemed to be saying. He got down on his knees the way grown-ups do when they want to make little of their height, appear on the level to kids.

I couldn't take the defection. "Coffee?" I asked, with six sugars. "Or maybe you'd like some grape juice in a Big Bird cup?"

"Coffee would be fine."

"Knock knock," Stephanie said to Ken.

I fled to the kitchen. Knock knock. Who's there? Boo.

Boo who? Oh, please don't cry. Knock knock. Who's there? Atch. Atch who? God bless you. Stephanie standing on her head flaunting tiny panties was quintessential Stephanie, a massing of genes unique in the history of the species. Stephanie pitching knock knock jokes was just another smart-ass New York baby, just another little sister of an eight-year-old. Which did I want her to be? What business of mine was it to give a fig for her being? Maybe I was jealous because Daisy didn't yet have the knock knock knack as slick and pat, was stuck on a crazy lazy fazy Daisy plateau?

Ah, jealousy. The great green boogie in the soul's nose. The sick, sweaty feeling I'd had every time I thought of Nora in the old days, no matter how often Jack said it was Nora who ought to be jealous of me, who would be half dead with jealousy if she knew of my existence and what I meant to him. The professional jealousies I'd felt when the kitchen was my life. Those shameful little jealousies I felt on Daisy's behalf if one of the other kids counted higher or sang nearer my key to thee or was quicker to share a cookie. The worst thing was that sometimes I was jealous of Daisy. Not for her; of her. My own beloved daughter. At that moment, for instance, because I thought she interested Ken Huysman more than I did.

He'd said I was interesting, but had he meant it? He didn't know the half. The night I tore the veal into shreds and ate it from the pan and what was I doing making veal, $9.95 a pound, but you see Daisy had said she wanted veal, real veal, a real veal meal deal, and so there we were and there it was, sizzling and buttery and juiced with lemon, just a squeeze, so carefully crafted you'd have thought the man from *Guide Michelin* was coming to dinner, and Daisy said she didn't want veal, she wanted cereal, and I poured crisps and crunches and milk into a bowl, and she said she didn't want cereal, she was Snoopy and wanted a bone. And I felt so helpless and drowning and mad and stupid and GUILTY because if we'd been with her father there would have been bones, and I drank two glasses of red wine, two glasses of ordinary Beaujolais, and she barked and called me Charlie Brown, and I ate the veal right out of the pan, butter dripping, the whole three-quarters of a pound of it, unappetitive me, and then I threw the pan to the floor, that heavy black frying pan, what did Larry's downstairs neighbors think, and I cried and I wanted to hit her, but I didn't.

Go ahead. Tell me it's normal. Tell me every parent throws pans.

Jealous, you see, because she can do things I can't do; has wings; may live forever. This ordinary child who loves Snoopy. Would she still love Snoopy when Ken finished with her? I ground coffee beans. Would she still love me? I poured coffee into the welcoming filter. Ken, Ken, go away. Come again some other day.

And next to her I wasn't interesting at all. Merely elaborate. Details up to my kazoo. But grounded. Mortal. Just another great woman.

A jolly atonal ruction made itself heard in the kitchen. "Ring a ring o'roses . . ."

I calmed, came down to the concrete. My head hurt. Not yet a Fiorinal's worth of pain; caffeine should cure. For what felt like the hundredth time since dawn, I watched the kettle. Almost time to think about lunch. Thank the gods there would always be lunch. "Pockets full o' posies . . ." A big bowl of iced raw vegetables might be a hit, and not violative of the rules, a tipoff to my talents. Carrots and celery and cukes, and there was enough roast chicken left over from the night before, even if Ken stayed.

I knew I should tell Ken about the time in New Hampshire with the clams. I knew I should tell him about my parents, about the color of the moon the night I embezzled sperm to grow a Daisy.

The kettle hissed. I let it come to full boil, then turned off the flame so the water could cool a bit. When I made bread, I listened to the rumblings of the yeast. For coffee, I followed instructions. I put the canister of coffee beans back in its proper place. I neatened the roll of blue paper towels, hung hand-high from the wooden cabinet next to the sink. My eyes lit on a telephone number dashed on the back of a twenty-five-cents-off coupon for Thomas's favorite brand of cat food. How like me—the unimportant paper towels just so, the essential telephone number carelessly dealt with. 929-9423. Veins pulsed. I dialed. "Ashes, ashes . . ."

My mind rehearsed. Hello, is this Mrs. Major? Hello, is Mrs. Major there? Mrs. Major, who are you? What do you want with me and my daughter? Mess around with us again, Mrs. Major, and we'll be sending flowers to your mourners. "All fall down."

Busy. I hung up and tried again. Busy again. I poured just enough water into the filter cone to dampen the grounds. I got the chicken out of the refrigerator so it could come up from the chill. I thought about the warmth of the day and bacteria and put the chicken back on ice. I dialed 929-9423, steeling myself for the irritation of the busy tone. This time there wasn't any answer.

929. 929. My first New York number, when I'd lived just off Washington Square, had been 929-9263—WAX-WANE in dial-speak. Proper call letters indeed for that moony phase of my life. Mrs. Major of Greenwich Village—a onetime near and not so dear neighbor? But how—? I'd left New York the day after I'd conceived. "One for the road," he'd said, as he'd always said, as I'd banked on his saying. No one could have known.

I got out the telephone directory. I fondly fingered a raggedy corner of the cover where Daisy's teeth had gone exploring. Majoda, Majol, Major. Mrs. N. Major, the flower man had said. There was a Norris Major, D.D.S., on Fourteenth Street, with a 691 number. Had I ever been drilled by a Dr. Major? Not to the best of my recollection. And if I had? Daisies to my daughter, with a card from a father who knew her not, made no sense whatsoever.

The great joke was that, once again, a part of my mind

wanted to call Jack. He would call the president of the telephone company, and the president of the telephone company would have someone check out the secret directory that listed the telephone subscribers of Manhattan in numerical order. And then I'd know—what? And Jack would know what Jack must never know.

In the living room, London Bridge was falling down. I had a moment's peace. I thought, This must be what it's like to belong to a real family. Mom's in the kitchen making coffee, Dad's in the living room romping with the kiddies. What Heidi and Jackie and Elizabeth and a million other women experienced every day. Did they know how lucky they were? Not to have someone to share the burdens, to have someone to share the joy. Because if Daisy was wonderful in the living room while I was in the kitchen, the act wouldn't go unwitnessed, wouldn't be wasted.

I tried the mystery number again. Again that hollow ringing, and no answer. Somewhere in a carton in Vermont, I had my old address book, great bulging ratty thing; I tried to scan it at a distance. I had seen that number before. It had never been important to me, but I'd seen it.

And Ken liked his coffee very hot. I lit a flame under the pot as the new brew trickled down. I tried the 929 number again, expecting nothing much at all. A man answered on the second ring.

My lines flew the coop.

"Is Mrs. Major there?" I managed.

The man laughed. "No, and not Mrs. Minor either."

"What?" I heard traffic. Fourteenth Street after all, and the window open?

"Would you believe Mrs. Farm Team? How did the Yankees do last night?"

"Is this 929-9423?"

"That's what the card says." His voice had a lilt I couldn't quite place. County Cork, one generation removed? Or Nepalese temple fingers hash for breakfast, maybe.

"The card?" I thought about cards in flower boxes.

"This is a pay phone, darlin'."

"A pay phone," I said dismally. "You're kidding me."

"Am not. Sixth Avenue, west side, between Tenth and Eleventh, one short block from that stunning historical monument, the Jefferson Market Courthouse branch of the New Yawk Public library. Which branch does not open until one pee em, as I just discovered to my shock. When I walked by the phone and heard it ring, I thought, jumping Jupiter, it's the mayor, calling to explain."

"A pay phone," I said again. Who—?

"Don't you hear the roar, darlin'? There."

"I thought you had the window open."

"Such a sweetheart. What are you doing tonight? Can you cook? Are you into latex?"

I hung up. I turned off the range, a few seconds late—the coffee was already at the simmer. Telephones and coffee pots were not my friends that day. What did the latex crowd do, anyway? Rubber sheets, was it, or rubber underwear? Even in the days when nearly everything sexual had enticed or challenged, latex had just sounded hot. As a child I sweltered resentfully inside my rubber anorak. Still, the time had been when I would have hailed a taxi and headed for the phone booth, for no better reason than that I didn't really want to. Thank you, darling Daisy, for saving me from such trips.

Chicken salad for lunch? Jack always ate chicken salad for lunch. No, my first impulse had been better—cold raw veggies, and the chicken left on the bone so the kids could pick it up.

I poured two mugs of coffee, steaming as ordered, and carried them into the living room.

"Hi, Mom!" Daisy's greeting was huge and syrupy, her head cocked, her eyes pure Kate Greenaway, as though we'd been parted for months. She went for my knees.

"Easy, girl," I said, mindful of coffee. Ken relieved me of both mugs. "Having fun?"

"We're having tons of fun. Ken says I'm bright as a button."

She danced away from my knees. I gave Ken a look, partly to ask for my coffee, partly to chasten him. One thing to want to take my girl to the moon, another to teach her triteness. "Bright as a buffalo, are you? Bright as a banana?"

"I'm bright as a wastebasket. I'm bright as a pen. I like this day. Is today my daddy's birthday? I'm going to draw him a picture—" heaping down on the floor next to a shoe box full of markers. "I'm going to draw him a face. Does my daddy like faces, Mom?"

"Everyone likes your faces, honey," I managed. "Your faces are terrific."

"I'm going to make him a purple face," Daisy said.

"Poo-poo face," Stephanie said, flinging red hair about.

"It is not a poo-poo face." Daisy stroked silver eyelashes onto the purple lids. Every day a new sophistication. Was I going to let Ken intervene in the natural order of things? But yours isn't a natural child, Mrs. Mozart.

Nick said, "Ken, can we go see James now?"

"In a couple of minutes." Ken sipped coffee. "Perfect," he said to me.

"Happy birthday, dear Daddy." Daisy waved her drawing about. She laughed. "Blow out your candle, you old mustache." She blew.

"I want to see James," Nick said.

"Because women don't have beards, you see," Daisy said.

"Now?" Nick tugged at Ken's khakis.

"But Nick," I intervened, "James is sick. You can't visit him, honey. You'll see him tomorrow, probably. Maybe even this afternoon in the park, if he's better."

"Ken said—" Nick stopped. His finger went alongside his nose.

"What I said," Ken told me, casual as a button, "was that if we went to see James without bringing our bodies along, we couldn't catch whatever he had." Before I could do more than swallow, he said to Daisy, "This is some drawing. I love the nose. And the funny silver hair."

"My daddy has funny hair, because it's his birthday. He can blow out two hundred and a million candles." Daisy turned to me, incandescent. "It used to be Iceman's birthday, but now it's my daddy's birthday. Isn't that good?"

Was it good? Or was it merely the end of the world? For sure it was the end of the temporary peace I'd bought with my lies of omission. I should have told her the truth from the start, the whole truth. Or I should have made up some gaudy lie.

Daisy handed her drawing to Ken. "This is for you, until my daddy comes."

"Your daddy's never coming," Stephanie said to my girl. "I asked my daddy when your daddy was coming, and he said never."

Coffee erupted from my cup and scalded my hand. "Damn!"

"Mommy?"

"I'm all right, honey, just a little burn. Stupid me." I squeezed back tears. "I'm absolutely all right."

"Do you want me to kiss it, Mom?"

"Would you, baby? There, that feels much better," though it didn't feel better at all.

Ken was at my side. "Ice water. Immediately."

I shrugged off his solicitous touch. I was more interested in Stephanie. The tiny redhead had backed up against the sofa, jammed two fingers into her mouth. She knew I had burned myself to keep from burning her. That goddamned Henry. But it was my own fault, wasn't it, for sending out murky messages? I deserved to burn.

Daisy grabbed the purple face and crumpled it. My burned hand felt as though it had been bludgeoned.

Nick said, "I gave my daddy a tie for his birthday, but Jackie paid for it. It had tennis rackets on it." He looked at Ken. "Can we visit James now? Please?"

Ken looked at me.

"Okay!" I all but screamed. Anything to shut up the daddy talk. Anything. Let Ken play his little game. That was all it was. Like Mr. Rogers on TV taking kids to the Land of Make Believe. And today, boys and girls, we will all pretend that our minds can be in one place and our bodies in another. Golly gosh. What fun.

Anything to bring the spring back to Daisy's face. I would see that crumpled drawing in my mind if I lived to be a hundred. Daisy, Daisy, let me be enough for you, ultra-mom, parent-plus, just us chickens, what's bad?

I put my wounded paw to my mouth. Stephanie and I would suck.

"That hand worries me," my friend the doctor said. "You could blister. Get infected. Half an hour in ice water—"

"I'll ask Elizabeth for ice water. When we get to her house. Let's get on with it."

"Jill—" He reached out and touched my hair.

"Let's get on with it," I repeated, but without quite so much steel wool in my voice.

Ken drew a few deep breaths. "Nick," he said, "tell me. How do you go to James's house?"

"Sometimes I go with Jackie or my daddy, and we stop at every corner, and we wait until the WALK sign comes, and then we cross."

"That's certainly a good way to go," Ken said. "Do you ever go any other way?"

"Once we went in a taxi like Paddington with tip-up seats because it was raining, and I waved to everyone like Paddington because Paddington is my favorite bear. When I was a little boy, I slept in a crib that had Paddington bear."

"That Paddington is some bear," Ken said.

I resisted an urge to eat my fingers. It's only a game, I told myself. Only a game, Mrs. Mozart. I put my aching red right hand on top of Daisy's head, bathed it in the starlight of that remarkable silvery hair.

"What if you want," Ken asked Nick, "to go see James without your mommy or daddy?"

"I just go." As if that were as ordinary an act as drinking a glass of water. "One two three. What do I see? I see James, and James sees me."

"Of course. That's the way to do it." Ken pushed back his oh-so-boyish shock of khaki hair. I saw sweat on his forehead. "That's the way to travel, all right. But you know something, Nick? I can't go to James's house that way. Jill can't go that way. Your parents can't. I don't know a single grown-up who can just go the way you kids can. We have to walk out the door, trudge down the hall, go into the elevator, press buttons, walk through some more doors, walk down the street—isn't that silly?"

Nick shrugged his shoulders. His finger went alongside his nose. He looked disbelieving. Grown-ups who could stay up as late as they wanted and watch as much TV as they wanted and turn on stoves and go on trips in airplanes and decide what's for breakfast—how could it be that they couldn't do this little thing?

"Why can't you, Mom?" Daisy looked at me pityingly.

"I don't know why, darling. My feet are too heavy. My mind is too heavy."

"I don't know why, either," Ken said. "But I know I'd like to be able to travel that way. Wouldn't you, Jill?"

"Sure," I said. And I wanted to live forever and be God—the whole bit. Who didn't? Never again to boil the coffee. "Sure I would."

"What I was wondering is," Ken said, "do you kids think you could take us to James's house with you? Take us your special way? You see, I thought if you all went together, you could maybe take us with you. We're both pretty thin for grown-ups."

"The kind little blue engine could take you," Daisy said.

"I think I can. I think I can. I think I can," Stephanie said.

"I wouldn't take the umbrella man," Nick said. "I don't like the umbrella man."

"I don't like the umbrella man," Daisy said.

"I don't like the umbrella man, either," Stephanie said. "He's yukky."

"I'm not yukky, am I?" Ken dared. "Jill isn't, is she?"

"No way!" my loyal girl declared, and the others agreed, even the red-haired witch.

"My butterfly could take you," Nick said. "My kind little butterfly." He giggled bashfully. "Because Jackie has to fly in airplanes, but I just go on my butterfly. Zoom, zoom, fasten your seat belts. My butterfly can go to London. That's very far away. That's even more far away than Staten Island."

I thought Ken would burst with ecstasy. "I'd just love to go to James's house on your butterfly. Wouldn't you, Jill?"

"Oh, yes," I said. "Travel by butterfly, avoid gridlock."

Ken punished me with a glare. Play the game or leave the room, he beamed. I made a face. I closed my eyes, I sighed, I thought about daddies, I nodded my capitulation.

"Let's sit down in a circle," Ken said. "Let's hold hands and go visit James together and tell him we hope he feels better soon. Daisy, you sit next to me and hold my hand, and Jill on the other side of Daisy—hold her hand gently, Daisy, that's the one she hurt, and then Nick on the other side of Jill, and, Stephanie, you sit right here between Nick and me."

Stephanie kicked the leg of the brown leather couch, but she obeyed; we all obeyed.

"Good," Ken said. "Now let's all try to breathe in the same rhythm. Big, deep breaths, like this." He inhaled and exhaled mightily. I flashed back to a thousand and one Greenwich Village events—tantric yoga, meditation, incense, candles, smoke—a thousand and one attempts to get off the wheel. I'd believed in nothing, including my own disbelief; I'd had to try everything once. In and out. In and out. The old in and out. Making love with Jack had been the closest I'd come to going. How should we live, O Lord? In and out. In and out.

THE PLAYGROUP 143

The circle breathed as one.

"Wonderful," Ken said. "In and out. Innnnn, outtttt. What wonderful kids you are. So strong. I know you can take us to James's house. Because—look. In, out. In, out. Big breaths. I see Nick's butterfly, waiting. It's so beautiful. I close my eyes and I see that butterfly. Nick, those colors are fantastic, and the wings are so big and powerful. That butterfly could take us anywhere. In, out. In, out."

I closed my eyes, the last of the circle. I saw a butterfly made of Indian silk, shot through with gold. I saw the never-before-seen color, the lost chord of crayons, that belonged between blue-green and green-blue.

"Look at the blue-green, green-blue silk," I heard myself say.

"And purple," Daisy said, and I saw the purple.

"And blue like Kandinsky," said the daughter of H. and H. Kahn, and I saw Kandinsky's piercing cerulean blue.

"Yes!" Ken said. "Nick, what's your beautiful butterfly's name?"

"Lokomo," Nick said. The name fluttered across my tongue as he said it.

"Lokomo," Ken said. "Let's breathe it. Lokomo."

Hands melted into hands. The circle swayed a little. I knew the rhythm came from Ken but it seemed to come from me, too.

"Lokomo in, Lokomo out."

He's making a mantra of it, that's all, Ms. Rational thought; but butterfly wings brushed my cheeks, and the thought turned to dust and blew away.

"Lokomo," Ken said. "Let's all say it together. While we breathe. Lokomo. Lokomo. Lokomo."

I can stop this anytime I want, I thought. The conductor will let me off if I ring the ding.

Lokomo. Lokomo. Lokomo. Lokomo."

We have always lived in the Lokomo. Because this train is my cocoon and I need no other home.

"Lokomo. Lokomo."

Blue-green, green-blue, and the air smelled vanilla. The breaths were breathing me now. Smoke me, Lokomo. Lokomo, my love. I don't know where I end and you begin. Come me, Lokomo.

"Take us to James, big butterfly Lokomo," Ken said, from a thousand worlds away. "Take us. Take us. In, out. In, out. Lokomo. Lokomo. Lokomo."

The floor was a pillow of air, slowly inflating. I held Daisy's hand even tighter. I willed our cells to cement forever.

"Lokomo. Lokomo. Lokomo. Lokomo. Lokomo."

"But James is asleep," Elizabeth laughed, getting up from her cracked green leather chair.

I dropped to the floor with a panicky bump. My eyes flew open. I was in my own borrowed living room.

"But James is asleep," Nick was saying.

"I don't want to play anymore!" Stephanie said. Her face crumpled. "I want to go home. I want my Banky."

Ken picked up Stephanie and rocked her to calmness. I was all over Daisy. "Baby?"

"Hi, Mom," my girl said, bright as a peanut butter sandwich.

"That was fun," Nick said. "But silly James is sleeping." He made big snoring sounds. He laughed. "Let's give Lokomo a carrot."

My head was reeling. My heart was speeding fair to bust. My breaths seemed to come from my toes, via Cincinnati. I saw triumph all over Ken's face. Had we? Had we? Or what?

Then I saw something that made me shriek.

My right hand, my burned hand, my sure-to-blister-hurting-like-hell hand: smooth, cool, ivory, and the pain completely gone.

17.

Nora Keefe listened to the whine of the elevator, wine to her ears, as it carried away the person of the considerably richer Ms. G. Arthur, rental agent extraordinaire. The sound diminished. It disappeared. Nora sighed her relief, but the sigh went down the wrong way; she choked, she coughed.

It's over, she thought. My life is over. I have rented myself a death cell.

Dear Jack. Please have my body burned and the ashes scattered over the tulip beds.

There would be no greenhouse after she died, though. Jack would have it torn down, giving no thought to the bulbs. His new wife, the fragrant young public person he would marry after a season of proper mourning, would not need a greenhouse. She herself would be fertile soil. Little Jack Horner sat in the corner eating his Christmas pie. He stuck in his prick and it did the trick and he said, "A father am I."

Nora looked at the telephone. It was white, like the woven rug beneath her feet, like the cushions that broke the shock of the pink silk sofa. She could wave the white flag if she wanted to. There was still time. She hadn't yet committed the irrevocable act. She could call Jack at his office, the way dozens of citizens did every day. She could call him and say, "Help," and he would help. He would come for her and take her home, no questions asked. He would soothe her, tease her, feel sorry for her. He wouldn't want her, though.

Until she gave him Daisy.

When he saw Daisy, when he realized what he had wrought, what they had wrought, the child of his dreams until now unknown, rescued from that slut who held her, the rekindling would happen. The three of them—the joy of it. Then he would say yes to Ireland, would say yes to everything good. Daisy would play at his feet, and Nora would wear perfume again, behind her knees. Come to me, darling. I will be all the women you need. Lover, friend, the mother of your child. I will give my clothes to Betty DuPont and buy daring silks. Jack, I dream of a second wedding. To signal the start of a new life. Daisy can be flower girl. Dr. Howard can give me away because I'm well now.

A church bell chimed for noon. Saint Patrick's, was it? No, it must be something nearer to penetrate the thick walls and sealed windows, something right at hand in her new neighborhood, her true neighborhood. Noon, and she wanted tea, the two cups of milky Irish that were her only lunch.

She walked into the kitchen. Expensively appointed, big exhaust hood over the range, eye-level ovens, two of them, copper-bottom pots gleaming on the wall, but a mean rectangle for all of that, an apartment kitchen, with a single window. And the cupboard was bare. Did not yield even a box of nasty teabags. Nora pined for the Greenwich Village townhouse kitchen where she took her sad little meals in airy splendor. She missed the tins of tea, and the Irish pottery, and the smells of Betty DuPont's cleaning potions, and Jack's special knife for carving smoked salmon.

I will never see any of you again. I will never see another human soul. They will find me here, rotting, when the neighbors complain of the stink. Put me in the compost heap, Jack. Put me close to the core, where the fires burn hottest. You can fix that, can't you? One little phone call to the commissioner of death. I won't be asking any further favors.

Tea would give her strength. There had to be a grocery store in the neighborhood, on one of the avenues. Going to a grocery store would be quite the adventure. Dr. Howard would be proud. At home, fifty-five blocks away, she lived a life which did not include marketing. Jack ran here for Irish bacon for his breakfast guests, there for Nora's tea and tinned soups, and somewhere else for whatever Betty DuPont indicated was needed to keep the place together. Mrs.

DuPont could have done the shopping, but Jack liked the convivial Village markets, the excuse to press the flesh. He was always running.

Nora double-locked the door to the apartment with the keys she had bought for $3,000. The keys jiggled in the cupped palm of her hand—expensive keys, on a cheap wire ring, the kind that locksmiths throw in for free when they duplicate keys. She thought of the key ring in her bag, sterling silver, with a small charm of a house dangling from it, seed pearls making a door for the house, emerald chips describing the windows. Jack had given it to her for their first wedding anniversary. Before the horror had happened. The whores. Whores for him, and hers for whom? Home is where you bang your hat. She put her new keys in the bag with her old keys. She heard them scream as they met.

She took the elevator downstairs. She walked the length of the cool lobby. The gray-haired doorman touched his cap. He greeted her by her new name. He asked if she wanted a taxi. Nora had sent him fifty dollars in the hands of Ms. G. Arthur, enough grease to win her a welcome without making her a wonder.

"I'll walk, young man," Nora said, very Mrs. Mayor of Greenwich, used to tramping the fairways.

She stood outside the building for a moment, looking across the avenue to the playground where Daisy spent her afternoons. A stone wall marred her view, and a great marble frieze of soldiers; but it didn't matter, Daisy wasn't there. Three o'clock, Mr. Kojak said. That was the magic hour. She went on staring anyway, at trees and nannies and dogs and a vendor hawking his wares from a cart bedecked with a red-and-white umbrella. All right, Daisy dear, one pretzel, as a special treat, but then we're going to go straight home and brush our teeth.

She found a Gristede's on Madison Avenue, just off Sixty-sixth Street. She lingered outside the windows, staring at expensive blue tins of imported butter cookies, then she got herself into the store. She almost panicked at the sight of the narrow aisles, but she couldn't stand there, people would notice her. She took a wagon as her armor. She plunged in.

She found the tea and plucked a green tin labeled Irish Breakfast. It wasn't the special Ceylon that Jack bought for her at Schapira's on Tenth Street, but it would do. She headed toward the dairy section.

She saw a young mother, blue-jeaned, with a girl sitting in the kiddie-seat of her wagon, little legs dangling.

But I have to shop for Daisy, Nora thought with sudden joy. I have to stock up for my baby.

She peered into the other mother's wagon. She saw milk in half-gallons, toddler size disposable diapers, graham crackers, apple juice, bendable straws—yes, this was the shopping list she had always wanted to tick off, the wagon-load her arms had ached to push.

She went up and down the aisles, as much at home as if these were the aisles of her greenhouse. She bought two kinds of graham crackers, honey and plain; she stood marveling in front of the cereals, deciding finally on puffed rice and puffed wheat because she knew them and frosted chocolate alphabet cereal because it seemed so exotic; she picked out the juiciest peaches she could find, and a heel of watermelon; she bought a gallon of milk, a great plastic jug; and half an hour later there went into the brimming wagon a family-size tube of toothpaste, enough to last them a lifetime.

18.

The telephone startled Elizabeth out of sleep. She groped for the ringing thing. "Hello?"

"Elizabeth?" It was her father. "Are you all right?"

"Oh, Daddy, I was asleep—" She yawned. She shook her head. "Sorry. Hi."

"You're not ill, are you?"

"No, I'm fine. James is having a nap, he was sick this morning, but it's nothing, don't worry, and I just conked out in my old green chair. Bring me some coffee, will you?"

"Here it comes, right through the wire—" the way he used to send love and kisses when she was a child, the many times he was in a different city.

"Oh!" Elizabeth said.

"Elizabeth?"

"I just realized I had the strangest dream."

"Do you want to tell me?" James Dobbs asked politely.

"It's floating away, butterflies and the Playgroup—" She knew her father didn't really want to hear her dream and, anyway, the sooner she forgot it, the better. "How's Washington today? Hot?"

"As depressed and depressing as it was yesterday. Am I getting old, Elizabeth, or is this the most foolish and venal White House yet?"

"I hope they're not tapping your line, Daddy."

"I wish they were, darling. Now and then one of the movers and shakers pretends to consult me, but, face it, I'm an old fart, a footnote to history, and the type is fading. I could tell my opinions to the *Post*, and nobody would care. You're sure my namesake is all right? I could take the shuttle up."

"I promise you, Daddy. He'll be running all over the park this afternoon." Her voice went a shade tart; James Dobbs was more solicitous a grandfather than he'd been a father.

"You sound edgy, Elizabeth," he pressed. "Sure there's nothing I can do?"

"Oh, Oliver and I had some unpoetic words."

"Do I dare hope for a divorce?"

"Daddy, don't."

"And your remarriage to a grown-up?" James Dobbs said.

"Are you sure you used to be a diplomat?"

"And a damned good one. Always told people the thoughts they really wanted to think but didn't dare to. And

I knew when to let something drop, and I'll let the subject of your marriage drop. For the moment. Heard anything from your sainted mother lately?"

"You asked me yesterday, do you know that?"

"I did, didn't I. And you said, quote, 'Not in months, thank heaven.' Close quote. See? I'm not getting dotty."

"You're not missing her, Daddy, are you? What happened to the senator's widow?"

"She started telling me her dreams. Well, you sound like yourself now. Are you ready for some news?"

Elizabeth tensed. "You've found Kelly? Is it terrible? She's not dead, is she?"

"Not by any means. Alive and well and living in Australia. I used up twenty-six favors finding that out."

"Australia!" Elizabeth said.

Her father said, "Do you recognize the name Kenneth Huysman?"

19.

He recognized her because he never forgot a face. It was his business not to. He hadn't seen her in the flesh before, but he'd seen all the pictures of her that reposed in *The New York Times* morgue: engagement, wedding, and a handful of public events in which her husband had a featured role—a fund-raiser for Adlai Stevenson, the opening of an Irish festival of the arts in Brooklyn, an Easter parade (she'd worn a raffish straw boater), and, the most recent shot, a celebration of the fifth anniversary of Israeli statehood, in 1953.

When she'd hired him, over the phone, she'd said she was a recluse and they would not meet face to face. For a dozen years—long enough for him to woo, wed, and divorce a woman she never even knew about—they'd talked several times a week, talked sex mostly, sometimes in steamy detail, with a punctilious formality that was never breached. They were always Mrs. Keefe, Mr. Kojak, holding each other at wire's length. He knew more about her, though, thought more about her, than he did about the long-departed wife whose alimony Mrs. Keefe was paying.

Now here they were, not quite face to face, but only yards apart.

Or was he wrong, taking a perfect stranger for her because he was expecting to see her surface in this neighborhood, had been hoping and dreading that she would surface? He didn't think he was wrong. The beautiful face of the old clippings was embedded in the terrible mask she wore. But, merciful saints, she was a ruin. Forty-eight, with the beauty of the twenty-year-old still visible, and what she looked like more than anything else was a seventy-year-old woman who had spent her life carrying rocks up mountains.

For a moment she seemed to be looking at him. He drew back into the trees. He wondered what sort of mental picture she had of him. She must realize he was nearby, working in her interest, carrying out her orders. He wanted to reach out to her but he couldn't because she would send him away and then he wouldn't be there when she needed him.

He needed her need of him. His wife had never needed him. She thought his work was slimy. Even now, she didn't need the alimony, she was living with a building contractor, big bucks; she just took it to bleed him a little. Mrs. Keefe was different. She was a lady. She'd stuck by that miserable cheat of a husband, though if ever a woman had grounds, it was Nora Keefe. Arthur had sent her photographs meant to test her mettle; she'd never complained. She wasn't interested in divorce, she'd told him from the start. She wasn't interested in storing up weapons for use against her husband. She just wanted to know. She knew, all right, down to the juices and shadows.

The pictures of the child had been different. They had made her need more than knowledge, they had drawn her forth. Arthur Kojak looked at her standing meditatively, uneasily, in front of the big apartment building on the corner, the two laden shopping bags from Gristede's dragging her downward. He tried to patch in the pieces of the puzzle, to fathom exactly what she was doing. Bringing food to a sick friend who happened to live in the neighborhood? She didn't have friends. For a moment he doubted his own powers to know a face. Nora Keefe, here, with groceries—was it possible?

The doorman rushed out to the woman, reaching for the bags. Mrs. Keefe for certain, Arthur Kojak decided all over again. Because anything was possible. A lifetime in his business had taught him one lesson, if nothing else: when people were pushed to passion, their givens, their limits, went out the window.

His stomach churned. The smell of hot dogs and sauerkraut from the nearby vending cart nauseated him. He wondered if he'd made a terrible mistake, telling Mrs. Keefe about Daisy. He'd only meant for her to need him more than ever. He'd thought she would surface for a look at the child, then retreat again, let him be her eyes and ears, but the shopping bags didn't look like retreat.

Mrs. Keefe had been hurt so much. He didn't want to see her suffer more. He didn't want anything to happen to the child. She was a beautiful little girl, the happiest child he'd ever seen, a shining clown of a kid. The mother deserved what she got, doing the things she'd done with Mr. Keefe, her mouth everywhere, a threesome once; the child was an innocent. Well, he'd tried to scare the mother into taking the child away, at least he'd done that. He'd had a dark sixth sense, and he'd warned them. And he'd be right here, ready, at the alert, in case Mrs. Keefe needed him, in case anyone needed him.

20.

I turned my hand this way and that—as though if I looked at it in the right light, from the right angle, I might find traces of the burn. I patted my hand, I rubbed it, I stuck the fingernails of my left hand into it. Nothing could have soothed me more at that moment than pain. I had to find that burn, feel it, or I had to turn in my mind, I had to concede that reason had lost the war and wild things ruled the universe. Daddy, help.

"My father," I said to Ken Huysman, "was the most rational being I ever knew, and my mother close behind. They were magicians, did I tell you that? You know about magicians. They think that everything is laws, everything is tricks. Magic is the one thing there isn't."

"They were professional magicians?"

"Oh, professional. They were farmers to the IRS. We had a big place up in Vermont, pigs, the works. I still have the house, though I let the farm go. They certainly weren't amateurs. The winters are long in Vermont. They got to do a lot of practicing. They performed all over the country. They were amazing."

"The Amazing Evertses. I can see it now." Ken's hand described a marquee.

"They called themselves Wilhelmus and Martina. In ordinary life they were William and Martha. Bill and Marty. They died in a plane crash when I was nineteen. Private jet. Coming back from a charity performance. My mother hadn't wanted to go, she had the flu, but she was the kind of woman who always went. I loved them. I miss them."

We were in my bedroom, sprawled teenishly on the big bed. I'd left the door wide open, not in the interest of virtue but because the sound of Daisy laughing with Stephanie and Nick was holding me together.

"They sound wonderful," Ken said.

"Are yours? Wonderful?" I rubbed the nub of the bedspread my cousin Larry had picked out, awful beige cotton thing.

"I think so. My father's a mathematician. The sexy side of math—probability and all that. There's a magic of a sort, don't you think? Of the acceptable sort?"

"Sure," I said.

"My mother has a restaurant, a little place up in Westchester, seats twenty people, she cooks one meal every night, and either you take it or you go somewhere else. You'd like each other. My father, too."

"Dutch food?" I asked. "You're Dutch, aren't you?"

"I am, and she does—I'll take you there some night for her Rijsttafel, nobody makes it better. She does other things too. Northern Italian, Creole, she's all over the map. Are you Dutch?"

"Wilhelmus and Martina? What else? Half and half. Both my grandmothers. I'm Dutch Jewish, Dutch Reformed, French-Canadian, and Polish. How's that for a one-woman United Nations?" I rolled over. I moaned. "Ken, how can we talk like this? As though nothing had happened? Or maybe nothing did? Tell me nothing happened. Tell me, darling. Say it was all some lovely joke, surprise, surprise. I mean, maybe I didn't burn my hand. I just imagined I did. So of course it's better. Because it was never worse. Jesus God, I just don't know." Sobs came, from deep in my shoulders.

He knew where to find the wellspring of the pain. "It's okay, Jill." He kneaded my shoulder blades. "I'm here."

I sat up. I knuckled away the tears. "You're here. Marvelous. I can't tell you how consoled I am. I have the antidote, says the man who gave the poison. The antidote, *c'est moi*. Spare us." I shook my head. I hugged my knees. "My daddy would tell me to look for the facts," I said, in a bright little voice. "Are there any facts in the room? All facts will please stand up and be counted. Okay. One—" ticking off on my fingers—"I have a right hand. Fact. Two, I spilled very hot coffee on it. Fact. Three, it hurt like hell. Fact, of a subjective nature. Someone else might not have felt hurt at all. Four, my hand turned pink. Fact."

"Your hand turned bright red," Ken said.

"Red. Okay. And there, it seems to me, the facts end, the possibilities begin. Am I doing this right, Daddy? Possibility number one. I wasn't burned very badly, so naturally enough, my hand quickly healed itself. Possibility number two. You made such a fuss over my hand, made such a point of its being the hand that Daisy was holding, that you hypnotized me into believing the hand would heal, and my belief sent a lot of blood rushing to my hand, and that's what cured me. Because of course at the same time that I want to believe Daisy is just another wonderful little kid, it's the last thing I want to believe, and you know this, you know I want to believe she could lay hands on the Treasury building and cure the economy, and you played on my longing. Possibility number whatever—no, don't say a word, let me finish—you made such a fuss over my hand that Daisy felt bad for me, and wanted to heal me, and her desire somehow translated into fact. Possibility number— oh, I don't know, the hand fairy came and kissed me, and I died." I started to cry again.

"Jill." Iceman put an arm around me. "It's all right. Nothing bad happened. The opposite. Pain is bad, healing is good. Start here. That's a fact, isn't it?"

"It's a value judgment," I sniffled. Where was my mama with the tissues? I hadn't cried since their funeral. It's awful to cry without your mother around.

"Is it your value judgment as well as mine?" Ken's voice was tough now. "It is, isn't it? Pain is bad, healing is good."

"But if she did it, if she healed me, she could as easily hurt me, couldn't she? Couldn't she? I'm so scared, you can't imagine. Oh."

"What?"

"I just had a fantastic idea. I'll heat up some coffee, I'll bring it right up to the boil, and I'll pour it on my other hand, and I'll see how long it takes to heal. The objective correlative. Daddy would be so proud."

Ken shook me, gently, as I'd shaken Daisy once or twice, to bring her home from monsterland.

"I was thinking about working again," I sighed. "Didn't you wonder if I worked? Don't ask me what I do. I never tell. The children sound happy. Should I go look at them. They might need pretzels. We didn't really ride on a butterfly, did we? On the astral, Fifth Astral— Nice game, though. Must keep it in mind for the next rainy day."

Ken suggested I take a nap. He would tend the flock.

"Oh, can't," I said. "Against the holy writ of the Playgroup. And thou shalt not leave the children in the hands of strangers. They'll have my head as it is. The other mommies. Do you blame them? They hate me because I make my own bread."

"Would you call James's mother?" Ken asked. "Find out if he's sleeping?" He might have been asking for a glass of water, his voice was so by-the-by, but I heard the eagerness beating below the placid sea.

I looked at the bedside telephone. "Are you and Elizabeth in this together?" I burst out laughing.

"The objective correlative," the good doctor said.

"I love her so much," I said. "My flower."

"If you love her, be brave, call Elizabeth."

"Fuck you. I will." I pulled the telephone across the bed. I dialed Elizabeth's number. "Busy." I yawned. I'd climbed the Matterhorn, in my sneakers. "What if he is asleep? Coincidence. Proves nothing."

"But if he's awake, you're free."

I dialed again. This time she answered. I said, "Hi. It's Jill. I was just wondering how young James is feeling."

"How sweet," Elizabeth said. I held the receiver away from my ear so Ken could hear too. "I think he's fine."

"Running around?" I asked eagerly.

"Napping, actually, but his color's good. I bet he wakes up ravenous and raring to go. How are you doing with the kids?"

"Just grand," I trilled. "Thanks, Elizabeth," though what was I thanking her for? "I won't keep you. Enjoy your morning off." I hung up.

"So," Ken said. He looked horrifyingly pleased with himself.

"So nothing. Did she say anything about how nice it was for us to drop in? No. Of course not." I stretched out my arms and legs, I nudged him off the bed. "Because nothing happened. Would you go away now? I want to color with the kids. There's a lot to be said for coloring. The simple things, you know?"

"I've never seen such a woman for denying," Ken said. "I bet you run from love like a marathon winner. Who's Daisy's father?"

"Go away," I said.

"Are you really divorced, or what?"

"I'll scream," I said.

"The woman who loves truth."

"I said I loved reason. I never said I loved truth. I'm not that terrific."

"You have to leap sometimes. If they'd shown Sir Isaac Newton a plane, he would have said it couldn't fly."

"Planes don't fly. They drop out of the sky, and people die. Go away, Iceman."

"What time shall I pick you up tonight?" he said.

"Go away. I hate you. I do."

"Five o'clock?" he said.

"Five-thirty," I said.

21.

"I was wondering," Arthur Kojak said to the tall gray-haired doorman in the braided tunic, "if I might have a word with you on a delicate matter."

The doorman let his eyes travel over Arthur's face, over the unprepossessing shirt and slacks, down to the fist with the rolled twenty-dollar bill peeping out.

"You want a taxi?" The doorman moved to pluck the twenty.

"Your facetiousness is hardly appropriate under the circumstances," Arthur said sternly. "There are grave matters at stake here."

"I don't touch matrimonial," the doorman said. He put his hands behind his back and rocked on his heels, challenging.

"Don't you? I'm proud of you." Arthur gave the man the twenty-dollar bill. "This is yours, for not touching matrimonial. If we all kept our hands off other people's marriages the world would be a superior place, I say."

The doorman pocketed the bill without a word. Arthur felt a twinge of panic. The house phone rang. The doorman turned to answer.

"Yes, Miss McIntee," he heard the doorman say. "Yes, ma'am. I'll keep an eye out for it. Yes, ma'am, I'll bring it right up. Thank you, Miss McIntee."

He turned back, and Arthur noticed a small enameled American flag pin among the braid, and he took a plunge.

"Do you love your country?" Arthur asked.

The doorman fingered his flag. "This is the greatest country on God's earth."

Arthur nodded fervently. "It's so heartening to hear someone unashamedly patriotic." He moved a step closer, put on a confiding air. "You know about next door, don't you?"

"The Yugo embassy? Sure."

"It's not the embassy," Arthur said, as if he were disclosing secrets. "It's the Permanent Mission to the U.N."

"The U.N." The doorman made a spitting motion, though no product actually hit the gleaming black-and-white floor of the foyer. "That's what I think of the U.N., if you'll pardon my French."

Another twenty peeped out of Arthur's fist. "Your country needs your help."

The doorman sniffed noisily. "We've got the senator's brother, a federal judge, and a former undersecretary of the Treasury living in this building. My country needs my help, and it sent you? With a pocket full of small change?"

"My good man," Arthur said, "I will overlook your egregious behavior in the interests of the greater good which we both wish to serve. Let me be brief. A woman, gray-haired, looks to be in her late fifties or sixties though she's actually younger, traveling under many aliases, including Nancy Kennedy, Nora Keaveny, and Nellie Kincaid, is believed to have recently moved into this apartment building, probably this very day. She may be staying with friends, or she may be subletting. No matter. What we need to know is this: Is the apartment she moved into on the side of this building adjacent to the Yugoslavian mission?"

"You mean—"

Arthur held up a cautioning hand. "I am not at liberty to go into details. I'm sure you can appreciate the security aspect of the case. So if you can just tell me if her apartment is adjacent to the Yugos—"

"But the Hollenbachs, I'm sure they're not—"

Kojak cut him off again, hiding glee. "Not their fault, probably. These things happen. I suppose they put the place in the hands of a rental agent. Which of the aliases is she using today, the sly devil?"

The doorman shook his head. "I don't feel—even under the circumstances—"

"Fifty," Arthur Kojak said.

"It's as good as my job," the doorman said. "Who do I turn to, then? I love my country, but the government—that's a different matter. I don't even know which agency you work for."

"You're better off not knowing," Arthur said. A stretch limousine stopped at the curb outside the building, and he said hurriedly, "A hundred."

"Let me see it."

Arthur produced a crisp hundred.

"Mrs. Mayor," the doorman let slip. He looked at the limousine and shook his head. "Rock stars. Hippies. They rent it by the hour, and they think they're important. They smoke dope in those cars. Worse." The car pulled away, and he said, "From Connecticut."

"The rock stars?"

"Mrs. Mayor." He took the bill. "I'd like to be of service to my country, gratis, but you know how it is. Three kids. She's not from Connecticut?"

"Her cover," Arthur said importantly. "She's Swiss. A real pro."

"You'd never know it to look at her," the doorman said. "Though I thought those shopping bags were suspicious. A little heavy, you know?"

Arthur nodded.

"There isn't going to be any trouble, is there?" the doorman asked. "You're not coming after her?"

"Heavens, no. We've got her just where we want her. No trouble at all. I'll be keeping an eye on things, and now that we know we can count on you—"

"Nobody gets by me. Nobody."

"Exactly," Arthur said. "She'll be gone tomorrow, I predict, as quietly as she came. Meanwhile, screen everybody—delivery people, the works—and if she wants a taxi, get her one with a sober driver and good springs. Safe, that's the seminal word. We want everything quiet and safe." He pressed another twenty into the doorman's hand. "If anyone from the Yugoslavian Mission comes over and asks you questions, what do you tell him?"

"I tell him I don't do matrimonial," the doorman said.

22.

Afternoons when the weather was fine, the Playgroup often converged, kids and mothers together, at the red and blue playground near Sixty-sixth and Fifth. Each time we went I had to steel myself to the trees, but we went.

You know those things, I think. The words feel old to my

fingers. You know what the playground looks like, red seesaws with blue handles, blue mothers with red hair. You know about me and the trees of Central Park. I didn't take Fiorinal that afternoon. I would wrestle the trees bareheaded. What were trees next to where I'd been?

The weather was fine, and we went to the park at three o'clock, the way we always did, as though nothing had happened, nothing was going to happen. Kids are like that. They bounce terrific. Then, for Daisy and the others, nothing extraordinary had happened. Magic is in the eye of the beholder. Butterflights of the fancy were everyday stuff to these kids. "What did you do this morning, honey?" "Nothing." "Did you have fun, sweetie?" "Sure." The STOP REQUESTED sign flashing on the new Fifth Avenue buses when somebody pressed the signal tape—now there was a connection to inspire awe, an event to be exclaimed over and dwelled upon.

I am calm today, but I wasn't that day. I wasn't in any hurry to face the other mothers. I thought they might read in my eyes what their kids had neglected to report. "What did you do this morning, Jill?" "We flapped our wings and went to visit James."

The pretzel vendor waved at Daisy. She didn't wave back. I waved at the pretzel vendor. He didn't wave back.

Daisy ran down the path to the playground shouting, "Kids!"

The whole gang was there. James looked as bloomy as the others. Daisy zoomed to the sandbox. I sat down on the bench, between Elizabeth and Heidi. Heidi looked as though she'd been hanging paintings with her teeth. On second glance, so did Elizabeth and Jackie. I suppose your serene correspondent did too.

"The show all set?" I asked Heidi. "They going to be standing in line around the block to get in when the reviews hit?"

"Henry's still rearranging the walls," she said. I swallowed my anger at hearing Henry's name. I would tell him firsthand what I thought of him for giving Stephanie ammunition to gun down my girl. Heidi laughed in a knowing wifely way. "He'll be at it till ten of five. I had to get out. I wasn't being any use to anyone. Whoo. Anyone want to go for a little jog-o? I've got nervous energy to burn."

"You?" I said. "Since when?" Heidi had shown up at the playground one afternoon in purple jogging silks, left Stephanie in my care and headed toward the famous track around the reservoir, and had returned half an hour later by taxi. Too awfully boring, she'd said.

"This is international thinness day. What do you think? Have I lost any?" She stood up, sucked in her gut, and bunched her flowing shocking pink shirt tight around her waist.

"A gutless wonder you are," I said.

Jackie looked up from the copy of *Gourmet* magazine she forced herself to subscribe to, poor uncookie. I was tempted, for one wild moment, to break cover and tell her how to do it in the kitchen—or how not to do it and not feel guilty. "How did you stand it when you were pregnant?" she asked Heidi.

"Are you kidding? It was heaven. I was legally fat. I don't think I've ever been so happy with my body. Weren't you?"

"I was," Elizabeth said. "I felt wonderful. Except that Oliver hated my body. And I only gained twenty-two pounds over James's birth weight."

"He did?" Jackie shook her head. "Bob loved mine. I was the one who didn't like it. Isn't that awful? If you and I get pregnant again, Elizabeth, we should do a husband-swap."

"Before or after the insemination?" Heidi said. She giggled. "Sorry."

"Overheard at the playground," I said.

"Jackie, do you really fool around?" Heidi asked. She threw back her flaming head in a fresh spurt of giggles. She slapped her own cheek. "What's got into me today?"

"Which is the question?" Jackie asked. "What's got into me or what's got into you?"

We all whistled. Jackie wasn't exactly famous for her wit.

"What the bazooly," Jackie said, more her normal line of country. "We've got an open marriage. It's not a secret."

"Everybody talks big," Heidi said.

"Not me," Elizabeth protested.

"Oh, you, you're driven as the snow," our giggler said.

"You don't talk big, either," Elizabeth said to her.

"Because Henry would die."

"If you talked big, or if you actually had affairs?" Elizabeth pressed.

"Either. God. They don't come any straighter than Henry. But at least we have a single standard."

Elizabeth didn't appreciate the remark. She announced that she didn't happen to think sex was what marriage was about.

Jackie groaned.

"Everything is about sex," Heidi said. "Look at our kids." We all looked. "That's sex, isn't it? Tell me the Playgroup would be as successful if it were three girls and a boy or three boys and a girl. Right, Jill?"

I jumped. The ladies had a way of leaving me out of the talk when it turned to sex, though I thought the existence of my daughter was fairly decent proof that I too had shared a bed. I suppose they were being sensitive to my current celibate state and tactful about my past. I hadn't wanted to lie about Daisy's father but I hadn't wanted to tell the truth so I'd spoken (fairly enough) of a separation too painful to discuss. They probably imagined I had an ex-husband stewing in prison or lying aphasic in a hospital for the incurably sad.

Sweet women. Look how I'd repaid their friendship.

I mustered breeziness. "Sure, everything's sex. This is a total non sequitur, of course, but I'm bringing a person of the male persuasion to the opening tonight."

"Two openings for Jill," Heidi said. Then, "Whoo, I am hopelessly raunchy today. You know Mr. Lucca? Our tenant? The dignified Swiss bibliophile? He was coming in when we were going out, and I told him—right in front of Stephanie—that I figured he had to be selling rare erotica, or how could he pay our rent? I thought he would die."

"Are you on Quaaludes?" Jackie asked.

"Nope. Cross my heart and hope to die, stick a needle in my eye."

Thus the grown-ups, that fine June day.

The sprinkler went on. The sprinklers of Central Park are one of the Seven Mysteries. Gremlins turn them on and off, according to the number of birds on the wing divided by the number of clouds at right angles to the Plaza Hotel.

Four small people rushed out of the sandbox, yelling for permission to get wet, tugging at T-shirts as they came. How mothery we all got then, sneaking in kisses as we helped the kids peel down to underpants, admonishing them to come out the second they felt cold. (Some chance.) Gorgeous little silky-skinned buggers. Had the morning really happened? I looked at my unburned right hand—my disburned right hand? It was just a hand, I decided. And the nasty phone call had been from some harmless besotted adolescent—the perpetually blushing after school checkout clerk at the supermarket, the one whose line I never stood in if I had a box of tampons in my basket. The trenchcoated man looking up at our living room windows was just another honest American hoping for a vacant apartment. As for the Green Witch flowers—well, better not to think about the flowers. If I didn't think about the flowers, or about butterflies with purple seat belts, maybe they wouldn't think about us.

Our kids had the sprinkler to themselves. The air was bright with the sounds of other kids, at a safe remove. I waved at a mom I'd chatted with one waitful day at the pediatric dentist's office (no cavities for Superbrush), but she didn't approach the bench. Other mothers avoided us Playgroup mothers the way their kids stayed clear of our kids.

A gray-haired woman came into the playground. She got center stage in my mind—maybe her tentative steps, her air of not belonging. She looked to be of the age for grandchildren, but not of the posture. Had those arms recently held? Could that anorectic body produce a lap? For sure she wasn't a nanny, did not have it in her to deliver a kind but final "No." Now and then a woman her age would sit in the sun, would talk about children grown and moved across the country, grandchildren only heard from near Christmastime. Maybe she was one of those women. They bored, but there were worse intruders—the derelicts who showered in the sprinkler until some mom flagged down a cop, the mind-benders who bought their pants to match their hair.

Our eyes met. My spine flamed. I inched toward the lip of the bench.

"Jill?" Heidi said.

The gray-haired woman covered ground, stood between the sprinkler and us.

"Jill?"

"Who is that woman?" I said.

"Bette Davis?" Heidi said. Jackie laughed.

"For real. Do you know her? Elizabeth? Jackie?"

Nobody knew her, nobody had seen her before. Elizabeth volunteered to go to Madison Avenue to get coffee for us all.

"Iced for me, please," Jackie said. "Milk, no sugar."

"A Tab," Heidi groaned. "My soul cries out for a real Coke."

The woman was still eying me. She seemed to be trying to smile.

"Have you ever seen anyone so lonely-looking?" Heidi said. "That dress belongs in the Metropolitan."

"See how beautiful women are when they get really thin?" Elizabeth asked Heidi, with plain malice. The woman might have had flesh surgically removed, she was so thin. "Jill? You want anything?"

"Coffee would be terrific," I said automatically. "Black." Then, "No, never mind." How could I look at coffee? Even iced, it might do awful things. Cure a wart, or something. "I brought apple juice for Daisy. I'll steal a sip. She never finishes it. But I'd love a paper. The *Times*, the *Post*, anything. I haven't listened to a radio today. So much as looked at a headline. Has the stock market bottomed out yet? Is there still an England?"

"There's going to be a Democratic primary for mayor," Jackie said.

Heidi, Elizabeth, and I all turned and stared. Jackie was hardly a political soul. Until that moment I would have given odds that she didn't know New York City had a mayor.

"There is?" I said helpfully.

"At least, someone's trying to force one. He's got to get a lot of signatures to be on the ballot, right?" She signaled uncertainty with her eyebrows.

"Right," Elizabeth said.

"I know him," Jackie said. "The man who's running against the mayor. Who wants to run." Now she used her eyebrows to inform her rapt audience that she knew the man pretty well.

"Aha," Heidi contributed.

"A lawyer," Jackie told us. "One of those professional Irishmen, you know? Charming like you can't believe. Very powerful." The eyebrows instructed us to feel the Irishman's charm and power secondhand. Easy enough for me to obey. Even before Jackie dropped his name, I knew to a certainty I'd felt his charm and power firsthand, for a lot of years. The man who would be mayor could only be Jack Keefe.

23.

"That was sweet," the long-haired young woman said over and over again. She visited little kisses on Jack's silvery hair. "Mmmmm. Sweet."

"You're a grand girl, you are," he said, very Big Jack Keefe. He got hold of her and faced her away from him and put his arms around her, partly to stop the visitation of kisses, partly because from the back, all that clean caramel hair streaming down, she conjured the Jill of a dozen years ago.

They'd met at "21," at the noontime Democratic fundraiser Olivia had sent him to. The man who would be president had been there, but the man who would be mayor, his news so new, had been the focus of attention. The political groupies lined up for his inspection. He'd picked the most Jillish, and when the pundits and powerbrokers had looked to have their fill of him, he'd taken her off to her apartment in a tall thin white building in the East Eighties.

He sat up, swung the long body out of bed.

"Where you going?" the young woman said. "Can't we relax for a minute?"

"I have to wash," Jack said. "And so," slapping her on a lean buttock, an almost Jill buttock, "do you."

"What a fetishist," the woman groaned. Jack had been adamant about ablutions before they went to bed.

"And you should be grateful I am, with all the dread herpes and things afloat in this city. Now when I'm mayor herpes will be illegal, by God, and there's the end to it."

The woman laughed. "Well, I'm very careful, if it's any comfort. In fact, my gynecologist says I'm phobic, so you don't have to worry about getting an infection from me. I'm fine."

"So was the woman who gave me gonorrhea," Jack said soberly. "Or so she thought. And a sorry business that was, with dread consequences for innocent people. Don't worry—" into the young woman's alarm—"that happened nearly thirty years ago. Before you were born." He kissed her nose, a thin nose like Jill's, but with more tilt.

"Thirty years ago. Wow." The young woman shivered. "Didn't your marriage—oh, scratch that one. But how many lovers have you had? You sleep with everyone, don't you? A thousand women, I bet. And if every one of those women had, I don't know, ten lovers, and every one of those men had ten lovers—" She threw her arms open wide. "I had one year of college math, but I don't think it takes very long before you've covered the waterfront. So if you had an infection and didn't know it—" She sat up. "Let's wash!"

They washed each other, and mere hygiene turned into a romp that landed them back in bed. It was three-thirty before Jack had his clothes on, was saying that he would call one of these days.

"What's my name?" the young woman asked, at her doorway.

Jack kissed her nose again. "You're pretty."

"What's my name, Big Jack?"

"Margaret, never Maggie, Klingman." He reeled off her telephone number.

"I'm impressed," she said.

"The politician's art, my sweet. You're a grand girl. God bless."

He arrived back at his office to a tongue-whipping from Olivia, who could sniff out his bed romps better than any wife. He went through his telephone messages. The White House had called. Jill hadn't. He called Washington, and the cardinal, then decided to call his house to let Nora know he'd done the dirty deed, he'd declared. The telephone rang and rang. He looked at his watch; he remembered Nora's early bath, wondered if he should worry. She was probably out walking, he decided. Not her usual hour for a walk, but she'd thrown her day off by rising when she had. Or maybe she was having a nap. Very likely that was the story. She was having a nap, and she'd turned off the telephone. He would give her a ring later on. He asked his secretary for tea, though it wasn't officially time, and he went on answering calls.

24.

Daisy slipped and fell under the sprinkler.

I was on my feet in a second, but I didn't get to her so quickly that the gray-haired woman didn't get there first. She knelt right down on the slimy cement, she let the cool water pelt her, she put her arms around my girl and lifted her out into the sunshine.

Daisy's knees were scratched and bleeding. "Mama," she wailed.

The woman kissed her knees, then I was there, claiming, clutching. I looked at the woman over Daisy's head. She was licking her lips, she was sucking in Daisy's blood as if it were the rarest of wines, and she didn't care if I saw.

I couldn't say a word. I just held my love and stroked her until the sobbing stopped.

Stephanie and Nick and James gathered silently around.

"Is she all right?" Heidi called from the bench.

"Fine," I called back.

The woman licked blood. She stared.

"I want to go back under the sprinkler," Daisy said, in a pouty little voice, as Jackie approached with a towel and Daisy's clothes.

"We've got to clean those knees, darling."

"I don't want the hurting stuff." Her mouth turned down.

"We've got to wash them and make sure there isn't any grit in them, that's the main thing."

"I don't want to go home." The other Playgroup kids had gone back under the sprinkler, and Daisy looked longingly at them.

"Maybe I can help," the gray-haired woman said. She

had a strange, unoiled voice, a voice that sounded as though it hadn't been used for years. "My wonderful summer palace is right across from the park and, goodness gracious me, I've got I don't know what in my medicine chest. Hydrogen peroxide, Methiolate, all those goodies." She laughed. "My granddaughter stays with me sometimes, you see, so I'm all prepared. My little Lily." She looked at my girl with hot eyes. "She's three and a half, just like you. What's your name?"

"Daisy."

"Daisy! Another flower! I don't believe it." She began to sing. "'Daisy, Daisy, give me your answer, do—'"

My flower smiled. She stuck happy fingers in her mouth. She loves that stupid song. Every dry cleaner and pediatrician and babysitter had sung it to her.

"'I'm half crazy, all for the love of you—'"

"Thank you," I said, "but it's time for us to be going."

"What's your name?" Daisy asked the woman, as I stood up, holding her tight in my arms.

"I'm Mrs. Mayor, dear. Will you remember that next time you see me?"

Next time she sees you in a pig's ass, I thought.

"Mrs. Mare," Daisy said happily. "Like a woman horse."

"A woman horse, of course," Mrs. Mayor said.

"A horse of course you Norse," Daisy chirped.

"A horse, of course, you Norse, in the gorse," followed us out of the playground.

I hurried Daisy home. Lokomo couldn't have flown us faster. But not fast enough; never fast enough.

I kept seeing that ancient tongue licking blood from ancient lips, my Daisy's blood.

If only. If only. If only. If only.

25.

Nora's hair was still wet, her heart still hot. She had touched Daisy, held her, locked eyes with her, kissed her, tasted her pain, drunk her blood. See a child and let her lay, bad luck you'll have all the day. See a child and pick her up, all the day you'll have good luck.

The mother with the curly dark whorish hair offered a towel, but Nora shook her head no thanks. That towel might have been anywhere, between those shameless legs—anywhere. Nora stood in a puddle of sunlight, trying to draw heat to her skin, wrapping herself in Daisy thoughts. Jill had whirled Daisy away because Jill knew where Daisy belonged, where Daisy longed to be. Handy Spandy, Jack-a-dandy, loved plum cake and sugar candy. He bought Jill at a grocer's shop, and out came Daisy, hop, hop, hop. Daisy had cried for Jill, but they were taught to do that, could be untaught in an afternoon. Jill knew.

The other mothers were ignoring her now, and Nora knew they wanted her to go away, but she wasn't going to go away. Public property. Let them call some uniformed ape and complain that she wasn't a member of the uterine sisterhood, that her tubes were dead and she stank. She'd learn them a lesson or two. "My husband, this city's next mayor—" she would begin with great dignity, and they would smile at her then, beg her forgiveness, offer her space on the bench.

Whores, and judging her. Extraordinary. The red-haired mother, putting on such a tender clucky face as she urged her reluctant daughter into clothes—she clearly did it with every delivery boy, went back into the cold room at the market to do it with the butcher. The dark-haired mother was worse. Nora had heard her mention Jack's name, and laugh. Nora had never seen pictures of her in bed with Jack, but Mr. Kojak couldn't be everywhere, at every keyhole in New York, he had to stop to take a pee now and then.

"Come on, fellows." The dark woman was helping both boys to get dressed—she was an old hand at threesomes, no doubt. The blond mother had gone off somewhere—to the zoo, Nora guessed, to meet Jack for a quickie. But Jack didn't have assignations at the zoo, Mr. Kojak had told her. Maybe blondie liked peanuts.

Nora would have bet a hundred dollars that the mothers had been with Jack all together, a pig pile, oiled and squealing, while the children lay drugged in a closet.

They felt strangely familiar, these three children—not half so close as Daisy, but not like the shriekers on the slides. Because her Daisy had touched them? Or because of the closet?

"Nick! James! Cool it!" They were undoing their sneakers as fast as the dark woman was doing them, and she was getting angry.

"Can I help you?" The words oozed out of Nora's mouth. Not for nothing the big man's wife all these years. "Can I help you?"

She moved toward the bench. How proud they would have been—Jack, Dr. Howard, Mr. Kojak, Mrs. DuPont, all her barriers and brakes and buddies and fuddies. How proud her tulips would have been if they had witnessed. "Can I help you?"

The name of the game was the name. She would have to tell Dr. Howard. They could patent the idea or something. Nora Keefe talked only to flowers. Nora Mayor bloomed in any old basket.

Though it wasn't just the name that gave her power to reach out to strangers, was it? Daisy's blood in her mouth was everything. For thou art the power and the wine. If we'd had Daisy from the start, my Jack, you would be president now. See how good I am with a crowd? I am beautiful, but women do not hate me because I nicely share my husband. If the nation could vote in bed!

"If he'll let you," the dark-haired mother said doubtfully. "You know how kids are with people they don't know."

Nora knelt down at the bench, in front of the blond boy. "Well, thank you for coming to my shoe store, young man," she said gaily, right into his sullenness. "And what may I sell you today? A pair of sandals in gray? Nice argyle socks all full of rocks? Brown tie shoes as old as the news?"

The red-haired girl said, "Saddle shoes all full of poo?"

"Stephanie!" her mother gurgled.

The dark-haired boy said, "Slippers with flippers?"

The blond boy laughed.

"Sneakers with squeakers?" asked Nora. She got the sneakers over his socks and went about tying double knots.

The blond mother came back, toting a brown paper bag patched with wetness. "Did Jill and Daisy go?" She dropped a kiss in the blond boy's hair. She gave Nora the coolish smile mothers give to strangers who are tying their little boys' sneakers.

Watery, Nora thought, too watery for Jack though pretty, but he'd probably done her anyway, just to be kind.

"Daisy took a tumble under the sprinkler," the red-haired mother said. "No big deal, but Jill took her home to clean up her knees. Wait till these kids start skating. Knees, knees, knees." She gurgled, she giggled. Nora wanted to vomit. "We ought to be going, too." She hoisted her daughter onto her lap. "Henry will have my head."

"Don't you want your Tab?" the watery blonde asked.

"Sweetie, do I ever."

Nora watched her dig change out of the pocket of her pink shirt. Carrot top is a friend of mine, she will do it anytime, for a nickel or a dime, fifteen cents for overtime.

"Fifty cents?" Carrot top said. "Sixty?"

"Seventy-five, and Daddy says it's going to get worse. The worst White House in his memory, he says. Drink deep."

If you were president, Jack, the fountains would spurt gold, the streets would be paved with cupcakes.

"There," Nora said. She patted the well-tied sneakers. "They won't come off in a hurry." She bestowed her vote-getting smile. "I'm Mrs. Mayor. Nora Mayor," patting her chignon. "I'm spending the summer here to be near my granddaughter."

The mothers said nothing. They smiled vaguely. They were waiting, she knew, for her to crumble to dust, be swept away by the man who raked the cigarette butts and glass out of the sandbox.

I won't go, Jack, I'll campaign for you until I drop.

The little red-haired girl looked at her and said, "Do you know the umbrella man?"

The dark-haired boy said, "Lokomo hates the umbrella man."

"Oh, but the umbrella man is kind." Nora's hand went to her throat. A strange grief was rising up in her. "The umbrella man is our friend."

Carrot top snickered. The dark whore raised an eyebrow. Butter-wouldn't-melt blondie handed the dark one a tall cardboard drink container. "Yours is a big buck."

"Oh, bazooly—" patting pockets, digging through her carryall—"I came out without a cent. I'll ask Bob to give it to you at the opening." She said to Nora, "Do you really know the umbrella man?"

The blond woman made a face. "I'm not going to the opening."

"Why ever not, Elizabeth?" the red-haired woman said. "It's going to be such fun. Very glittery crowd. Whoo."

"No," Nora said carefully to the dark one, "I just have a feeling the umbrella man is good. Did I—" fluttery—"say something wrong?"

"Jackie, I'm going to the jungle gym," the dark boy told his mother.

"Okay, honey. Be careful."

The other two ran off with him. Nora saw the children at large in the playground draw back to give them room. Oh, yes, she thought.

The mothers looked at her as though to say, The kids have gone, now you go, too; but she didn't go. She wouldn't sit until they asked her, but she wouldn't go. Would stand there until the sun went down if she liked. When Jack was mayor she would ask him to christen the playground after her. The whoremothers would eat their hands every time they saw the sign: Welcome to the Nora Keefe Memorial Playground. She would die in the gladdest second to live on as torment to them.

"Oliver was going to sit with James," the watery blonde was saying, "but he—he's got a—he can't."

"Can't you leave him with Mrs. DuPont just this once?" the redhead asked.

Names tickled Nora's brain. She stifled an exclamation. Elizabeth . . . Oliver . . . Mrs. DuPont. The watery blonde must be the Mrs. Gray for whom Mrs. DuPont kept house every day but the Mondays she gave to the Keefes. Elizabeth and Oliver Gray, and little James. Mrs. DuPont had tried telling of James's cuteness one day until Nora had made it quite clear that such tales left her colder than cold.

And it was Jack who had brought Mrs. DuPont into their household the day he found the mouse in the oven. Had known of her existence because he'd been in Elizabeth's watery oven? He'd said it had been Oliver Gray who'd recommended her, one day at the Downtown Athletic Club, but when did he tell the truth if a lie would do? I will stand here with your public, Jack, until the crown is ours.

"I'll take James," the dark-haired woman said. "I'll be home anyway with Nick—I'll bring him back to our place from the park, if you like, and you can pick him up after the opening."

"Oh, Jackie, how nice, are you sure? Why aren't you going yourself?"

"What am I, a culture maven all of a sudden? Hey, you know me, my idea of a great Tuesday night is to take off my shoes and not go farther than the bathroom. You're not insulted, are you, Heidi?"

"Listen, sweetie, if you can make twenty zillion trips to Paris and never set foot in the Louvre, I guess I can't be.

Though I trust—" severely—"that when the time comes, you'll put Nick's art education in my hands."

Nora thought the dark one would blow away, she liked that idea so much.

"You bet I will," she trilled. "And Bob can teach Stephanie tennis. And James, too," she said to Mrs. Oliver Watery Oven Gray.

"Bob is coming, isn't he?" the red-haired one said.

"Well, sure. Got to have the family represented. Anyway, he doesn't walk across the Atlantic twice a week, he likes getting out." She winked, and Nora shuddered. "Now you girls keep an eye on him. So do I get James tonight?"

"That's lovely of you, especially after yesterday. Look, let me ask Mrs. DuPont to bring over a pile of fried chicken around six. She makes the best fried chicken."

Nora stared at the jungle gym, at the swings. One little girl had been swinging for half an hour straight, how did their stomachs take it? Mrs. DuPont had made her fried chicken for Jack and Nora once. Chicken arteriosclerosis, Jack had called it.

"I can make the kids' supper," the dark mother said, sniffily.

"Of course you can, but why should you have to? You won't have to feed enough hundreds of people this weekend? If you'd rather, I'll have Goldberg's send over a pizza. I'm just being selfish, honestly—I don't want to be too horribly in hock to you."

They hate the dark one, Nora thought, and she knows, but she won't go away—just like me. She wanted to reach out a sisterly hand; then the dark one yawned, and Nora saw her stretching her mouth to swallow Jack, and the sisterly hand turned to wood.

The red-haired mother got up. "You two work out this fascinating problem." She yodeled for her child. She came face to face with Nora, standing there diffidently but so definitely. "Our lady of the sprinkler!" she said.

"I do hope little Daisy's over her spill," Nora said. "It

would be a shame—" a bit breathlessly—"for her mother to miss your opening. An art gallery, is it? Not that I mean to pry. She looks very artistic—Daisy's mother. But then all you young mothers do so much. Very different from my time. My daughter does a grand job under the circumstances, though I do wish she didn't have Lily in day care, and now that I'm here, maybe she'll feel she doesn't have to. Because the mayor—there's nothing like family, is there? Even mayors have families. Presidents do. Do you think Daisy's all right?" Her heart pounded.

"Oh, she's the most resilient kid in the bunch," the red-haired mother said.

The dark-haired mother said from the bench, "Jill's not going to miss that opening, don't worry, not after dropping a hundred fifty bucks at Charles Jourdan."

They don't like Jill, Nora thought. They don't like each other at all. Ding, dong bell. Pussy's in the well. They know what they do when they're not here. They despise one another. Who put it in? Little Jackie Thin. Who took it out? Little Jackie Stout.

"Charles Jourdan?" Nora said.

"Shoes," the dark woman said. "To die for."

Clouds sailed across the sun. Nora's thin body shook. Would you be so kind, Mrs. DuPont, as to fetch my Aran sweater? When my husband is mayor, there will be no winter here. We will beat our snowplows into swords and sell them to angry nations. There will be no clouds in summer except when we are sleeping. Don't be frightened of the thunder, darling, the flowers need the rain.

She said goodbye to the mothers. She hurried out of the park. Jack, I don't know if I'm ready. I thought it would take a while. God moves in merciful ways. Do you like graham crackers, Dr. Howard? Ms. Arthur will be upset if she finds crumbs on the couch. Jill in her streetwalker's shoes, leaving her baby behind.

She stood at Fifth Avenue, waiting for the light to change, watching the taxis stream by, pointed toward

Greenwich Village. You can't go home again, Mrs. Mayor, the 3:25 to Greenwich has been deranged.

She gathered her lies about her as she nodded to the doorman at the building she had bought for her girl, as she floated through the lobby and rose in the elevator. The pains were beginning now, slight and far apart but unmistakable. She let herself into the apartment. She went directly to the child's room. She took off her shoes and arranged them toe to toe, then lay down on the bottom bunk bed, on the Mickey Mouse pillow and sheets. The pains were getting stronger. She reached out supplicating arms to the teddy bears and the trucks. She thirsted for tea, but the books believed in empty stomachs. She rubbed her belly. She took deep breaths. One was supposed to count, she had read. Dear Dr. Howard, will it hurt awfully much? Do not shoot me with damaging drugs, no matter how much I beg you. Pain lasts only a minute, a child is forever. It's coming. I think it's coming. Is it a boy? I will love a boy but I do hope it's a girl. Oh, is it really really a girl? She looks so much like me, I can't believe it, forgive me for loving my own beauty. Daisy, darling Daisy, let me hold her, you needn't wash her first, our blood and shit are one, isn't she lovely, Jack, really she looks just like you, we will all sleep together tonight, don't be afraid of the thunder.

26.

Heidi Kahn had a headache. Her mouth was parched and tasted mildewy. Her body was still going fast, but her mind had gotten lumpy, her temper snappy. She'd yelled at Stephanie to put away her toys—yelled like an ordinary harassed cut-off mother, the sort she most disliked being. Stephanie had cried. Now she was sulking on Heidi's chaise longue, stroking her old pink blanket, sucking her fingers. Heidi would have to make peace with her before Mary

Girard picked her up to take her to Jill and Daisy's. Heidi didn't want to have to say soothing things, take time to cuddle. She wanted to sit on the toilet by herself, and take a shower by herself, and do magic at her dressing table by herself. She wanted to shuck off her mothering body and mothering mind and get perfectly glamorous and brilliant for Henry and the horde coming their way in an hour.

She rose above her mood and ruffled Stephanie's red hair. She kissed the small nose. She gave Stephanie an old *New Yorker* and a pair of snub-nosed paper scissors and told her to cut to her heart's content. Joy for the kid, peace for the beast, Heidi thought. She went into the big cool blue bathroom that adjoined her and Henry's bedroom.

What goes up must come down. She got onto her scale—a proper doctor's scale with weights and balances, calibrated to the quarter pound—and put her hand on the sliding metal cylinder that would deliver the verdict on her body. And—all right. Down she'd come, a whole pound and a quarter, down to one eighteen and three-quarters, maybe one eighteen and a half if she pushed out all her breath—no, one eighteen and three-quarters she stayed. Good enough. Because it had fled from the gut, her middle was truly flat, she could dress like a person for the opening, she would do Henry and the paintings proud.

"Mommy? Can I weigh myself?"

"Sweetie, I'd like some privacy, if you don't mind." Dexamyl had what her old friend Mark had chastely called a powerful cleansing effect. Heidi wanted the bathroom to herself, and now.

"First I'll weigh myself, then you can be private."

"Okay, okay. Hurry, please, sweetie."

"I'll weigh myself with Banky, and then I'll weigh myself without Banky," Stephanie said.

"Come on, Steph, just get on the scale, will you? Dammit, this scale is here twenty-four hours a day, why did you have to pick now? There. Whoo. You weigh twenty-nine pounds. Terrific. Dr. Miller will be impressed. Go wait in the bedroom now, okay? Daddy'll be up in a minute. I want to get through with my shower."

"I want to have a shower with you."

"Stephanie! Jesus! Get out and let me use the toilet. Have a heart. Mothers are people too. Go sit on my chaise and cut the hell out of that *New Yorker*. We'll shower together tomorrow. Go." She propelled her daughter out of the bathroom and closed the door, hating herself, yelling at herself not to hate herself, mothers have some rights.

Was there a clingy stage at three and a half? Heidi thought back to Julie at that age, she consulted the various pundits whose words were stored in her brain as water beat down on her head and body. Thank all the gods that were for the existence of showers. She turned knobs to make the water hotter and stronger. Three-and-a-halfs were famous for saying no, for pushing, not pulling. Silly, though, to worry, to overanalyze. One cling didn't make a stage. Maybe Stephanie was coming down with something, whatever James had, or maybe something had upset her. Sure, the brouhaha with Julie and Amanda that morning, the still unexplained storm that had sent Julie into hysterics, Amanda spinning home to have breakfast with her mother. Heidi stepped out of the shower and reached for towels. Julie and Amanda had patched up their coolness sufficiently to plot another night together, but Heidi was only marginally consoled; there was a trouble still to be dealt with, a trouble involving both her girls. She vigorously toweled her hair, too impatient, too wrought, too late, to give it the gentle pats her stylist prescribed, as if her hair were tender leaves of freshly washed Bibb lettuce. She turned on her hair blower. She turned it off. "Stephanie?" She opened the door.

"Hi, Mom." Stephanie was stretched out on Heidi's chaise, her blanket over her, fingers in her mouth.

"I love you." Heidi bent down to kiss her daughter. "Don't mind my wet hair."

"Can we play hairdresser?"

"Not today, sweetie, I just don't have time, I have to blow it myself. But I'll leave the bathroom door open." Heidi sat down at her dressing table, shifted the blower into overdrive, and blew her hair into a perfect frenzy. She stroked moisturizing cream onto her face. She waved at her daughter's angled reflection in the dressing table mirror.

She heard door sounds. "Is that your father?" she called out.

"It's nobody." Stephanie giggled. "Hi, nobody."

"Hi, nobody," Heidi said. Where was Henry? She'd hoped he'd have time to stretch out on the bed for ten minutes. She dotted her face with ivory foundation, then blended it over her face with knowing fingertips. "Stephanie, want to watch me do my eyes?"

"Nobody's home." Stephanie giggled again.

"This offer will not be repeated," Heidi said playfully. Tomorrow she had to call Julie's school to arrange for Julie's class to come to the gallery to see the new show. Then she had to throw herself into setting up separate rooms for the girls. She'd wanted Julie to make that leap, but she hadn't wanted it to happen the way it had, with trauma and tears. Stephanie would be wrenched. Heidi would have to make it up to her—maybe a kitten? Henry would kick and scream, unless they could figure out a civilized way to deal with the litter. Jill kept her cat's litter box on the fire escape. The Kahns would find a way.

She reviewed her reflected face. A painterly palette . . . masterful brushwork. Henry was right. Hers was a face the German Expressionists would have lined up to paint. She would like to have been painted by Gabriele Münter. There was a great artist and a great woman, staying on in the house she had shared with Kandinsky to guard his paintings from the Nazis even though Kandinsky had left her for another woman. I love Henry that much, she thought. He loves me that much. We love the children that much. Dear God, I do love the children, even though I wear forest green mascara. I think I will start lighting candles Friday nights. I want to be flagrantly Jewish. Hanukkah isn't enough. Is it the Weimar Republic all over again? Who can afford to buy paintings anymore? Thank God we own the building. If times get very tough and they come after us, I want to be outrageously Jewish. Just don't ask us to hang Chagall. There are limits.

"Hi, sweetie. How does your old mama look?"

"Naked." Stephanie stroked Banky.

"Ha ha. Such a wit. Well, clothes is next. Clothes *are* next? I think I'll wear that green dress your father likes so much. Since I happen to be so Slenderella tonight. You know, it's exactly the green of the tree in the Münter we've got in the show." She put her hand on her closet door.

"Mama!" Stephanie screamed.

Heidi whirled around.

"Mama, don't open your closet!" Tears were streaming down Stephanie's face. She clutched her blanket.

"Steph?" Heidi knelt by the chaise. "Steph? What on earth?"

"Mama, I'm so sorry. I didn't mean to do it. I didn't mean to," Stephanie sobbed.

"Sweetie? Did you break something? While I was in the bathroom? It can't be as terrible as all that. Things are only things." She put a tissue in Stephanie's hand but Stephanie didn't use it. Heidi kissed the tears.

"I'm so so so so sorry."

"Tell me, Steph. I won't be mad, I promise. Use the tissue, please."

"I cut it up so hard." Stephanie's eyes blinked frantically. "I don't think it'll go back together. I tried, I really tried, but it wouldn't go."

Heidi got up on the chaise and stretched out next to her daughter. "What did you cut up, sweetie?"

"Your dress." Fresh tears came coursing down the small fat cheeks.

Cold ribboned across Heidi's chest. "My dress?" She looked at her closet door.

Stephanie slowly pulled *The New Yorker* out from under her blanket and handed it to Heidi. Heidi opened it up. She saw shreds. She saw confetti. A full page ad from Saks Fifth Avenue was now only a woman's head.

Heidi was so relieved that laughter came belching out. "Oh, sweetie. It's just a magazine. I told you you could cut it. At least you left the head. Don't feel guilty. Save that for when you're a mother."

"I cut it up so so so hard," Stephanie sobbed.

"Listen, Steph, I've been a perfect beast today, I know, and Daddy's been busy, and you had a hard time with Julie this morning—but that doesn't mean we don't love you with all our hearts. If I think about Daddy or the opening or clothes, it doesn't mean I've stopped thinking about you. Underneath, I'm always thinking about you. You know that, don't you?" She hummed like bees in Stephanie's hair, an old joke of theirs. "Because you're my honey girl, my sweet sweet sweetie. May I get dressed now?"

"Oh, no, please, Mama, don't open your closet. I'm so scared."

"What's to be scared of? Are you afraid something's in there?" She had an insight. "The umbrella man?"

"No, no, no. Don't open it."

"I have to open it, Steph. Want to come over with me, holding hands, so you can see there's nothing bad in it?"

"You're going to hate me. You're going to kill me."

"Oh, but sweetie—never! You're my love." Heidi rocked her until she felt a measure of peace return to the room. She wanted to get on with dressing, but she didn't dare move.

Henry walked into the bedroom. "Hello, my ladies."

"Hi, darling!" Heidi thought she'd never been happier to see him. "Everything all set below?"

"Just about. The bartender showed up with those paper napkins that have poodles drinking martinis on them, and Marguerite is having an esthetic breakdown, but that looks to be the last crisis." He took off his sleeveless cashmere sweater, started to unbutton his rumpled white shirt.

"Marguerite just can't stand the idea of a woman behind the bar." Heidi hugged Stephanie to her. "Tell me what makes people tick, will you?"

"Clocks make them tick," Stephanie said.

Her father swooped down on her. "Do I smell tears? What's going on? Has Banky been crying?"

"Stephanie doesn't want me to open my closet," Heidi said.

"She doesn't, doesn't she?"

"Because I cut up her dress so hard, and I'm so sad," Stephanie said.

Heidi handed him the mutilated *New Yorker*. "Cut it up with my blessing, I hasten to add."

"I want to put it together again, but I don't know if I can," Stephanie wailed. "Can I have a TV?" She put her face into her hands and sobbed.

"No," Henry said cheerfully, "but you can have a new record player, if you like."

"I already have a record player."

"You share that one with Julie. Suppose we got you one all your own."

"Could I have my own *Peter and the Wolf*? Without any scratches on it?"

"Sure." Henry looked at Heidi. "All right with you?"

"Oh, consult me now," she said, but she wasn't angry. She loved his sensitivity to the girls' moods, his deft way of defusing tension. "And your own *Hansel and Gretel*, if you like."

"Mom, I'm so so sorry about your dress."

Henry inverted *The New Yorker*. Confetti trickled down to the chaise. "You know what this is?" he said to Stephanie. "A cut-up magazine, that's all. Your mother's dress is fine. You're a good girl. It's all right to open the closet."

"I don't want to go to Daisy's house. I want Julie to babysit me. I won't be a bedbug anymore."

Henry ran a hand through his thinning hair.

"Can you lie down for ten minutes?" Heidi asked. She wanted to lie down with him, to tell him that she was glad to be his wife, the mother of his kids, that she would never again grumble about his grumbly side.

"I don't want to go to Daisy's house because I don't like Iceman and Lokomo." Stephanie was close to tears again.

"I thought Iceman and Lokomo were your friends," Heidi said.

"Well, today there was a different Iceman. His name was Ken. Not a pretend Ken. He sat in a circle with us. We did things."

Heidi and Henry exchanged glances.

"What kinds of things?" Heidi asked cautiously.

"You know. Scary things."

"We don't know, baby girl," Henry said. He sat at her feet. Heidi went on rocking her.

"We went to see James on Lokomo. Because Jill burned her hand. I don't like Jill anymore."

"I never liked Jill," Henry muttered.

"Henry!" Heidi stroked Stephanie's hair. "But James was sick this morning, sweetie."

"Well, we didn't catch anything because we didn't take our bodies. Can I go to the opening? Please? I'll be so good. I hate Jill. Jill let Iceman take us. It made my stomach hurt. I don't want to be in the circle. The circle killed your dress. Can I go to the opening?"

Heidi fought to stay calm. One hand went to the steadying coolness of Henry's shirt sleeve. "Sweetie," she said to Stephanie, "you'd be bored in five minutes. You can come to openings when you're six. You know what? You won't want to come. Julie never wants to come. Hey, here's a terrific idea, don't you think, Henry? How would you like to go to Nick's house instead of Daisy's? James will be there too. Daddy or I will walk you over. I think they're having pizza for dinner."

"What a smart mother you have," Henry said.

"Is that okay, Steph?" Heidi asked.

Stephanie nodded.

"That's my sweetie. Now go wash your face with lots of cold water. You can use our bathroom—special treat. Any towel you like."

Stephanie hopped down off the chaise and went into the bathroom. Heidi and Henry reached for each other.

"Let's take a trip," Henry said. "As soon as school is over for Julie. Let's take the girls to Venice. Marguerite can run things."

"Henry, I do love you so much. What on earth do you think they did with this Ken person?"

"A séance or some crap like that? I'd expect that from Jill."

"You're so judgmental. Positively Victorian. Just because she's divorced."

"Divorced, my eye," Henry said. "I wouldn't be surprised if she didn't know who Daisy's father was."

"Henry!" Heidi leaned against him to cancel out the scold in her voice. "I suppose that's the end of the Playgroup."

"I never liked the Playgroup. I think Stephanie should go to school in the fall." Henry chastely kissed Heidi's cheek. "That didn't rearrange the artwork, did it? You're very beautiful tonight. Bony but beautiful. If we go to Venice, you're going to eat pasta noon and night."

"Henry, you don't really want a fat old broad for a wife, do you?"

"I want you healthy. Are you on one of your starvation kicks again? What did you have for lunch?"

I will throw those pills away, Heidi thought guiltily; I will throw them down the toilet. "The real question," she said, "isn't what I had for lunch, it's how we're going to get Stephanie into a decent school this fall. If we really decide to send her."

"We don't have pull in this town? Come on. All we have to do is tell Frank Herrup he can buy the Klee, and she's into Snooterly."

"Someday, you know, my Henry, you're going to call it

that in front of Frank. Anyway, we're not selling the Klee."

"I'm glad you have your priorities intact."

Stephanie emerged from the bathroom, shiny of face. Heidi called Jackie and Jackie said she'd be delighted to have one more body—what the bazooly. Heidi called Jill and said, in a voice giving nothing away, that there had been a change, Stephanie wouldn't be coming over, she'd explain all to Jill later.

"You still want her here?" Henry said.

"I want to know what happened this morning. I better call Mary Girard before she leaves the dormitory. Oh, Henry, it's all my fault. Jill's been very weird about the kids lately, and I didn't pay attention, I didn't take her seriously."

"Never mind," Henry said. "It happened, Stephanie ventilated, we got the message, it's over." He picked Stephanie up. "What do you say, sprout? How about letting your mother and me get dressed in private? You go pick out a couple of books to bring to Nick's. Jackie does know how to read, doesn't she?"

"Henry!" Heidi scolded.

Stephanie went to her room.

Heidi took off her robe. She opened her closet door.

27.

Albert Cunningham, who did not do matrimonial, had that let-down feeling. Nearly two hours since Washington had appeared to enlist his aid, and the enemy had not struck. Mrs. so-called Mayor was safe in the fourth floor apartment she'd sublet from the innocent Hollenbachs (or were they so innocent? Those university people; and five-year-old Harry didn't look like either parent, had maybe been given to them for cover; Albert would take a careful look at their luggage tags when they came back from their so-called vacation in Japan). Mrs. so-called Mayor was safe upstairs, and not a dragon had dared the portals. No suspicious packages had arrived. No gentlemen bearing poisoned umbrellas had come claiming they were elevator inspectors. A tall man in a foreign agent trenchcoat had walked by the building twice, but no one who dressed that much like a spy could possibly be a spy. Albert wondered guiltily if he'd taken more than he should have from Washington. The day wasn't done by any means, though, was it? Young Gary Purdys wouldn't be taking over the door for another four hours yet. And there was always tomorrow—though Washington had made action sound imminent. He'd get his chance, one way or another, to display a hundred forty dollars' worth of heroics. Never mind about the so-called legacy of Tito. The Yugos were Moscow, and Moscow wasn't sleeping.

Albert got out a chamois cloth and shined up the oval copper tub of dried flowers and leaves reposing beneath the intercom phone in the outer lobby. Cleaning and polishing were not among his duties, but he was senior man at the door, and he felt that disorder in the lobby shamed him. He did not like finger-printed copper, any more than he liked Gary Purdys's habit of unbuttoning the top button of his tunic. Mrs. Cohn in 20-A always noticed the gleam of the tub, let Albert know it brightened her day. Albert had no problem with Jews. Israel, God bless it, was a thorn in the side of Moscow. He had no problems with anyone, except the enemies of freedom. He wondered why Washington was so set on keeping Mrs. so-called Mayor where she was instead of grabbing her. Maybe they were doubling her. Or maybe they had someone inside the Yugo Mission who would feed her disinformation through their adjoining wall.

The intercom sounded—the service entrance. Albert flipped on the closed-circuit TV. Mrs. Nkruma was returning from the park with her Pekingese. Young Gary Purdys had once said to Albert that the Nkrumas and that little blond dog were practically miscegenation. Albert had gotten angry. He didn't care about the Nkrumas' color. What bothered him was that Dr. Nkruma worked for the United

Nations. The Nkrumas lived on the fourth floor, across from the Hollenbachs. Albert buzzed Mrs. Nkruma in, thinking.

He put the inner door on the buzzer system and went back to the washroom behind the mailroom. He spun open the combination lock that kept his cubby private. He got out the pistol he had on hand for the times, every two or three months, when young Gary called in sick, and Albert stayed on an extra stretch, into the dark and dangerous hours.

He brought the pistol back to the outer lobby and concealed it among the dried flowers and leaves in the brightly gleaming oval copper tub. He went on thinking.

28.

Mary Girard, will you forgive me? You were dear that afternoon, arriving timely and plump in your scruffy jeans and sneakers, staring worshipfully at my, yes, Charles Jourdan sandals—not the pistachio confections that had stunned me my first day in New York but a giddy enough pair at that, three shades of red banding across the toes, thin two-inch vermilion heels straight as a Victorian spine. Dear you were, and competent looking, with that brisk round cheery student nurse's face of yours. You came bookless and without boyfriend, ready to serve with all your being. Stupid little bitch, if you—

I'd had my qualms throughout the day about leaving Daisy in the evening. I'd gone so far as to pick up the phone and dial the first two digits of Mary's number. I would take my life off the hook and bar the doors. Daisy and I would cozy up under my quilts with chicken-and-watercress sandwiches on homemade pita bread. We would read and draw houses with chimneys and play ferocious Go Fish and solicit each other's opinion on the issues of the day. I would make my apologies to Heidi and arrange to see the show another time. I would tell Ken Huysman: No.

But—you know me. I was no respecter of my qualms.

The opposite. I had to prove to the watching world that fear did not own me. I had to thumb my rational nose at the assaults of the day. They weren't real, after all, like yeast or steel or angles, like my new French shoes.

Mary made leaving easy. The other Playgroup had confessed to similar feelings. Mary was that little bit better at managing our children and our homes than we were ourselves. I trusted her with all my being to get Daisy out in case of fire—I was sure she would even get the cat out. I knew that peanut butter would not grout the precious little windpipe when Mary was around. Crisp messages would be left if anyone called. The living room would be a shade neater than Mary had found it.

She came. She stared at my shoes. She declined to have a cold drink.

"Mary," I said, when Daisy was off in her room, "I have to tell you, a man called early this morning and tried to scare me. Started asking if the doors and windows were locked. I called the cops. They had no real suggestions—didn't seem to think he was anything but a crank. What will you do if he calls back?"

"Maybe you should hope he does. If he calls tonight, he won't call again, believe me." Mary, beaming, reached inside her blue button-down-collar shirt, where five or six gold chains of varying thickness terminated in objects hidden from public view. I half expected her to produce a cross to be brandished in the presence of evil—not our Mary. She came up with a tiny silver whistle. "I blow this right into the phone," she said, "and he'll be on his way to Manhattan Eye and Ear, screaming."

"Doesn't that violate your oath?" I asked, as she tucked the whistle back inside her shirt.

She pointed across the room. Daisy was standing in her doorway feeding the doll named Grouch with a special little trick bottle that looked to empty of milk when she turned it upside down. How my parents would have smiled at that bottle. "There's my oath," Mary said seriously.

You see? Anxiety felt stupid, indulgent, when Mary was around. I found myself saying to her, "I've been thinking about doing some work again." My heart kicked up its heels at my words. "Would you be interested in a steady arrangement? You could take Daisy to the park. Or play here if the weather's bad. Friday morning would be good." The Playgroup didn't meet on Friday. Daisy sometimes had withdrawal symptoms. A regular date with Mary, whom she adored, would ease the pain. "Say ten to one?"

"I've got clinical all day Friday. Dumb summer schedule. I could give you Thursday afternoon."

"I'll take it." I had the Playgroup Thursday mornings, so separating out in the afternoon would be a burden I could bear. "Terrific."

Mary didn't ask what kind of work I did, any more than she'd asked for theories about the evil phone call. I'd noticed before that she never freighted her mind with unnecessary cargo. A giving, uncluttered person. Mary, I'm sorry.

Daisy came running over with Grouch. "Mom, let's play that you're the babysitter and Mary is the mom, okay?"

"Okay," I said, catching her up, hugging her hard. "Then I have to finish getting dressed before Ken gets here." I had showered, I'd pulled on silky pantystockings, I'd stepped into my fabulous shoes, to help my feet get over their shock before they went public. The rest of me was robe and unpolished face.

"Oh, hi, babysitter," Daisy trilled at me, as I set her down. "I'm sure glad to see you."

"Hi, Daisy," I said. "I'm sure glad to be here. We'll have fun when your old mother leaves. Hi, Jill," I said to Mary. "You look terrific tonight. What's for dinner?"

Mary cleared her throat.

"Pasta salad," Daisy prompted, "with shell pasta because shells taste better than elbows. And ham without any— any—"

"Nitrites," Mary guessed. She'd been under our roof before. She gave me a suspicious glance, quite outside of the game. Like every other nursing student I'd met, she mistrusted "healthy" food.

"Oh, good," I said. "Pasta salad and ham. My favorites."

Daisy threw her arms around Mary's knees. "'Bye, Mom," she said. "Have a wonderful time. Don't come home too late or your taxi crab might turn into a pumpkin. I mean, your trashy cab!"

Mary patted Daisy's head. "Okay," she said, with all the mommyness she could muster. Games weren't her strength. "You do everything your sitter tells you, right?"

"Right, because she won't tell me anything!" Daisy went spinning across the room in that way she had, spiraling into her laughter.

"Well, now you know what's for dinner," I said to Mary. "The pasta's in the white ceramic bowl in the refrigerator, and you can't miss the ham. You know where the carving knife is, don't you? Of course you do. You know where everything is. I'll leave you to it. Daisy missed 'Sesame Street' this morning so she might want to watch it now, but she might not. Maybe just 'Mr. Rogers' and 'The Electric Company.'"

Mary nodded, and kept on nodding, until I wound down and went off to my own room. I would not, I vowed, I absolutely would not show Mary the emergency telephone number list again (posted conspicuously in the kitchen), the syrup of ipecac on the top shelf in the medicine cabinet in the bathroom. She knew my safety net down to its holes. I ought to check the expiration date on the ipecac, now that I thought on it. I'd bought it while Daisy was in utero, happily ingesting amniotic fluid; by now it was probably more toxic than anything else she might swallow.

I fooled around with makeup. I put on a red-and-white-striped cotton jersey dress that Daisy had liked in a window on our way home from the market. I had a playground tan, and no one could say I wasn't thin enough for jersey. I wasn't the Jill of old, Jack's Jill, with hair to here and drop-dead clothes; I didn't want to be. I suited myself as I was. I would do for the doctor. The mothers of the Playground would proudly claim me in public as one of theirs without worrying for their husbands.

I put fresh sheets on the bed I'd changed three days before.

Do I have to go on? I could use a nap. If only Mary had stood me up for some thrilling young man. I must get to work on *How to Cook for Your Daughter*. Don't put food on their plates. Let them serve themselves. They feel in control this way. We had a hinged serving spoon, a double spoon, that opened and closed like jaws; Daisy named it Alligator. She liked taking string beans with it. She always liked vegetables. In Vermont we had a garden. I let her work with me in the kitchen from an early age. Taking fava beans from their pods and putting them in a steamer is every bit as much fun as eating crayons. She was good about washing her hands. Don't overcook the carrots. Children like crunch.

Ken arrived at five-forty bearing flowers. "I'm restoring the balance of nature," he said. "A man who takes flowers from a household has to bring some back, don't you think? You don't have an absolute ban on flowers, do you?"

I said I didn't. I started to take them with a properly gracious smile.

"They're for Daisy," he said. "You get me."

My girl carefully opened the florist's wrapping. There were no Gerbers—no daisies at all, the clever man. He'd managed, in the middle of Manhattan, to find a bunch of flowers that looked as though they'd been culled from an early summer garden—ranunculus, zinneas, snapdragons, sweet William—delicate blossoms, softly painted, just right for a child.

"Sweet Kenneth William," I said.

"Oh, boy!" Daisy said.

Mary went to the kitchen and came back with four small pitchers and bottles full of water, the better to occupy Daisy as I departed with Ken. "How do you want to arrange them?" she asked.

"Let's put all the reds together. In that bottle."

I knelt down next to her. "Good night, darling. Have a fine time with Mary. I'll be here when you wake up."

"Good night, Daisy," Ken said. "See you very soon."

Daisy clung to me. "You could be here for breakfast," she said to Ken, "because I make such good coffee."

Mary blushed.

"You do make the best coffee," Ken said.

"I'm going to wake up bright as a bottle," Daisy said.

"I'd like to see that," he said.

I stood up. Daisy fell over the edge into little girlhood. "Don't go, Mama." She clung to me. "I'll be so lonely."

"But Mary's here, girlfriend." I hoisted her. I put my cheek to her cheek. "Thomas is here."

"And my mice might come." She brightened. "Thomas never eats my mice."

I hugged her. This wasn't the moment to pick on the make-believe gang.

"And my new friend might come," Daisy said.

"Which new friend?" Mary asked.

"My new horse friend from the park. Mrs. Mare."

We all laughed. Such a loving girl. So different from her prickly mother. "Long wave the Daisy," I said. One more hug, and I put her down.

"I'll call when we get to the restaurant," I told Mary. "We'll be at the gallery for an hour, I'd guess. The number is next to the kitchen phone. Where the emergency numbers are."

Mary nodded and nodded.

I checked that my keys were in my bag.

Daisy got down among her flowers. If only. If only.

Mary, I'm truly sorry.

29.

At 5:45 P.M., Daylight Saving Time, Elizabeth Gray dialed Kelly Smith in Melbourne, where it was 7:45 the following morning, and on the chilly side.

30.

Heidi was in a mist, in a well, in a war. She didn't want to come home. She urged her head into deeper pillows. I know it was only a dress, but it wasn't only a dress, it was the fabric of my life. Cut into the tiniest pieces, the cookbooks would say a fine dice, green confetti like the green specks of thinness inside the Dexamyl capsule.

Stephanie couldn't have done it. Couldn't have. Those blunt little nothing scissors, her fat beginner's hands. Couldn't have. Heidi swam backward through the mist. She hadn't mentioned the green dress until she was out of the bathroom. Stephanie couldn't have known. No one could have done it. It couldn't have happened. It had happened.

"Henry?"

He was sitting on the side of her bed, weightless as a doctor. Henry, in his new navy pinstriped suit, balding, going thick around the middle, the most beautiful man she knew. Looking at her with eyes that ate at no other table. Had only two lovers in all his years before they met. Waited for her, almost.

"Hi, darling," Henry said.

She had never seen him so sad. His mouth was stroking downward. She took his wrists in her hand so their pain could flow together.

"Stephanie couldn't have done it," she said.

"I know."

"She did it, didn't she? Didn't do it, but did it." She wanted to laugh at her silliness; but she'd forgotten how to laugh, the machine had turned cold. "Where did life go?"

"Heidi," Henry groaned. "Heidi, Heidi. We'll get through this somehow. I love you so much. I love the girls so much."

"Where is she? I need to see her." Her voice spiraled. "Where is she?" Heidi tugged at pillows. Her hands were made of custard. She finally built a wall and slowly unpeeled her spine and propped herself up against it. "My baby. Is she in her room? Did you say anything? You didn't say anything, did you?"

"Of course not. She has no idea. I went to ask if she was set to go to Nick's. She was lying on the floor with Banky, fast asleep. I put her to bed. Clothes and all."

Heidi felt hysteria bubbling up. "Wake her, Henry. Wake her. Wake her. I have to tell her I don't hate her. Henry!"

"Let her sleep, darling. She looked so peaceful. We can't do her any good right now."

"Is she dead?" Heidi shrieked.

"Shhh. Shhh. She's just sleeping. Just a tired little girl dreaming of teddy bears." Tears started down his cheeks.

Heidi reached for him, pulled him to her. "Like confetti," she said softly. "Like confetti. She couldn't have done it. I was right here. Looking at her. When I said. That I wanted to wear the green dress."

"I know. I know."

"I was in my closet an hour before. Everything was fine."

"I know."

"Henry?"

"What, darling?"

"I think I did it myself, I must have done it myself."

"Heidi, no, I don't think so, I wish—no."

"I took a pill," she said. "Please don't hate me. Please. I couldn't bear it. Tell me you don't hate me. I took a pill. To be thin. I'm so sorry. I shouldn't have done it. I'll never do it again. Please. Don't hate me. Dexamyl. I was a little crazy all day. My body was here, my mind was there. I must have done it myself. Somewhere we'll find the scissors. Tell me you don't hate me."

"I don't hate you. I'm sad that you took a pill, but I don't hate you."

"Please, please don't hate me."

"Easy, Heidi. Easy, darling." He kissed her forehead, her cheeks, her lips. "I love you."

"I've failed. My little baby." She started to sob. "What did I let her become? What is she? Why does she hate me? Why does God hate me?"

"Nobody hates you, dearest. Whatever is going on, it's not your fault. We'll get to grips with it. We'll get to the other side. We're all in it together, and we'll get out of it together. Do you think you can sleep?"

Heidi slid back down along her pillows. It's not a school day, is it? I have to call my mother. I forgot to pack Julie's toothbrush. No, I remembered at the last minute. I will light the candles every Friday. I will teach the girls the words. We will cover our heads. I nursed Julie for six months, Stephanie for nearly ten. I have not withheld my body. I have a right to think about dresses. How can I think about dresses? I will never wear bacon again. I had an abortion once. If I hadn't had the abortion, I wouldn't have Henry, the girls wouldn't exist. I want a rabbi.

"I want a rabbi," she said.

"A rabbi?" Henry said. "All right. Whatever."

"I want a kosher closet."

Henry smiled. "I'll find you a rabbi."

"One who doesn't play golf," Heidi said. "May I please have some water?"

He got her water from the bathroom. She sat up again. She heard a distant buzzing and humming. "What time is it?" she asked.

"Almost quarter to six."

"My God. It's started. Downstairs. What are you doing here?"

He kissed her forehead again. "Silly question."

"I've got to pull myself together. You go back to the gallery. I'll be down in ten minutes. How's the crowd?"

"Big," Henry said. "Excited. You don't have to go down. I don't have to either. Marguerite can manage. And Eric. There will be other openings."

"Of course we have to go down." Heidi's voice was gay. "We have to see Jill, don't we?" She swung her legs out of bed. She wobbled to the bathroom. She thought of Stephanie's book of *Bambi*, the pictures of the baby deer unfolding spindly legs, being nosed to his feet by his mama. Nose me, Mama. You never told me these things happened. Heidi brushed her teeth. She glossed her lips. She came back into the bedroom and put on her purple robe.

"How do I look?" she asked Henry.

"Beautiful."

"Let's go," she said.

"Shall I get out a dress for you?" he asked.

"Oh, I'm not afraid of the closet. I don't want to wear a dress. It's a Dior robe, you know."

"Dearest, you can't go downstairs in your robe."

"They'll think it's the latest thing."

"Heidi, you can't. It makes you look—unhappy."

She sat down on her chaise, sank into it. "I want to go away," she said.

"We will, darling. Venice. I meant it. I'll get Marguerite to start making calls first thing tomorrow. Or someplace else if you'd rather. Do you want to visit your mother?"

"I want to go away alone. Just you and me. Not the girls. I don't want to see them again. Oh, Henry, no, I didn't mean it, I didn't, I'm just so scared, I'm so scared. It's the pill. I didn't mean it. I swear it. I want a rabbi. I love them. I didn't mean it. If God had wanted me to have the other child, I would have had it, wouldn't I? Take away the pill. I'm so scared. I must have been the one who cut the dress. I must have been. Maybe Mr. Lucca did it. Him and his feelthy pictures. I didn't go to bed with Mark. We didn't even discuss it. He found me the abortionist that time. I was a stupid kid in college. Did you remember Stephanie's night light? We will never overcome this moment. It will stain us forever. Please go downstairs. I love you. I'm so unworthy. I love you the way Münter loved Kandinsky. I wish I were still nursing. If I could give Stephanie milk! I would give her anything. I'm going to lie down in her bed. Banky and me and baby makes three. I will kill the person who killed us. Don't call a doctor. Really. The pill is almost used up. I just need to lie down with my baby. You go to the opening. Get photographed with the mayor. He used to play shortstop for the Yankees. Jackie slept with the mayor. No, she slept with the other one. The man who wants to be mayor. Where did you hang the Münter?"

"Right where it started," Henry said. "Between the Dove and the O'Keeffe. Can I get you anything, dearest?"

"Just take me to my baby. I want to be there when she wakes up. I will feed her the milk of kindness. Henry, I hate myself. If I wear a robe all my life, will Stephanie be okay? Did you call Jackie to say she isn't coming?"

"Yes," Henry said.

They walked down the hall hand in hand.

"Did the poodle napkins go?" Heidi asked.

"The poodle napkins went. Marguerite ran out and found dark blue ones. Kandinsky would approve."

Stephanie was snoring gently, fisting her pink baby blanket. Heidi eased her over, then lay down beside her, put an arm around her. Henry kissed his two redheads. He stood in the doorway, watching, until Heidi's breathing grew deep and even. He went downstairs.

31.

Arthur Kojak was waiting when Mrs. Keefe walked out of her building. She headed east on Sixty-sixth Street; he followed. She crossed Madison Avenue, head down; he followed. She paused in front of a shoe store on the far corner, big windows with rounded corners, Charles Jourdan in bold white letters over the windows; he crossed to the opposite side, to keep from being mirrored in the windows. He shook his head as she lingered; he felt a fond little smile pushing at his cheeks. Mrs. Keefe hypnotized by shoes—unlikely. But women surprised you that way. His wife had liked shoes. She'd liked getting pedicures. She'd liked watching Arthur's face when he got the bills. Now Mrs. Keefe was walking on. He followed.

At Park Avenue he wanted to shout, to grab her arm. Traffic was turning every which way, and Mrs. Keefe seemed heedless. She stopped on the esplanade, and this stop he understood—there were neat rows of waxy red begonias, she wanted to say hello. He knew she had a greenhouse, was often in it when they talked on the telephone. Now and then, when he'd sent pictures that had pleased her especially, she would get just a little chatty, she would talk about her flowers. Once she had said, "I have to go upstairs and take this on the extension. I can't talk about that woman in front of my tulips."

Not Jill that time. A singer—a tall black woman with tricky breasts and a heart-shaped ass. The things Mrs. Keefe had been through.

She let the traffic lights complete a cycle, then crossed the other half of Park Avenue. Her pace slowed. She paused in front of a building and tilted her head, as though to admire the details over the windows. She put her fingers to a wrought-iron balustrade one house down.

She got to 114, Jill's building.

Arthur crossed the street to her side, cutting back a few yards to stay a safe distance behind her. He didn't like the distance. He wanted to hear her mind. He wanted her to feel his presence, to know she could count on him. He didn't dare cut in, not yet; there was still the chance that she would dismiss him.

She stood there looking up, looking at the doorway.

Go home, Arthur silently begged her; but he knew she wouldn't. He didn't really want her to go. She had a right. After all she'd been through. To some joy.

She looked at the buttons next to the tenants' names. She raised her hand, then let it fall away.

He could open the door for her, Arthur thought. His hand closed around his special keys. He could get her through the front door. He knew she wouldn't hurt the child. A woman who cared about the sensibilities of tulips. She was as fragile as a flower herself. She had been so good with Daisy in the park. He had been there, among the trees. He had seen her pick Daisy up, get her out from under the sprinkler, moving twice as fast as Jill because she knew what love really meant. He had wanted a child himself but Mrs. Kojak had said no. He emerged from the shadows. He walked straight to 114.

"Let you in?" he said, in his jolly super's voice, one of his dozens of voices. He pulled out his ring of keys. His mouth was sucked totally dry the way it got at the dentist's office when they put in the saliva ejector. He couldn't believe he was standing so near to her—he could touch her if he wanted to. She smelled of sweet talc, a gentle elderly smell. Her skin looked as though it would fragment if you blew across her face, like the puffballs he'd huffed at in the summers of his boyhood. He tried three keys, without any luck. "I'm the super's brother," he said. "Laid up with a bad back. I'll get it in a minute." He got it.

"Tell your brother the yews need watering," Mrs. Keefe said, as he held the door open for her.

"The what?"

"The yew trees. In those tubs."

"It's going to rain. Any minute," he said.

"They have dense branches. Rain may not penetrate to the soil. Tell him to take a hose to those tubs and soak them."

He watched through the grillwork over the front door as she walked across the lobby to the elevator and summoned it down. He wondered if he'd done wrong. Neither right nor wrong, he decided. He went back along Sixty-sixth Street, west to Fifth Avenue, and took up his post among the trees opposite the big apartment building. He was getting hungry, and not for vending cart junk. He wished Nora and Daisy would come home.

32.

Jackie set the pizza out in the living room because she wanted to watch the six o'clock local news on TV, she wanted to see what Jack Keefe looked like when he made his big announcement. "Boys! Pizza's on! Come and get it." The mayor of New York—to think of it. Well, Bob would be glad of one thing. She would finally register to vote. She hoped she wasn't too late to vote in the primary. "Get it while it's hot!"

The boys came galloping in, neighing, snorting, until she told them enough was enough, time for a little hay. She sat them down on the floor in front of the couch. No need for tomato sauce on the couch, right? She slid triangles of pizza onto plates.

James said, "Ride a cock horse to Banbury Cross to see a fine Daisy upon a white horse."

Nick said, "Ride a cock horse to Danbury Cross to see a fine Daisy on a crazy horse."

"Yeah, Nick," Jackie said. "Yeah, James." She clapped.

"Mom, why is a woman horse called a mare?"

"It just is, honey. Shhh, they're starting. Want me to cut your pizza?"

The boys said no. Jackie watched impatiently as the anchorman went on about a scandal in the Water Department. Who cared? She took a bite of pizza. "Good, isn't it?"

Nick said, "I'm a little worried about a mare."

"You promised," James said to Jackie.

"Promised what?" A commercial came on. Cars—sure, just what they needed. She saw that the boys weren't touching their food. "Is it too hot? Blow on it. This is a picnic, right? We don't have to worry about manners."

"You promised that Daisy wouldn't go away like Megan," James said.

"Well, it's not really something I can promise, but I don't think she will."

"What do you call a man horse?" Nick said.

"A stallion. James, are you okay?" He was pale again. She hoped he wasn't going to have another bout of whatever had felled him that morning.

"I'm sad about Daisy," he said.

"Honey, what's to be sad about? You'll see her tomorrow morning, right here."

"I wish I'd kicked her," James said.

"James, you want something instead of pizza? I could make you scrambled eggs."

Nick pushed his plate away. "You should have kicked her in the head, James."

"Boys, boys. If you don't want to eat, okay, but calm down. Hey, here it comes. Come on, cozy up." She patted the couch to either side of her. She put out her arms. "See that man? I know him. Isn't that fun?"

"He's a stallion," Nick said.

"Jesus Christ!" Jackie laughed. "Where on earth do you boys get it from?" She shook her head. Bob would break right up. She hugged Nick and James. She waved at the television screen. Jack Keefe looked exactly the same. She could almost taste champagne. That beautiful silvery hair. "I will not lie back and watch the heart's blood drain out of New York," he was saying. A stallion. What a riot.

"Goodbye, Daisy," James said.

"Goodbye, Daisy," Nick said.

An absolute riot, Jackie thought. She could hardly wait for Bob to come home and share the joke.

33.

"Who dunnit?" Ken asked.

We were standing in front of a soft-edge oil of houses on a sweep of snowy road, pine trees in the foreground, blue mountains stretching out in the background. All around us the H. and H. Kahn gallery throbbed. Flashbulbs popped. People exclaimed one another's names. Waitresses were offering up seedless baby avocados and fried squid on rounds of semolina bread. Ken and I may have been the only two people looking at art.

I checked my catalog. "Gabriele Münter. It's called *Houses in Winter*. Do you like it?"

"Very much. Do you suppose it's because I knew it had to be painted in 1935, and guessed it was German, or is the message there in the painting? That air of absolute peace, but it looks so fragile. You just feel that a cataclysm was rumbling up. Who's Gabriele Münter, do you know?"

"Kandinsky's mistress. A great favorite of Heidi's. Heidi says Münter taught Kandinsky how to paint, though the received opinion has it the other way around. I don't understand why Heidi isn't here. Or hateful Henry. I hope nobody's sick. Do you suppose Stephanie—oh, there's Henry now. And here comes Bob Geritano. Nick's father. Sweet. Hi, Bob."

I introduced Bob and Ken. They shook hands. Bob told me I looked smashing.

"Like a forehand?" I told Ken that Bob was a tennis ace. Ken said he played squash and wished he could play tennis in the summer but he couldn't make the switch. They talked about their rackets. I thought they looked cute together. Ken in cord that didn't match his hair and a very proper blue-and-gold-striped tie, Bob flashier—but not finer to my eyes—in a navy blazer and open-necked blazing white shirt that showed off his lustrous darkness. So sincere, both of them. One rode butterflies, one didn't. I thought that Bob might strangle Ken if he knew about the morning, but how could he ever know? Even if he heard, he wouldn't hear. They started talking kids and sports.

A waitress offered champagne.

"Thanks, I'll stick with this." I was drinking Irish whiskey, neat, in a wine goblet swadled with a blue cocktail napkin, the six-for-a-dollar kind of paper napkin. An event, all right. I wondered and wondered where Heidi was. Henry was busy with a couple who clearly considered themselves important, maybe actually were. I didn't want to intrude.

A waitress offered slices of air-dried beef wrapped around cornichons and pickled onions.

"I'll have one with an onion if you will," Ken said to me.

Bob and the waitress smiled at our newness. Bob and the waitress smiled at each other. Where was Elizabeth? I had a notion about Bob and Elizabeth. I filed "One with an Onion" in my chapter title file. For *How to Cook for Your Next Lover*?

A flurry happened at the door. Photographers moved across the room as though remote-control devices impelled them. Henry Kahn left the couple who thought they were important and sailed into action.

Do you want to know the funny thing? I wasn't surprised when I saw the towering self, the grand silver head, the blarney grin. Jack Keefe was New York. Had I really thought to come back to the city and not encounter him? As likely to miss the skyline, never get fanned by a taxi, not overhear a Yankee game on a stranger's radio. To see him at Heidi's gallery, on a day laden with events, seemed so much of a piece with the all-in-all that I wondered why I hadn't foreseen his entrance through that doorway.

"Who's that?" Bob Geritano asked, as the commotion grew.

"Jack Keefe," I said, easily enough. "He's putting up a primary fight for mayor, if you didn't hear the news."

Bob smiled a funny little smile. Sure; the famous open marriage. Jackie must have told him she rather knew the man.

"Jackie's never going to believe this," he said. "She's going to kick herself all over the place for not coming tonight."

"Is your wife political?" Ken asked.

"She's not fussy. You get very lonely flying."

I squelched a smile. "She's a stewardess," I told Ken.

"I know. Those 747 butterflies."

I kicked his ankle. He put an arm around me.

"I think I'll go shake his hand," Bob said.

Something in his voice, his manner, made me want to hug him and pat him and say everything would be okay. He was a good man. For a moment I envied Jackie. Her life so resolved. But when did resolution ever make me happy? If something came in a simple package, I didn't believe it was serious, I didn't believe it was real. Enigmatic men in cord were more my style. Men who ran for magus.

"I'll introduce you," I said.

"You know him too?" Bob said. "Mr. Keefe is all right."

I didn't say anything. I linked arms with Ken. I watched Jack finish up with Henry and move into the crowd.

He saw me.

My matter-of-factness vanished. My adrenal glands pumped insanely. There were so many threads between us, I could have twisted them into a tightrope and walked across air to him. But I had felt that rope around my neck. Not for nothing had I left New York. I stayed where I was, stood linked to Ken.

The room saw how purposed he was. The seas parted. He came to me.

"Broadway Joe?" he said. "You look as though you could use a steak. Or would you be more in the mood for Chinatown?"

Oh, he was good. We were alone, just the two of us, no one else in the room, on the planet. We'd been out of touch for mere seconds. We were the sum total of what mattered.

He didn't move me. Not a bit. Daisy had taught me deeper magic.

"You've got me confused with someone else," I said. It was so nearly true. Then I threw my arms around him for a bear hug, an old pal hug, a dreadful insulting juiceless G-rated hug. "It's great news, Jack. Great news. This is Ken Huysman. This is Bob Geritano. Jack Keefe."

There were handshakes and murmurs.

"I see you still have a taste for the Irish whiskey," Jack told me. "But why did you go and do a rash thing like cutting your hair?"

"I fell on hard times and had to sell it." Then all at once I'd had it with his proprietary air, his assumption that Ken and Bob didn't really matter to me or to the great scheme of things. I wanted to rock him, to break him, to put him in my slingshot and zing him away. I said, "If I'd been braver, I would have cut off my legs. Everything you liked."

"Mr. Keefe," someone called from the crowd.

Jack gave me the look I had hoped for.

"Mr. Keefe, over here, sir. Andrew Storrs, *Paint* magazine. If you're elected mayor, what will be your policy vis-à-vis municipal funding for the arts?"

Jack braceleted my wrist with his blunt fingers. "Well, now," he said to the press, "Washington has told us it's up to local government to feed the people. And I say, by God, that we will find a way to feed their eyes and ears and hearts and minds and spirits as well."

"But at your press conference this morning, sir, you made fun of the mayor's plan to pipe music into the subways, even though he's got impressive documentation in terms of the psychological benefits."

"With all due respect to his documentation," Jack said, "that's just plain daft, isn't it?" He got a ripple on that one. No one else could roll out "daft" the way Jack did. I tried to shake my arm free of his grasp. Ken wasn't laughing. "Because," Big Jack said, "we'd spend a million dollars on a hundred committees with this one saying it should be Beethoven, and that one saying it should be Frank Sinatra, and the work force would be in chaos because people would stay on past their stops to hear the end of a movement, and—" waving his arms like a conductor, smiling, looking tall and silvery and certain—"with the exalted incumbent in office for another term, would there be a subway system to pipe the music into? We'd have three trains in operation, and they'd be late. We'd all be going to work on foot. The mayor would do better to buy every citizen a Walkman."

He turned his back on the crowd. He let go of my wrist. "Your heart is so hard to me? After everything we were? I love you the way I did the day we met and every day since."

"Please." My arm was free, but my chest was in bondage. Ken and Bob had stepped aside, were pretending to be engrossed in a chat about public television and kids.

"I know we can't go back," Jack said, "but let me hear that you remember our golden days the way they were. I'd rather have that than Gracie Mansion." He couldn't stop the merry snort at his blarney, and I couldn't keep back laughter, and for one instant the world went away and everything old was new again.

I panicked. I tugged at Ken and Bob. "Did you know," I babbled at Jack, "that you once met this man's wife? Jackie Geritano, curly dark hair, beautiful cheekbones, eyes like Sophia Loren's—is that a fair description, Bob?"

Ken put an arm around me, steadied me against the tremors at my core. I leaned into him, into safety, into a future built around a child he loved, a child Jack had said he could never let me have.

"Eyes better than Sophia Loren's," Bob was saying. "You met her in Paris. Five, six years ago."

"You think I'm so full of ambition I've squeezed out the memory of those eyes?" said the man who would be mayor. "Jackie Geritano. Paris. Please send her my regards. And may I say, you're a lucky man."

"You son of a bitch," Bob said, "you don't remember her

at all. It was Dublin, not Paris. You poured champagne on her tits. And you don't remember." His eyes filled with tears. He walked away.

"I think, by God, that I just lost a vote," Jack said.

I handed Ken my drink. I said I'd be right back. I took off after Bob. I caught up with him at the door.

"I'm sorry," he said to me. He kept on moving.

"What for? You were wonderful. You're a lucky man, he was right about that much, and Jackie's a lucky lady. Bob?"

"What?" We were out on the sidewalk now.

"I won't say a word to her, if you want. Maybe it would be nicer if she thought he remembered?"

A black stretch limousine pulled up in front of the gallery. Bob stared at it.

"Money," he said. "Goddamn money."

"I know."

"You don't know at all. If I made more money, Jackie wouldn't be off flying every weekend. I sold her body to save my soul. Nice."

"Come on," I said. "Jackie gets tired, but she likes her work. Mothers need out from under."

"Out from under to Johannesburg? Sure they do."

Three men got out of the big car. One was the present inhabitant of Gracie Mansion.

"Good luck, Mr. Mayor," Bob called out, as the men walked into the gallery. "Beat hell out of Jack Keefe."

The mayor gave Bob a big wave.

"He doesn't matter a speck to Jackie," I said. "You know that, don't you? You're the only one she cares about. You and Nick."

"You're a good person." Bob kissed my cheek. "I always thought you were a little—" He upped his nose.

"Snooty?"

"Not snooty exactly. It's just that you're always a little bit someplace else. You'd make a terrible tennis player. But you're nice."

"I'm a hopeless tennis player."

"Say good night to Ken for me," he said. "Thanks, Jill."

I stood outside the gallery for a while, watching people go in and out, feeling the summer air, reading the shops of Madison Avenue, smelling the buses, thinking that the sky was getting dark too early—rain was going to come. I wondered if Jack and the mayor were confronting each other, or shaking hands, or what. In the old days I would have hustled back inside to be a part of the action. Now I just wished I could sneak home, invisibly, and watch Daisy and Mary at dinner. Or maybe they were through and had gone on to stories and poems. Daisy always got Mary to read the books I couldn't bear (but refused to be an absolute censor and heave)—*Br'er Rabbit, Mickey Mouse's Picnic*. Daisy would be sitting on Mary's lap, cozying up to her breasts—missing mine? Mine missed her. Ken came out.

"Did you think I'd fled?" I said.

He laughed. He put a confident hand on my shoulder. "The air is a hell of a lot better out here. Want to walk for a while? You show me your favorite buildings and I'll show you mine? Go have a drink somewhere?" He looked at his watch. "I reserved a table for eight, but if you're getting hungry, I bet they'd take us earlier."

"I'm kind of worried about Heidi. I can't imagine why she isn't in there. Can we go back in for a bit? I'd like to see the rest of the paintings. I'd also like to have another drink and tell Henry to go to hell, though I don't suppose it's the moment."

"You can come back and see the show tomorrow, can't you? All summer, as far as that goes. Who can concentrate on anything in there tonight? Your friend Mr. Keefe and the mayor are having a good time. Keefe just said if the mayor is reelected, next year in New York will be like Munich in 1935."

"Oh, fun."

"Until tonight, I thought Daisy looked just like you."

"Ken, don't."

"And Nick is what we would call first generation offspring—"

"It's going to rain," I said.

"It is, isn't it? I think you're fantastically brave. Want to stop by your place for a raincoat?"

"A little hard on Daisy, don't you think, doctor? Two goodbyes in one evening? Anyway, you don't have rain togs. I'll take my chances with you."

He kissed me.

He kissed me.

He kissed me.

He kissed me.

Iceman oh Jesus God how—

"Jill."

"Ken."

"Darling."

"Shhh."

He kissed me and I was seared and we were sealed but were not seers.

The nights of complexity blasted forever out of mind, the chasm crossed in a single lip.

"Dearest."

"I know."

"Shhhh."

"Do you?"

This tired old bounced-around mama new as a plastic maidenhead ready to be broken on the crosswalk.

"Jill."

"Niceman."

"I never."

"Me neither."

We moved apart in the interests of a cleaner New York. We stood there on the sidewalk holding hands awaiting a call from Hollywood or maybe a Pulitzer Prize. A Heisman Trophy?

We got Elizabeth instead, in layers of white, cutting

across Madison Avenue, pearls bobbling, blond hair bouncing.

I waved. I wondered if she would notice. Us.

"Jill, hi. I'm so late." She looked distraught. Her eyes were shadowy in the wrong places. That awful Oliver, I thought.

"Never mind," I told her. "The fun's just started. The mayor is in there, and Jack Keefe. Special unscheduled preprimary debate. Not to mention a lot of paintings. Don't miss the fried squid." I was breathy, girlish. "This is Ken Huysman. Ken, this is Elizabeth Gray. One of the famous Playgroup mothers," as if he didn't know.

Elizabeth of the many embassies put out a hand, then let it drop. She stared. She gawked. She had a thing for khaki hair, maybe? "Ken Huysman?" she said. "Ken Huysman?" she said again.

"I know," I said. "Shades of Iceman. It knocked me for a lollipop the first time." I laughed, God help me.

Elizabeth shut me up with a look. "Ken Huysman the psychologist?"

"You know his work?" I asked merrily.

Elizabeth looked bewildered. Elizabeth looked thrown. "Are you—do you—have you known him for long?" she asked me. "Are you in it together, then?"

Her delicate face contorted. Pain? Rage? Muddle? I couldn't decipher the message, but I knew it was bad news. Ken's grip on my shoulders didn't keep my knees from trembling.

"We met yesterday," I said. Hard to believe, but there it was.

"Oh, heaven." Elizabeth bit her lip. She was pale as February. "Good heaven."

I looked from her to Ken and back again. Ken's face was a mask. "Somebody tell me something," I said.

Dark clouds hammed it up in the sky. Thunder rolled across my temples, inviting the usual pain. The hot new Yankee shortstop came out of the gallery, trailing women. I wondered if I could slip into the ranks and slide away.

"We have to talk," Ken said to me. "But not like this. Let's go have a drink."

Elizabeth's pallor rooted me. I said, "Talk to me now."

He put both hands on my shoulders, turned me to face him. His eyes were set at extra sincere. "I had a relationship with Kelly Smith. We didn't part on great terms. I was going to tell you tonight."

For one exquisite moment I felt nothing but relief. The upset was over romance gone wrong? Easy.

Ken said to Elizabeth, "I know what great friends you and Kelly were. I expect you think I'm a bit of a skunk."

"A skunk!" She folded her arms across her chest.

"Look, truth to tell, neither of us has much reason to be proud of the whole business. Frankly, I'm surprised she told you about it—even you." He pushed back khaki hair; he favored us with the boyo grin. He was the Iceman I'd eyed coldly through the diamonds of a fence. "I thought she regarded me as her dirty little secret."

Elizabeth wasn't buying the disarmament proposal. "Oh, she didn't say so much as a word at the time. I knew she had a secret—she let me think it was my own husband. Better that than letting me know about you. When you think how I loved Megan." Her rounded voice was peaking and pitching. Rountree would have disowned her. "The truth came out today. Just now. On the telephone. Halfway around the world, Dr. Huysman, and she still shakes when she says your name."

One fact and another collided in my mind, blotted out all else. "Did you know about the Playgroup, then?" I asked Ken. "Before you happened to walk by the park and happened to notice the shining kids?"

"Did he know about the Playgroup? Tell her, Dr. Huysman. Has he invited you and Daisy to California, Jill? Or does he want to keep her here near the others?"

I looked at Ken. I rubbed my hand back and forth across my lips, angrily erasing.

He groaned. "Jill, I'm not the enemy. Come away with me and have a drink. I'll explain everything. Everything."

"Oh, God." I wanted to turn to powder, to go back into the packet they'd poured me out of, to be inert again. My eyelids closed. I would sleep standing up. Please somebody put me away.

I heard a shout from inside the gallery, the sound of breaking glass. I heard the sky break apart.

"Jill, I'm so sorry," the diplomat's daughter said. "I can see this is awful for you. We're not intimate friends, maybe you think I'm way out of line. But I know how much you love Daisy. Keep her away from this man. My father says it's maybe the most loathsome program ever promoted by Washington. Like training dolphins to carry bombs, only a thousand times worse. Teaching children to do the most hideous things with their minds. Jill? Are you okay?" The rain curtained down. She put out a motherly hand. "Jill? Come inside."

"No! No!"

Ken grabbed me for fair. "Jill, you don't for a single instant believe—"

"No!"

I ran. I ran the fastest race of my life, skidding and sliding in my giddy shoes up the slickening sidewalk of Madison Avenue, slicing through the sluicing rain.

"Jill! Jill!"

I took my shoes off, I hurled them at him.

"Jill! Darling! Jill!"

"If you follow me, I'll kill you. Go away go away go away!"

We faced off across Seventieth Street. The rain was bombing down. I knew my feet were in agony but I couldn't feel the pain. Somewhere a child barked.

"Jill, give me ten minutes. Five. This is madness."

"Go to hell!"

He picked up my bleeding shoes, he cradled them. "I'll

be at home if you need me. Do you hear me? I love you. I love Daisy. Do you hear me?"

I flagged a taxi. I poured myself in. I slapped a five dollar bill into the coin catch and sent the driver speeding over to Park Avenue and down toward my girl.

34.

Nora stood outside the door. She felt she needed to know its details. It was Chinese red, with six panels inset, and a little column of locks stacked over the doorknob like stones piled for a cairn. Five feet up from the ground and dead center was a peephole. Peepholes made Nora shudder. She imagined a rifle put to the hole and fired into her eye. A neat black plate with white lettering above the peephole said "6-E." E for East, E for Everts.

No sounds filtered out from 6-E. On the other side of the elevator, in 6-W, someone was playing *Pictures at an Exhibition*, thunderously. Real thunder bumped into the music, then went away. Nora had a theory about lightning and tulips, but she couldn't remember what it was. Her head was empty as a jack-o'-lantern. She had no thoughts, no hopes, no fears; she was simply there. She rang the bell.

"Who is it?" a woman called out.

Nora had a panicky moment. Was that Jill's voice? But Jill had to have gone by now, the way she had hurried home from the park, so eager to be free of her child and out in the world of men.

"It's Mrs. Mayor, dear," she said.

"Who?"

Not Jill, no; the voice wasn't half so sucky. But close enough so Nora could pretend to think it was Jill's. "Mrs. Mayor from the park, dear. Daisy's friend. Did you forget I was coming?"

The shutter on the peephole slid back. The door opened

the two inches its chain allowed. Nora saw a slice of face.

"Mrs. Everts is busy right now. If you leave your number, I'll ask her to call you."

Nora panicked again, then remembered a rule she'd read in a magazine. Sitters were never supposed to let strangers know the grown-ups were out. "How stupid of me," she said. "I'm late, aren't I? She's already gone to the gallery, hasn't she? And probably went off in a bit of a dither and forgot to say I might come. It's terribly important, you see. I lent her a—"

"Hi!" said a little voice from the other side of the door, as a silvery blur tackled the doorkeeper's knees. "Hi, Mrs. Horse, you gorse."

"Hi, Daisy dear, so near."

"You see?" Daisy said to the keeper. "I told you she was coming tonight. Because my mice already came, and now Mrs. Mare is here. You see? Open the door, Mary."

"Honey, I can't. Mrs. Mayor, I'm sorry, but Mrs. Everts didn't say anything to me about your coming. I can't let you in."

"But I told you she was coming," Daisy said.

"I've just got to get that book back," Nora said. "You don't understand." She threw tremors into her voice. "It's a matter of the greatest urgency. I'm sure I could find it in minutes. It's got a lavender cover. I'm not at liberty to explain, but I have to get it back. Young woman, do I look as though I've come for the family jewels?"

"I'll tell you what," the keeper said. "I'll telephone the gallery and ask her about you, okay? I won't be a minute. Here, Daisy, I'll leave the door on the chain, you can talk to your friend."

"Thank you," Nora said. Tell tale tit, your tongue shall be slit, and all the little jackey birds will have a little bit. "That's very kind of you."

A whimper wanted to be born. Was it all over, then? Nora thought of walking away, walking to the river.

Thunder cracked again. East is east. Hudson is west. I wonder which river drowns the best.

"Sing me the song," Daisy said shyly. "Please?"

Nora crouched down to meet the glorious eyes. "'Daisy, Daisy, give me your answer do. I'm half crazy, all for the love of you—'" Her voice broke. "Goodbye," she said. "I think I should go. Goodbye."

"But don't you want to know how my knees are? Because they really got hurted before."

"I know, darling. I know. Please tell me how they are."

"They don't hurt anymore, except a little little, because my mom really washed them, and Mary says I shouldn't have a Band-Aid. She's a nurse. Did you ever know a nurse?"

"Oh, yes. Oh, yes. I've known a lot of nurses. Once when I was in the hospital a long time ago I had a nurse named Mary."

"Did she take your temperature?"

"Yes," Nora said. She heard the keeper of the door returning. Would there be policemen, she wondered. She rose for sentencing.

"Mrs. Mayor, I don't know what to do," came politely. "I talked to someone at the gallery who talked to someone else who said Mrs. Everts had been there but seemed to have gone. I guess they've gone to dinner. She said she'd call me from the restaurant. But it could be, you know, awhile. Boy, it's pouring out there. Real cloudburst."

Purpose flooded back into Nora. "May I ask you a great favor, then? It's truly, truly urgent. If you could take a look for the book. Lavender. Oh, average size. But it's a very rare book you see, and on top of that, I left notes in it of a very important nature. It's called *Transplants*. Lavender, with silver letters on it. It's connected with some work Jill and I hope to do together. I must have it tonight. I do believe she said it was in her bedroom. Would you be an absolute dear and take a look?"

"Sure," the door mouse said. "I could do that. I'm really sorry to leave you in the hallway. I hope Mrs. Everts won't be furious."

Mrs. Everts, Nora thought. *Mrs.* Everts. "It's sad, but we do have to be so careful these days. I'm glad you're such a good watchdog for Daisy. She's quite my favorite little girl. If you'd just take a look for the book."

"You bet."

Nora waited a minute. "Daisy?"

Silence, then a giggle, then, "Hi."

"Hi. Want to play a game?"

"Yes! Do you want to play doctor? I could be the doctor and you could be the baby and Mary could be the nurse because she really is a nurse."

"I'd love to play that later, but I was thinking of a different game. About animals. Do you like giraffes?"

"Well, monkeys are my favorite."

"Monkeys are wonderful," Nora said. "Can you climb like a monkey?"

"Yes, and my mama says I eat bananas like three monkeys."

"I've got a great idea, Daisy. Why don't you pull a little chair over to the door and climb up on it so I can see what a good little monkey you are. Can you do that?"

"Of course, Mrs. Gorse."

"But hurry, darling, because it's just our private game and we have to play it before Mary comes back. Hurry."

"I like this game," Daisy said.

I have been in this hallway all my life, Nora thought. I have had no other home. Jack, do you remember? When you carried me across the threshold, through the red doorway? I thought I would never stop bleeding. Then later when they took all my bleeding away forever, I thought I would never stop dying. Twenty-one years old. Mary the nurse was not kind. I heard her call me a whore. She thought I had sold my children. In a way the truth was more shaming. So unbewitching a bride that my husband was happier lying inside the sickest cesspool. And for all the lives that you cost me, you dared to come whining to me that your penicillin shots made you sore. But you see, darling? How much I still love you? Going to the wildest jungles to find you fresh-baked monkeys?

"Hi, Mrs. Mare. I brought the chair. Hey, I made a rhyme, and it wasn't time."

"It's always rhyme time. Here's one more. Can you put the chair against the door? Closer. Closer. Yes, right there. Now can you climb up into the air?"

"One two three. What can I be? I'm a monkey in a tree."

"Darling monkey, here's one more. Can you open the chain that holds the door? Hurry, hurry, monkey dear. I think the tigers are coming near."

"How do I open it, Mrs. Horse? Because I never opened it, of course."

"Just slide it all along the slot. Hurry. The tigers are getting hot."

"One two three. What do I see? I see a chain that's nice and free."

Nora took her.

35.

Henry Kahn gripped the telephone. He groped blindly for his desk chair. He kicked his office door shut, but he could not block out the obscene sounds of escalating merriment on the main floor of the gallery.

The fear they all lived with had happened, had come horribly close to home.

"Mary, listen to me," he said into the telephone. "Get ahold of yourself, can you? She'll be all right. I know she'll be all right. We all have to stay very calm. Please. There. Better. Good girl. I'm going to send Mrs. Gray over as soon as I hang up. I'll make an announcement here that Mrs. Everts is urgently needed and see if anyone has an idea where she might be. Please don't start again, the least important thing is who's at fault. If I may be perfectly brutal, let's not waste time on you. Thank you. Now we'd better get off the phone in case that woman tries to call you. Please God, she will call very quickly. I will call the police from here. Mary, get a grip on yourself, you owe it to Daisy. Go wash your face with cold water. Make a big pot of coffee. Make a sketch of the woman, whatever you saw of the face, put in every detail you remember. Help is coming right away. We're going to get her back. She's going to be all right. Please God, she will be all right."

36.

Don't let it happen to you. Make your life a fortress. Keep your ipecac up to date. Avoid processed foods. Always wait for the WALK sign, no matter how clear the coast is, no matter if the coast is goddamn translucent, is pierced with the final light. Choose your playgrounds carefully. Check for safety matting underneath the sprinklers. Teach your children to be frightened. Train them to refuse to stay with sitters. Be sure they wash their hands after the toilet. Encourage rudeness to strangers. Do not permit games or rhymes. Start them on whole grains at an early age. Never buy French shoes. Beat the love right out of your daughters. Encourage viciousness to strangers.

The tenth circle of hell is the circle of friends waiting in your apartment to tell you your child is gone. Don't let it happen to you. You cannot imagine those faces. Pain and fear and guilt and hatred and a hideous excitement. Sobbing Mary and pale Elizabeth and why in the name of names of names was Big Jack Keefe there in my living room holding out pitying arms, waiting to catch my fall.

I knew. You know. Only one word, whispered. "Daisy?"

They laid it out for me as I stood there dripping rain and

blood and piss and the wetness at my breast could be nothing but milk unless it was the leaking away of my heart.

They brought me towels and robes and Irish whiskey and led me to the couch.

They told me to stay calm.

"Yes, we must all stay calm has anyone called the police would anyone like a drink excuse me for peeing on the floor but my cousin said the hell with the carpets do you know I believe I'm lactating could somebody bring a bucket I seem to have lost my shoes."

"Jill Jill Jill Jill Jill."

Jack told me the commissioner himself was coming though he was in bed with the flu.

"Well tell him to bring his floozy because we need a new babysitter is this pressure under grace or is it."

"Jill Jill Jill. Calm calm calm."

Mary threw herself at my bleeding feet but I would not stoop to kick her I would not sully my toes.

They brought me blankets against the snow and told me to send my mind down useful paths.

How could I send my mind when I couldn't find it?

That woman had drunk my girl. Was drinking her.

In the midst of the madness Jack held me in tender ways and truths came spilling out with the tears.

"Is she mine, Jill?"

"She's mine. You can't take this one away. Did you have her taken away?"

"For the love of God, how can you ask that?"

"You know how I can ask."

"Jill, if you knew how it destroyed my soul not to have children with you."

"It's the children we destroyed, your soul is running for mayor."

"If that's what you think, then I have to tell you. What I never told you before. Because I didn't want your pity. My wife couldn't have children. I brought home a dreadful infection when we were married only a year. If you knew what it did to her. Having thought we would have a dozen. I couldn't let myself have what I'd taken away from her."

"Jack, is it true? Oh, God. The woman I envied all those years. You kept a secret like that from me?"

"Such a nice tough love we had. One perfect thing in my life. Never any pity between us. But I know I have God's pity and forgiveness, or our daughter wouldn't exist."

"Does she exist? That woman is drinking her blood."

"Jill Jill. Calm calm."

Then he said could I do a sketch of Mrs. Mayor before the commissioner came because Mary was in no shape and Elizabeth who had gone to the Louvre at eight wasn't a whiz with a pencil.

I sketched and I sketched and I sketched and I put an arrow through her right eye.

Jack looked at the picture. "Holy Mother of God."

"But I forgot the alligator bag the kind you don't see any more that old old kind of brown on a shoulder strap we have a serving spoon named Alligator I would like to feed you to Alligator Mary only kidding the old old kind of bag with a clicky little gold clasp I saw her drink Daisy's blood I should have killed her on the spot."

"An alligator bag. Mary Mother of God have mercy on us all."

Elizabeth brought a tub for my lacerated feet. Jack trembled whiskey into my tumbler and his.

"Mrs. Major Mrs. Major Major Mayor Nora Mayor she sent the killing flowers from the Green Witch Florist in the Village do you still send flowers from the Green Witch Florist after an abortion, Jack."

"Nora Mayor. The Green Witch Florist. Lord Jesus be with me now and in the hour of my need." He broke toward the telephone. He dialed. He stood listening.

You whisper, you scream one word. "Daisy?"

But they were joking, weren't they? Playing a wonderful new game? Throwing a surprise party? She was really in her bedroom, waiting, laughing into her hands, thinking of songs to sing, we would smile at the pee on the floor, oh, I do like events so much, no one ever surprised me with a party, they must love me awfully much to go to so much trouble. I ran to her bedroom. I pulled open the closet door. I flung back the bedspread, I fluted among the dustballs under the bed. Then I saw her on the puzzle shelf. I picked her up and rocked her, I put her to my breast. Drink deep, little Grouch. Grandma is here. Mama is coming home soon.

"Jill Jill Jill. Telephone telephone telephone."

Should I answer it? Or play hard to get? What was the secret to being popular? If my parents hadn't done magic at parties, nobody would have come.

"Jill Jill Jill Jill."

I went to the phone. "Hello?"

"Jill, dear, is that you? Home so soon? It's Mrs. Mayor."

"Oh, hi, Mrs. Mayor, how are you?"

"Fine, thanks, dear, how are you?"

"WHERE IS SHE? GIVE HER BACK TO ME! GIVE HER BACK TO ME! IS SHE ALL RIGHT? CAN I TALK TO HER? GIVE HER BACK TO ME!"

"Jill, dear, shhh. Don't excite yourself. She's fine."

"Can I talk to her can I talk to her?"

"In a while, if you're nice. Tell me, does your uterus hurt?"

"It hurts. It hurts. Do you want it to hurt more? You can stick hot irons up me. Just give her back to me."

"You can have another one, you know. All the fucking you do. You can have another one just like that. Ask hizzoner, he'll come right over."

"Please, may I talk to her? Please, Mrs. Mayor? You can be our friend. You can come for dinner. Once a week. Twice. I'm a very good cook. You see? We won't hurt you. You're very nice. I know how nice you are. The nicest person ever. You wouldn't hurt a fly. Please, may I talk to her now?"

"You wouldn't call the police?"

"No, of course not, never. Who needs police? This is a family matter. You could be our best friend. You can live here if you like. Truly. I'll give you my bedroom. I'll sleep on the couch. Shall I come get you now?"

"You think I would sleep in a whore's bed? One death at the hands of whores is enough."

"I'm not a whore. I love you. You didn't take Daisy's raincoat. Did you dry her hair? She doesn't get ear aches like other children but we mustn't take chances. May I speak to her? I will do anything anything anything. I will dedicate my life to you. May I speak to her?"

"She's very happy with me. She's never been so happy. I gave her chocolate cereal. She never had it before. You're a bad mother. Daisy, dear, come say hi to Jill."

"Hi, Mama."

"Hello, girlfriend. Hello, dearest girl. I love you so much."

"Was that nice, whore? More than you deserve. Did you ever hear her happier?"

"Please, Mrs. Mayor, wonderful Mrs. Mayor, let me talk to her some more."

"She's going to tell you a poem. Would you like that?"

"Oh, yes, please. Please. Then may I come to get you and we'll all live together and be happy?"

"It's an old poem, but we changed it a little. We're quite a team, Daisy and I. You shouldn't leave her with sitters. They don't understand special children like Daisy. But you don't care, do you, whore, as long as you can go out and fuck?"

"Please let me hear her poem and come for you."

"I'll let you hear her poem. Then you sit there and wait for the next call. If you shoved lye up your cunt you might know the pain I felt. You should have given her chocolate cereal. She might have stayed at home. Here she is."

"Hi, Mama."

"Hello, my love. You be very good for Mrs. Mayor and

very strong and I'll be there in a little while. Can you tell me what the building looks like?"

"It's pretty big."

"Is it? And you're so big, and brave, and wonderful. If you need anything at all, ask Mrs. Mayor, and don't forget to say please."

"Well, my mice are here but I wish I had my yellow phone so I could invite Iceman to come over."

"I'll call Iceman for you, darling, all right? I'll ask him to get there as quickly as he can."

"Mrs. Mare said to tell you the poem. It's silly."

"Tell me the poem, darling. I know I'll love it."

"Two little blackbirds sitting on a hill. One named Jack, one named Jill. Fly away, Jack. Fly away, Jill. Come again, Jack. Don't come again, Jill."

37.

Nora clapped her hands over her ears to keep out the hideous wailing. "Mamamamamamamama—" relentless, not pausing for breath, giving no mercy, like an old Irishwoman keening at a funeral for someone lost at sea, the sound so penetratingly tragic that other mourners might envy the dead.

She had never seen anyone change so. Daisy full of jokes and kisses and the fun of the run through the rain, the fun of hiding under Nora's skirt to escape the closed-circuit camera when they went through the service entrance; then, after the call to Jill, the collapse into agony, the bellowing of her despair.

Nora carried the kicking, shrieking thing into the child's bedroom, set her down on the Mickey Mouse bunk bed, heaped her around with teddy bears, brought extra blankets, offered water, tried the alphabet cereal again only to have the box flung across the room with a force that astonished

Nora, causing a storm of chocolate frosted letters to break loose over the room and pelt onto every surface. Ms. Arthur would not be pleased.

"Daisy, dear, you don't need Jill anymore. I am your mother now. I'm your mother and you're my little girl, just the way we were Peter and his grandpa. Such a wonderful game. Life will be better than before. Did Jill ever give you a daddy? I will give you a daddy. You see, the truth is that Jill was your sitter when I was away, she was just taking care of you until I could come home again. Don't cry, dear Daisy. Remember how I held you in the park? Let me hold you now so you can feel that I'm your mother."

"Nooooo. Mamamamamamamama."

Nora tried graham crackers, songs, dominos, jumping up and down and making faces.

"Mamamamamamamama."

Nora tried shaking her.

"Mamamamamamama."

Nora tried shaking her harder.

"Mama."

Nora closed the door to the child's room and went to the master bedroom. Cry, baby, cry. Stick your finger in your eye. Go home and tell your mother you ate too much pie. Pussywillows never wept. Bleeding hearts didn't bleed. Transplants were always tricky but transplants were her special genius. If you love it, it will grow in foreign soil. Unless it was defective, of course. Came from a second-rate nursery. Cry, baby, cry. Stick your finger in your eye. Go home and tell your mother you had to die.

She went into the bathroom, took off her underpants, hiked her shirtdress up to her waist, and straddled the bidet. She washed away the afterbirth. It hurt less than I expected, Dr. Howard, but to tell the truth I found less fulfillment than I'd been led to hope for. One ought not to read magazines, I expect.

She dried herself with a pale yellow towel monogrammed *H* in deep yellow satin. She threw the towel into a corner.

She took the cap off the toothpaste she'd bought that afternoon and rolled the tube from the bottom. She leaned across the sink to the mirror. She wrote, "Jack Keefe for mayor." She dropped the tube into the toilet.

She walked by the child's room without pausing, without looking. She took the elevator downstairs. She said no to the doorman's offer of a taxi. She started through the downpour toward home.

38.

I went to the yellow plastic telephone. "Daisy's gone, Iceman. Snatched. Find her for me. You can use her any way you want, fair enough? You can use her to think the Kremlin into the Baltic, and I won't raise an eyebrow. Find her for me, Iceman. Bring her home. Let me hold her one last time."

Jack was vomiting in the bathroom. Mary was curled up small and weepy in a brown-and-gold stuffed chair that had raisins and crayons under the cushion and maybe (please, God?) snakes. Elizabeth was busying herself with coffee no one wanted.

"It's not like that," Iceman said, "but I'll come right away, I'll do what I can. I'll need the other children. Get the other children."

"No," Elizabeth said.

"Why not?" I started to weep. "I'll kill you, I'll curse James. How can you say no?"

"How can you ask me to say yes?"

Jack came out of the bathroom. He gargled down a belt of Irish. He said to Elizabeth, "You are the Elizabeth Gray for whom Betty DuPont works? Would you be so kind as to call her up and ask her to come over?"

"Bob Geritano won't say no." I kicked the couch where Elizabeth sat. "Heidi won't say no, will she? They'll get

Iceman and me there on Lokomo. Fuck you and your ugly kid."

"Jill, Henry told me tonight there's been some trouble with Stephanie. I wouldn't call Heidi if I were you."

"No."

"Calm down."

"Wait for the commissioner."

"Like using Laetrile to cure cancer."

"Ask me to do anything else."

"No."

I ate my fingernails. I ate Grouch. To have her safe inside me. I ate my robe and put on my jeans. I ate the clock that was eating my life.

The commissioner made his appearance. He was almost as tall as Jack. He was wearing a linen suit the color of oatmeal. His nose did not appear to be clogged. He offered his hand to Jack. "I'm sorry you have to go through this, old boy."

"You're sorry for him? You're sorry for him?"

"Jill, you cannot know how it grieves me to say this. I have every reason to believe that the woman who took your daughter is my wife, Nora."

"Your wife?" I rocked, I reeled as puzzle pieces flew through the air and assembled a picture of hell. "That woman is your wife? You drove her to this? I did? Daisy. My Daisy." I sucked my fist. "Daisy."

Jack reached out a consoling hand, mayor to mother for the front page of the *News*. "If it's any comfort in this terrible hour, let me say Nora is the gentlest of women. Your Daisy will not be harmed. I know it in my deepest heart."

"You have a photograph, Jack?" the commissioner asked.

"Not recent, Tom, but she hadn't changed all that much." He took a picture out of his wallet. A woman twenty years old.

I spat. I hissed.

"Jill, if you can find it in your heart not to hate her. . . . Think of her pain and how she must have envied you. And then my coming to the realization that this great city needed me for its mayor. Did she have detectives on us, I wonder. Olivia will hit the ceiling."

"Have you called your home, Jack?" the commissioner asked.

"Of course. No answer. I've asked our housekeeper, Mrs. DuPont, to come here. She has keys. If you could send her downtown with one of your men. May I ask for someone discreet?"

"The best, Jack. We'll help you however we can. How did you like our Yankees last night?"

"She drank Daisy's blood," I said.

"You must try to stay calm, Mrs. Everts. We know what an ordeal this is for you. Perhaps you'd like to lie down?"

"She said she lived across from the park. When Daisy hurt her knees."

"Friends in the neighborhood, Jack?" the commissioner asked. Elizabeth brought him a Scotch and water. "To our next mayor," he said, and drank.

"No friends, Tom, you know what she's like."

"A rental, then?"

"It seems so unlikely, but not more unlikely than the terrible deed. She keeps a great deal of cash in the house. Cannot go to banks, you see. Our housekeeper can check the safe when she goes down."

"Jack, did you ever really love me? Was there maybe one true moment?"

"I will love you until the day I die. I will make up for the pain. I will put up a swing at Gracie Mansion."

Betty DuPont arrived just then with eyes the kindest lights I had ever seen. She alone of the people there didn't hate me. The commissioner took her from me and sent her off in a squad car.

Jack had another drinkie poo.

The commissioner decreed that a team of officers would

start canvassing the doormen of the parkside buildings.

"No police. I promised. She'll hurt my baby."

"Plainclothesmen, Mrs. Everts. Trust us. We know what we're doing. Do you have a doctor you can call to give you something calming?"

My doctor was not made for calming but he was very good at coming and he came. The room got a little chilly. Elizabeth stood up and backed against the wall, clutching the draperies. Larry, forgive the fingerprints, you know how it is when the rain falls hard in New York.

"There's no time to waste," Ken said. "We've got to get the children here."

"No. You're evil," Elizabeth said.

"Listen to me, Elizabeth Gray. Your mind has been poisoned by a woman who wanted me to love her and I couldn't. I never knowingly worked for Washington. I was out in California. The human potential movement. Doing nothing less than saving civilization. I didn't know we were secretly funded by men who had other ambitions."

"No."

"I love the Playgroup children. I haven't met your son but I know he's beautiful."

"You made him put the garbage in Oliver's tennis bag."

"Garbage?" Ken's brown eyes signaled puzzlement.

"Oh, heaven, but Oliver is garbage, isn't he?" Elizabeth moaned. "If you knew how I've wanted to do something like that myself."

"Please," I said. "Daisy. Daisy. Every minute is a lifetime of hell."

"Why our children?" Elizabeth said. "Why did you pick our children?"

"I didn't pick them. They picked each other. This isn't the time for details. Let's find Daisy. When Daisy is safely home, I will tell you all the things you want to know, I will be your humble servant, you can wipe your hands on my mind. Will you think about how you would feel if James were in Daisy's place and Jill refused to help you?"

"Oh, heaven." Elizabeth started to cry.

"Would someone explain to me?" the commissioner said.

"You and Jack go into the bedroom and plan his campaign," I said. "You have no influence in this sphere."

"You can't ask me to give up my son," Elizabeth wept.

"Listen to me," Ken said, "and listen good. If Daisy dies, your son will be destroyed. There it is, simple and brutal. You think whatever I want him to do will cost him too much? Think of how he'll feel if Daisy dies and he learns he could have saved her. And he will learn it. I will make it my business to track you down wherever you try to hide him, and I'll tell him. Think of how he'll feel about himself, how he'll feel about you."

"He's all I have. You can't ask me this. Daddy will find a way to hide us. No. No. No."

39.

Arthur Kojak watched her wade hatless and coatless down Fifth Avenue, seemingly mindless of the wet. So thin; she would catch a cold, she would get pneumonia, in a week her lungs would be dead. She needed him now if she ever would. He could not stay away any longer.

He came out from under the trees of Central Park and crossed the avenue. He ran until he was nearly parallel with her. He couldn't tell if she knew that someone was close behind her; she would not hear his footsteps in the rain, but sometimes she just seemed to sense things. He didn't want to frighten her. After all she had been through. He cleared his throat. He said, "Mrs. Keefe?"

She didn't turn around or slow her pace. "Good evening, Mr. Kojak."

"Mrs. Keefe? How did you know?"

"Your voice is familiar to me, Mr. Kojak. Even when you try to disguise it as you did earlier this evening. Thank you for your assistance. There will be a bonus."

"I'm pleased I could be of service, ma'am."

He raised his big umbrella over her head. She didn't protest but she didn't take his arm. To their right, across the avenue, beyond the brick wall, the red and green turrets and barn roofs of the Children's Zoo loomed gay in the rain. Arthur wondered if Daisy had gone there, if she'd played in the gingerbread house and slid down the Alice slide into the White Rabbit's hole, if she'd counted the three little pigs. One, two, three. A passing taxi honked inquiry. Arthur signaled no. Two kids under a dripping scalloped canopy, rich kids, called out something Arthur could not decipher. He wondered if Daisy was dead. "Puddle coming, Mrs. Keefe."

"I have eyes, Mr. Kojak."

"Yes, ma'am."

They walked a wordless block. The Hotel Pierre was ahead on their left. Arthur longed to invite Mrs. Keefe to join him for a drink at the café. The Pierre had always seemed to him the hotel for the gentle, the pure, where a virgin bride might go in dignity. Its walls rose like great slabs of the homemade clotted cream he remembered from his boyhood. He wasn't wearing a tie, but one of the security men owed him a favor for declining to pay attention to an unworthy guest's indiscretion. Mrs. Keefe's saturated state would be overlooked because of her magnificent bearing. If Daisy was dead, the world would shout, in her defense. Would the mother weep or be stone at the trial? The happiest child he had ever seen. "Mrs. Keefe, would you do me the honor of joining me for a cocktail at the Café Pierre?"

"You overstep yourself, Mr. Kojak."

"I beg your pardon, ma'am."

Sixtieth Street; Fifty-ninth; Fifty-eighth and across. Stoplights and shop lights so bright in the rain. Mrs. Keefe came to a halt in front of the weeping windows of F. A. O. Schwarz. Arthur saw her reflected face bobbling strangely among a quartet of Raggedy Anns sitting around a table having tea. Her frail shoulders bent toward each other. He thought she might stand in front of that window until they came to get her. "Is she dead, ma'am?"

"I don't know, Mr. Kojak. I think so. I didn't know they were so fragile. My wedding service was Belleek. I have it intact to this day, not so much as a soup plate chipped. My African violets do not die. I offered her everything. She thanked me with tears and snot and hideous shrieks. A hybrid is only as good as the weaker parent. I do not fault my husband. If you could throw her away for me. Find a compost heap."

"I will do what needs doing, Mrs. Keefe. First we have to get you safe and dry. May I offer you the shelter of my home? A taxi across the Fifty-ninth Street Bridge, and in ten minutes we are there. Humble but comfortable."

"Mr. Kojak, I do not take taxis. I do not go to Queens. I have a home of my own and legs that take me there. I must see my tulips tonight."

"I'm sorry to bring up disagreeable matters, ma'am, but we have to think of the police."

"You think your thoughts, and I will think mine, Mr. Kojak. Please refrain from impertinence. My husband will deal with the police. The police are not an issue. I want you to throw the body away. I do not want that woman to have the body. My poor dead baby must not be slobbered over by whores. Throw her in the river. Bury her in the playground. Bury her deep."

"May I have the keys, Mrs. Keefe?"

"I thought you were the man who opened doors, Mr. Kojak."

"Inside doors are trickier, ma'am. It would save time if I had the keys. And, if I may say so, ma'am, you might be better off not having them on your person."

"I see. All right. Here they are. Mr. Kojak?"

"Yes, Mrs. Keefe?"

"I am carrying a good deal of cash. I would like to settle my account with you. If we could step into a doorway, I'll have no need of your services after tonight."

"It's been my honor, Mrs. Keefe. Your account is settled in full."

"Don't be foolish. You may need to run. Take this wallet. You'll find about five thousand dollars in it. I want you to have it. You have served me well."

"I can't, ma'am. I'll manage all right. You take care of yourself."

Their eyes met in the tall mirrored column in the middle of Schwarz's window. They watched each other watch the reflection of a squad car speeding downtown, skewing the dark with its whirling red beam.

She gave the briefest of shrugs. "As you will. Goodbye, Mr. Kojak."

"Goodbye, Mrs. Keefe."

40.

Jackie Geritano wished Elizabeth would come for James. James and Nick were acting up—not exactly making mischief but not exactly being good—touching each other too much and grinning strangely and making funny humming noises and cocking their heads the way they had on the ferry, as though they were hearing that far-off train in the night. She wanted James to go home, and Nick to go to bed, and then she had bed hopes of her own, co-starring Bob "the Lob" Geritano. He'd come home from the opening in a serious mood—not grim or depressed, just serious, and exceptionally tender, and she wanted to be alone with him, naked, stripped of their games and fantasies, absolutely open to him, ready to be imprinted so boldly by him that neither miles of ocean nor other men's bodies could erase or even smudge his mark. He was so good. He wasn't much of an actor—hadn't fooled her for a minute about Jack Keefe remembering her; had she really thought he'd remember?—but, bazooly, that was part of the special package, wasn't it? Bob's inability to lie, even in the interest of kindness? She felt foreign to herself, thinking these thoughts. It had been a day for foreignness, though, starting with "icky and sticky" in the morning, then the news about Jack Keefe running for mayor, and the peculiar gray-haired woman in the park who made her think of the witch in "Hansel and Gretel" with an appetite for tender children. Lying in bed with Bob, listening to the rain, knowing Nick was safe in his bed a few yards away—that would somehow bring the day around, would bring her home to familiar soil again. She wished Elizabeth would come for James.

She snuggled up against Bob on their living room couch. He put an arm around her. She had the latest issue of *Gourmet* on her lap—as usual, she was having trouble getting into it. Heidi had lent her a collection of short stories by women, and Jill had lent her a copy of *The Magus* because Jackie had told Jill she'd liked the movie; but what was the point of starting a novel or even a story when her head would travel 12,000 miles before she got back to it? She'd read on her vacation, in August. Let Bob pore over his tennis magazine. Right now his arm was entertainment enough for her.

"You want another glass of wine?" she asked him. They'd decided, for no special reason, to open a bottle of the special dry Lambrusco Jackie had bought at the airport in Bologna when a flight to Milan was diverted. It was keeping cold in the refrigerator.

"I'll get it," Bob said. "You're off duty now, remember?" He mussed her dark hair. "Feel like a couple of hands of blackjack?"

"I'm happy watching you read. Hey. What the bazooly?"

Nick and James were standing under the arch that linked living room and hallway. Nick was wearing his yellow slicker. James was wearing his Yankee warm-up jacket.

"It's time to go," Nick said.

"Go where? Are you kidding? It's pouring like nobody's business."

"Well, James didn't wear his slicker so you better bring an umbrella."

"Bring an umbrella nothing. Elizabeth will be here any minute. Nobody's going anywhere until then. So take your stuff off, boys, and settle down, okay? You want some popcorn?"

"We've really got to go, Jackie," Nick said, in his calmly stubborn way.

"My mom is busy," James said. "Moms get really busy sometimes. So do dads. My dad is a very busy man. He has his own bank. So we better go."

"Go where?" Bob asked.

"We have to go see Iceman. We can't get Daisy without Iceman. It's too big. It's really big, Daddy. We have to hurry. Please put on your raincoat and take us, please?" He started to cry.

"He's sorry he's crying," James said, "but Lokomo is nervous."

Jackie made a face. "You know I hate when you start with the made-up names."

Nick let out a whoop of rage. He picked up a green glass Venetian ashtray and hurled it against the wall. "I hate you!" he screamed, as glass exploded. He was going for a lamp when his father got to him and for the first time ever put hands roughly on him. "You want her dead!" Nick screamed at Bob. "You and Mama want Daisy dead! I hate you I hate you I hate you."

"Nick, how can you, honey boy? Come on. Come on. Come on." Bob picked Nick up and rocked him and shushed him as if he were a baby, until the shrill wet noises from the back of Nick's throat gave way to sobs.

Nick lay his head against his father's shoulder. He wiped his nose against the white cloth. His little body shuddered as if for cold and Bob held him the tighter.

"We went there by ourselves and we saw her, but we couldn't bring her back, it's too big." Nick snuffled, and James took hold of his feet, and Jackie moved in close because she'd never, not even in Sydney, felt so far from her son. "Please please please please can we go to Jill's now?" Nick begged. "I'll be so good. I'll eat green scrambled eggs. I won't splash water out of the tub ever ever ever. Please can we go before the umbrella man gets to her. Please, wonderful Daddy, please?"

"Icky and sticky" battered at Jackie's mind. She put one hand on Nick's back, one on Bob's. She dug out the cheery smile she presented aloft when the aircraft encountered turbulent air and the seat-belt sign went on. "The thing to do is call Daisy, am I right or am I right? So she can tell you she's okay. If she's asleep you can talk to Mary Girard and Mary will tell you that Daisy is snug in her bed and safe as all bazooly. Then we'll make up a fresh batch of popcorn and I might happen to have some presents in my closet I was saving for a rainy day, and how's this for a rainy day? Real wooden jigsaw puzzles from London, just like Prince Charles used to play with. Then we'll all settle down and relax and enjoy the rest of the flight."

41.

The man in the light gray suit said he was a New York City detective and flashed a shield to help make his point, but Albert Cunningham hadn't spent seventeen years at the door for nothing. He knew right where to go on Canal Street to buy shields that would fool the commissioner himself. He knew how cops walked, how they looked at you, how they smelled. If the man in the light gray suit was a member of the finest, Albert was a monkey's uncle.

Invoking the need for discretion, Albert drew the so-called cop over toward the oval copper tub of dried flowers where his pistol lay concealed. No, Albert said, none of the tenants had sublet for the summer, those who went away preferred to leave their places vacant. No, there weren't any gray-haired ladies visiting friends or relations in the building—there weren't any long-term visitors on the premises at the moment, period. Yes, he would know. He knew everything that happened in the building. He was senior at the door. He was on very good terms with the tenants and the other personnel in the building. Noon, midnight, weekdays, Sundays—if something happened in the building, Albert Cunningham heard about it.

The so-called cop gave him a hard stare. Albert's hand crept into the tub toward his little friend. He wasn't in any hurry to use it, but Moscow didn't fool around. The so-called cop gave Albert a number to call in case any recollections came to mind. He started for the door, then turned around. How much had the woman greased Albert? he asked. Then, almost casually, he mentioned that there was a missing child.

Harry Hollenbach, Albert thought grimly—Harry who didn't look like either parent. Wheels within wheels; factions against factions. He wondered who the smooth-talking thug really worked for, whom he was really after. He was Red Brigade maybe? If he thought either Mrs. so-called Mayor or the so-called Hollenbachs had been doubled by Washington—Albert put his hand on his gun.

The so-called cop said the Feds might be around to talk to Albert, then went out through the revolving door. Albert had to smile. The Feds, indeed. He wondered what impostor would be coming next. What a good joke on Mr. Red Brigade that a genuine Fed had got to Albert first.

42.

Heidi came to at the bottom of the deep green sea, groped her way to the surface, reached out for the warmth she knew was supposed to be there. Nothing. No one. She sat up, all awake in the shadowy room, her motherheart drumming. "Stephanie?"

Stephanie came gliding out of the bathroom. She stood in front of Heidi. "Let's go," she said dully.

Heidi had to hold back a cry of pain. Stephanie was there and she wasn't there. She was as different from the girl Heidi knew as she had been the frightening night two years before when she'd run a fever of 104. But that night had had an explanation—roseola—and a predictable outcome—a rash, a day of crankiness, and then total cure. This different Stephanie might be a stranger forever.

Maybe Vienna instead of Venice, Heidi thought; or was Zurich better these days? Frank Herrup would know who was best at restoring broken small minds. Julie would need help too. Heidi foresaw unprecedented reaches of panic and guilt. They would all need help. Maybe Jerusalem was the answer.

"We have to go now, Mama." Stephanie spoke in the bloodless monotone of the audio component in her computer spelling game. Her hazel eyes were heavy lidded and unfocused—nobody home. The little hand tapping at Heidi's was so chill and unfleshlike that Heidi bent and blanketed it with kisses; her lips grew cold and the hand did not warm.

"Go where, my sweetie pie? Come back into bed. Have a big old cuddle with Mama."

"We have to go to Daisy's house."

"No, no, sweetie, don't you remember? Daddy and I told you you didn't have to go. We changed the agenda. You were going to go to Nick's house, only you fell asleep. On the floor. In your clothes. So tonight is for staying home. Are you hungry? We could go cook up a storm. All your favorite things. Cinnamon toast and cocoa. That should warm you up."

"We don't have time, Mama. Lokomo says it's easier to fly on an empty stomach. Take off your robe and put on your jeans, okay? I'm not afraid anymore. They can't save her without me. I don't like her but I have to save her. Nick and James like her better than they like me. Iceman says I can bring Banky with me. I wish Julie could come. Julie can't do the circle but I love her."

Heidi gathered Stephanie onto her lap. She wished Henry would pick the moment to come upstairs. She felt that she'd slept for hours, but she still heard the thrum of the opening that was supposed to end at eight. She wished Marguerite would blink the gallery lights and send everyone away.

"No one's ever going to bother you again, my sweetest sweetie." She stroked Stephanie's hair. "Not Lokomo or Iceman or anyone else at all."

Stephanie puffed out a little laugh. "Mama, you don't understand. I have to go." She was the patient mother now, coaxing the balky child. "If you take me to Daisy's, you can bring me back home with you. If I have to go by myself I might not get back."

"Little girls don't go by themselves. Their parents love them too much to let them do that."

Stephanie giggled. "I can go. Julie knows. Boy, did I bug Amanda and Julie this morning." Now she sounded very much like a three-year-old. "Boy, was I a moth in your closet."

Heidi clasped her around, moaned out her name.

"All right, Mama—" breaking free, her voice in neutral again—"do you take me or do I go myself? I'll give you to the count of ten."

Heidi managed to pull out a jokey voice. "You will, will you?"

Stephanie tumbled over onto the sheets and lay down clutching Banky. For a moment Heidi thought Stephanie was out from under the strangeness, ready to snuggle up. She lay down next to her.

"Ten. Nine. Eight. Seven. Six. Five. Four. Three. Two. One." Stephanie's eyeballs rolled up into her head until only the whites were showing.

Heidi screamed as she had never screamed before. Henry came running.

43.

If only Alexander Graham Mozart had eaten a yellow plastic tulip and sunk beneath the weight of his mother.

Ken threw his arms around Nick and James. "Thank you for coming, men."

Thomas the big orange cat scratched Mary Girard.

James waved an everyday hand at the fainting Elizabeth.

Bob Geritano hugged me which was meant to be nice but why was he consoling me why?

Grouch, she's not dead, is she? Tell me, Grouch. Please, Grouch. Hold me. Hold me. She's not dead, is she?

I gave Thomas a bowl of real Devon cream, four dollars and ninety-five cents the pint.

"I hope Stephanie makes it," Ken said.

All the questions I didn't ask because I didn't want to know the answers.

I put out a pâté my girl and I had crafted over the weekend and left on the ice to ripen fresh baby artichokes studded down the middle giving the look of a flower in every slice I call it Daisy pâté.

Elizabeth screamed for everything to stop.

The commissioner took the first slice.

If only my cousin Larry had died on the drafting board.

Jack said he would put up a slide at Gracie Mansion.

Bob went to Elizabeth.

If you don't have fresh baby artichokes make a different pâté.

"Anyone have to pee, men?" Ken asked.

I told the commissioner I had bought it at Woolworth's.

The telephone didn't ring and didn't ring.

Tears on Grouch's plastic face.

Jack said to Jackie how sad they had to meet again under such terrible circumstances.

"Hey, who pulled my hair?" Nick said.

"This is it," Ken said. "Stephanie is here. Let's go to Daisy's room, men."

Elizabeth stood up all Rountree proper spine and said she was going wherever James was going.

Bob and Jackie said they were going too.

"Sorry," Ken said, "too much weight."

I grabbed his sleeve. I said just me.

"Not this trip. Too big. You stay here. Daisy will need you fresh. Please don't light that cigarette, commissioner. Stephanie, you do that again and I'll spank you next time I see you. Come on, men. Jill, I love you. Hang on. We'll do it. Let's go." He took the kids into Daisy's room and closed the door.

44.

She was dead.

Sweat broke out all over Arthur Kojak's body. He cradled the beautiful body and begged it to come alive. Over and over again he put his ear to her heart, he held a mirror to her mouth and nose to check for respiration. Nothing. Still as a doll.

He hadn't expected to find her dead. Unconscious, maybe; but he'd get there in time to save her, to save everyone. He'd cleanse the place of evidence pointing to Mrs. Keefe, then he'd telephone the glorious news to the frantic mother. In a week the event would have receded. Children healed quickly. Daisy would be the happiest kid at the playground again.

Like a doll, and he talked to it as if it might answer at any moment the way he'd seen children do with their dolls. Nothing. He closed the lids over the ghastly rolled-up eyes. He pulled a Mickey Mouse sheet over her face.

His hands were shaking. His whole body was vibrating. He had never known such pain. It didn't matter what he was feeling. He might still be able to save Mrs. Keefe if he kept his head. He went into the living room, the master bedroom. He saw nothing out of place. The master bath was another matter. He panicked all over again when he saw the toothpaste scrawl, "Jack Keefe for mayor." He took tissues and started rubbing, then took a washcloth, wet it, and went to work on the white smudgy swirls his rubbing had left behind. He fished the toothpaste tube out of the toilet and wrapped it in the washcloth and a yellow towel he found lying crumpled in a corner. He brought the bundle into the kitchen. He had to get rid of all the food and the Gristede's shopping bags. And the body.

He heard a sound. He froze.

Children calling out "Daisy."

From another apartment? But one didn't hear sounds from other apartments in buildings like this one.

He ran to the child's room. He opened the door.

The air was so sweet with the scent of vanilla, he almost swooned. A slipstream pinned him against the wall, a thick wild wind that whistled around the room like the beating of a thousand tiny wings. The air was blue and green and green and blue and purple and he knew it was the end but he couldn't scream.

They told him to lie down on the bed next to Daisy and he did. They told him to open his mouth and he did.

This won't hurt, said the butterfly, as it started sucking out his life and giving it to the girl.

She threw off her sheet and sat up.

The child who had been dead was laughing.

She said: "One two three. What do I see? The umbrella man is looking at me. May I have a pretzel, please? My mom will pay you tomorrow."

45.

Nora walked past the linen wholesalers and the foreign bookshops of lower Fifth Avenue, down toward the misty beacon of the Washington Square Arch. She hoped the rain would stop before morning. She worried when Jack jogged in the rain. She was asleep when he did his running, but she worried in her sleep, had dreams of him falling or catching his death of cold.

She got to Fourteenth Street. The light was against her. Everything was against her. She had not meant to hurt the child. She stepped off the curb. A taxi swerved around her. "Crazy broad!" the driver yelled, leaning on his horn. Nora kept moving into the traffic. She pulled petals off the daisy. She's alive . . . she's not alive. She's alive . . . she's not alive. The crosstown bus was coming fast. The street was a bedlam of horns. The eyes of the bus were hot and hungry. She heard a woman screaming. Someone dragged her to the curb and lifted her to the sidewalk. The bus said it would get her next time. But there wouldn't be a next time. Daisy was alive!

She felt the rain pull back. Tears came to take its place. Dr. Howard would be so pleased to know about the tears. Mr. Kojak was gone but Daisy was alive. She heard her tulips calling "Mama." She hurried the last two blocks. She smiled when she saw the squad car. Daisy was alive. She went inside.

46.

"Sixty-sixth and Fifth, northeast corner, apartment 4-A," Ken told the commissioner.

Jill and Ken broke for the door.

The telephone rang.

Jill paused long enough to hear the commissioner answer and say to Jack, "Your wife just got home."

Jill and Ken kept running.

47.

Stephanie sat up in her bed. "Knock knock," she said.

Heidi clutched Henry's hand. The little red-haired girl in front of them looked like their own real daughter. "Who's there?" she asked in a choked voice.

"Sin," Stephanie said.

"Sin who?"

"Cinnamon toast and cocoa would be wonderful now."

"Wonderful now, *please*," Henry said, then he swooped down on the bed and covered his daughter with kisses.

48.

"You've got to let us up there!" the woman screamed. "My baby! My baby! You know her! You wave to her every afternoon!"

For a moment Albert Cunningham was shaken. The woman was very convincing. But wasn't the entertainment business filled with pinks? Moscow could call on any of a hundred actresses.

A black car did a squealing slide into the curb. A man in a linen suit the color of oatmeal jumped out of the back seat and ran into the building.

"Police Commissioner." He flashed metal. "Four-A. Kidnapping. Let us in."

Now Albert felt downright insulted. This dandy the commissioner? Not in a hundred years. Albert just wished he could signal upstairs. The man who was Washington had come streaking in not twenty minutes ago. Two men in cops' uniforms were coming through the front door now, but anyone could get a uniform, uniforms were a dime a dozen. There were too many for him, but he wasn't going to let the country down, if he went he was going to take some of the enemy with him. He reached for his pistol. He aimed it at the man in the oatmeal suit. Sirens were screaming now, cops were pouring in, real cops, but it was too late to stop his finger, the lobby was roaring and smoking, the man in the oatmeal suit was going down. "That asshole shot the commissioner!" he heard a real cop yell, and, as the cops' bullets struck his shoulder, he thought it was probably as well he was going down himself.

49.

"Mamamamamamamama."

"Daisy dearest darling baby flower love my love my darling sweetest baby girl."

"Hi, Ken."

"Hi, Daisy."

"Look, Mom, there's the umbrella man, I tried to wake him up but I couldn't. You're not mad at me, are you?"

"No no no no never never never dearest darling baby Daisy girlfriend. Ken, oh, God, it's the pretzel vendor, he's dead. Can we get out of here?"

"I don't think anybody's going to make you sign a receipt. Let's go."

"Because I asked him for a pretzel but he didn't have any. Can I press the button? It doesn't have a one."

"Try *L*. For Lobby."

"He was very nice to me. He covered my face when I was dead because it's nicer that way."

"Dearest dearest dearest darling girl. You weren't dead."

"He didn't have any pretzels. Because it's dark, you see. Pretzels are for daytime."

"They are, aren't they? You know so many things."

"It was a little boring being dead. Can I have ginger ale when we get home?"

"All you want. Gallons and gallons. I'll fill the bathtub with ginger ale if you want."

"Why are they putting those men in the ambulance, Mama? Did they swallow puzzle pieces like Curious George?"

"I bet that's just what they did. Silly men."

"Silly billy men. You can put me down, Mom. Hey, the rain went away. Don't come again some other day. Ken, you have to wait for the WALK sign. It's very, very important to wait before you cross the street. Cars come very fast here. Okay, we have the light now. Both of you hold my hands. Look, I can almost see the playground. I'm really glad we moved here, Mama. There's so much to do. Because the buildings are tiptop tall and they really take care of you. I love New York."

July

1.

July, and hot, and Daisy's laughter was pure silver again. She'd had her rough moments during the first few weeks after Nora—clinging to me when she wasn't bawling me out over trifles, starting out of deep sleep; but if ever she'd earned the right to be cranky, it was then. Nora wasn't the only source of turmoil in her young life. The Playgroup, that pillar of her existence, had collapsed without notice, her beloved "kids" scattering over the globe. Ken—whom she loved—was nonetheless a stranger on *her* side of Mama's bed, was very much with us.

And then there was Mama herself. I could have supplied the material for a hundred children's nightmares in the wake of the Nora night. I had embraced unreason with a convert's hot-eyed fervor. I had raced from room to room, from telephone to typewriter, spewing panic and chaos all over my cousin Larry's apartment. I had believed everything anyone told me, as long as it didn't make conventional sense. The orderly universe I'd believed in until then had betrayed me, and I was going to show *it*.

Ken cheered me on. He said I was growing. He said my brand of rationality had been hopelessly narrow, an insult to the possibilities of life and hence not rational at all. He brought me bouquets of documents about the brain as miniature electrical generator . . . about the connections between psyche and soma . . . about the mathematical properties of promiscuity. I not only believed in the basic Playgroup syndrome, I believed all Ken's embellishments. One night he told me excitedly he was now convinced that Nora's very cells had been changed and charged by her squelched longing for children, that she was the primary source of the Playgroup's extraordinariness; and I believed him. I actually liked the theory. It seemed a kind of rough justice that childless Nora should alter thousands of little lives. And—though I would never forget the bad hours she'd given my girl—I had some feeling for the blows Big Jack had dealt her pride and I rather cherished the image of him as her cosmic messenger boy.

Heidi told me from behind her own mad mists that Stephanie had *thought* a dress of hers to pieces; and I believed her. There had been a first time for everything "impossible," hadn't there been? Electric lights? Cameras? X-rays? I believed Elizabeth's hysterical insistence that James had *thought* garbage into Oliver's tennis bag. I believe Jackie's babblings about Nick starting to retch because James was vomiting, two blocks away. Ken had me feeling right ashamed that once upon a time, in my arrogance, I'd only believed what I understood, as if mine were the ultimate omniscient mind.

I believed the crazed doorman who told me, from his hospital bed, that Arthur Kojak had worked for Washington. I believed Ken's Wagnerian tale about Kojak dying to give his lifespark to ignite my Daisy's stalled engine. I had no use for the police commissioner's statement, from *his* hospital bed, that Kojak was a second-rate private detective who'd been hired by Nora to track Jack's catting, that Kojak had died of heart failure. Nothing simple or superficially sensible for me!

Everytime it rained, it rained trenchcoats from wicked government agencies. All butterflies carried children on their wings.

And Jonah swallowed the whale.

I suppose the onslaught of credulity was overdue. Maybe it was the inevitable rebellion against my super rational parents as well as a reflection of how hurt I was by reason's betrayal of me. Maybe it was a chemical explosion triggered by the wildly sweet nights with Ken after four years of no desserts. Maybe it was the natural aftermath of coming home one rainy Tuesday evening to find my daughter gone. A mother has a right to be nutsy after living through that anguish.

I talked and I wrote, those last weeks of June, and I wrote and I talked, and I believed and I believed.

And didn't believe. I'd been a skeptic for thirty-two years, and no matter how I explained away my turnabout, I couldn't stop asking questions, I couldn't still my doubting voices.

Night after night I lay awake next to a sleeping Ken, trying to reconcile past and present mindsets, trying to make certain I understood what was what. I couldn't shake the feeling that I was leaving something important out of the equation. I had to find it if I wanted peace.

And one night I found it. Oh, my God. So simple. My father's beloved objective correlative.

I sat up in bed, my heart tripping.

Eleven little digits. 1-603-555-1212. New Hampshire Information.

I looked at Ken, his face calm in sleep, and I knew—as we always know on the verge of treachery—that I loved him. I silently begged him to wake up and keep me from committing the act that might put an end to what we were just getting started but he didn't wake up *because thoughts do not beam*. I kissed his shoulder, got out of bed, padded across the shadowy living room, and made my call from the kitchen telephone.

"In Rye Beach, please. A listing for a restaurant called The World Is My Clam."

Almost midnight, and the woman who answered at the restaurant said unnicely that they were about to close and I should call back the next day if I wanted information.

"Don't hang up!" I knew the name of a waitress, Shelley, because how could I forget that perfect name? I asked if she was there, and she was, and she came to the telephone.

"Ma?" she guessed.

"No, it's Jill Everts, in New York City. I don't suppose you remember my name, but do you remember, two summers ago, a mother who used to come in every week or so with a year-and-a-half old girl, beautiful little girl with silvery hair and big blue eyes, who loved scallops? That was me. And my daughter. Daisy. Remember?"

I heard hesitation, and someone yelling "Shel-ley" in the background, and the awful disco jukebox, and then she said, hurriedly, "Sure, I remember. Daisy. A cutie. She liked throwing your steamer shells."

"Yes! Shelley, listen. This is very important. I hate to bring up the most unpleasant subject on earth—but do you remember when the Red Tide hit that summer? Did anyone get sick at the World? Any of your customers?"

Silence, then she said, suspiciously, "Are you a newspaper reporter or something?"

My throat was all but closing with fear and hope. "No way. I'm just who I said I was. This isn't for anyone's ears but mine. I've had recurring nightmares. I'm trying to get to the bottom of them. Stop them. It's gotten so I dread going to sleep."

"Oh, wow. Well, listen, there's nothing to hide. Nobody got sick from here. We closed for a while like all the seafood joints did, but it was actually quite a ways north of here that the Tide hit."

I wanted to stand up and dance a jig. I was operating under my old rules again, though, and I pressed for truth. "You're sure?"

"I'm sure. I was working the day they reported the Tide, and I remember—I'd just eaten two dozen raw oysters when I heard the news. I mean, I seriously thought about going home and writing out my will! But I'm here to tell you about it, right?"

There it was. I thanked her, hung up, went to the refrigerator, got out the carton of apple juice, drank three glassesful, poured a fourth, and threw the empty carton in the trash. I went to the living room. I sat down in a corner of the couch. I flung the shackles off my mind and watched it happily race around in the dark.

In the dark, clarity was mine.

The day outside The World Is My Clam, when Daisy had shrieked that we mustn't go in—that had been the start of my downfall. My poor wounded single mother's ego had turned those shrieks into a religion. Life had thrown me a rum punch? I knew how to hit back. This wasn't any old child having a spasm of gas or a plain old tantrum—not my baby. When she cried, the universe was crying, the mountains and stars were sending a message. You see, Jack? You see, everyone? I couldn't marry the man I loved, I couldn't have a family though every dumb ugly boring girl I'd known in high school could; but I had something better. I had a baby who could *smell* the Red Tide. Maybe it was scary being the mother of Supergirl, but not half so unbearable as being the mother of Everygirl.

And I kept falling. Down, down, falling for everything.

How clearly Heidi had once seen my eagerness to believe our children were different from other children. But it was Ken who had keyed into my needs, and he took me all the way down. And we brought Heidi and the other Playgroup parents down with us.

There *wasn't* any Playgroup syndrome. I had no doubts that Ken truly believed there was—but his believing it didn't make it so. I could see him out in California, my tanned good earnest Dr. Iceman, motivated by his love of children, trying to find a way to preserve their natural magic. Then, when he'd found out that Washington was secretly funding his work for the crassest of military motives, his outrage and his fear for the future of the world had pushed him close to the edge. The only way he could function was to think that children were creatures of light who, guided by him, could keep the powers of darkness from destroying us all in war.

Nora was unhinged, a woman who lived in constant pain, but her condition wasn't some kind of contagion to be spread by Jack's peripatetic penis. How eager Ken had been to fit that ridiculous notion into his scheme, and how perfectly it had served my own needs. No, my egobound Jill, the love of your twenties was neither god nor demon—just another husband who minored in legs.

As for Stephanie and James moving matter with their minds, and Nick feeling the workings of James's body, I had believed these preposterous ideas because I had to believe that Supergirl had Superfriends. Sure, kids were more open than grownups, had qualities which even the most cautious observer might liken to ESP . . . but that didn't for a minute mean that scissors in a magazine could translate into scissors on a dress. Heidi had taken Dexamyl that day, and—peering through the darkness—I hadn't a shred of doubt that she'd cut up the dress herself in a ten-minute fit sponsored by the drug. Had I really believed that James had thought garbage into Oliver's tennis bag? Probably because I'd wished I had such powers myself! There were plenty of people who had access to his bag at the bank, and dozens of women who had reason to dump on him. Nick's retching when James was vomiting: there was a good old fashioned word to cover *that* one—coincidence.

Explanations had been there all along, if only I hadn't willed myself not to see them. I sat there in the dark living room, sipping apple juice, seeing them now. The whole Lokomo trip was just your basic mass hypnosis, but I'd had to make it more; I'd had to make everything more. I'd believed I'd badly burned my hand so I could believe it was miraculously healed by my girl like no other girl. I'd believed the kids and Ken "saw" where Nora had Daisy, though Nora had no doubt pointed out her apartment from the park after Daisy fell and we left. Finally I'd believed Daisy had come back from death because I needed to think I'd given her something even better than a daddy—immortality. Anything to counterbalance feelings of failure and feed my desperate ego. Anything to please the man with the khaki hair.

I still believed Ken was good. I still hoped he was our future. But I saw now that I'd been wrong in letting him move in with us so quickly. Daisy was all right, she knew the difference between Iceman the pretend and Huysman the real. Did I? I had to make sure my new found clarity wasn't just another blinding flash, that the lights were on for good.

I slept in his crevices and crooks all night. In the morning I told him the news.

2.

Daisy and I have moved to West Eleventh Street! Nora and Jack gave us their brownstone. They are in County Cork. Their postcards are litanies of tranquil names. They describe fishing at the estuary in Rosscarbery, shopping at the Golden Pheasant in Courtmacsherry, pubbing in Glandore. A Mrs. Goode in Castlecove is helping them to find a house to buy. They hope for a white one, with a garden.

It's all right, isn't it? That they're free and maybe happy? If I had hounded Nora through the courts, asked a jury to set a price on Daisy's and my pain, who would have come out ahead? I have Daisy and Nora doesn't, and Jack will not be mayor of Cork City—enough.

Ken has been calling every day, gently trying to sell me on his notions and connections. He found out that Jack and Oliver liked to share a woman now and then, that Heidi had an affair in college with a professor of political science who had gone to Columbia law school with Jack. I don't mind. Daisy and I are always glad to hear his voice, and I am immune to his message. Because *there was no Playgroup syndrome*. There were just four precocious darlings, no more and no less magical than any other kids their age.

I've been writing to the other Playgroup parents, but I don't know if I can bring them around. Tough though it was to convince them that our children were mysteriously bonded, it's tougher to convince them that we all were deluded! Or maybe the "Playgroup syndrome" is giving them the excuse to make moves they wanted to make anyway? Jackie had her tubes tied. She and Bob have bought a tennis club in Florida. Nick sent Daisy a toy alligator, a snapping head on a stick. Elizabeth took her James to Sydney to visit Kelly Smith and Megan. Elizabeth wrote me a long letter. She said maybe she'd been hard on Ken. Kelly was her absolutely dearest friend but she wasn't exactly mature about men. Still, Elizabeth is reluctant to come back to New York—because of Oliver as well as the Playgroup?—and may stay on in Australia a while. James sent Daisy a tiny stuffed koala. Henry sent me a conciliatory postcard of my favorite Paul Klee oil, a mosaic Mount Parnassus, but he and Heidi are checking out Swiss schools for their girls, and I know he will never again let Stephanie play with Daisy.

We don't need any of them. Daisy and I have been joyfully rediscovering each other as we traipse around Greenwich Village. She loves the showy markets of Sixth Avenue, the open air cafés around Sheridan Square. She plans to grow carrots in Nora's greenhouse. Later today we will make our first visit to Washington Square Park, where there's a playground and there aren't many trees. Only kidding about the trees. I'm not afraid of anything now. I threw my Fiorinal away. I haven't had a headache since the night when I called The World Is My Clam. They are temples of reason again.

My cousin Larry is coming back from London at the end of September, with a British bride. She has two small children. I recommended Mary Girard as a mother's helper. She should be on her feet by then. Betty DuPont will help out here at the house and be Daisy's sitter when I start to work again. I'm having a professional stove installed in Nora and Jack's big kitchen. I've ordered a marble topped pastry table.

I miss Ken. Daisy does, too. His latest theory is that we should marry, in his parents' backyard, while the weather is still mild. I would like to see him and my girl at breakfast again. I would like to watch the World Series with a husband of my own. I do love him, but is it a safe love? I wish he would become a sports writer. I'm going to wait until I'm absolutely, permanently sure.

3.

Washington Square is bright with the T-shirts of a hundred children.

Daisy and I stand near the famous arch taking in the scene. I see the big fountain wreathed in cement and a lone shaggy guitarist on its lip who seems not to know that the war in Vietnam is over; I see a drug dealer who is pushing loose joints but not too strenuously because it's too hot to strain; I see the all-wrong Boston red of the New York University library rising up on the south side of the Square; I see joggers and lovers and ailanthus trees and dogs running wild on the dirt where grass should be; I see the playground, a few yards to our left.

Our playground. Daisy tugs at me. I look at the shiny fence, clearly new, probably wrested out of the Parks Department by some earnest hardworking parents' committee, and I smile. I could tell those parents a thing or two about playground fences.

In we go.

Daisy climbs up a timberform, whizzes down the slide, skips over to me. "Was that sliding or was that sliding?"

I tell her it was sliding.

"I want to try that slide." She points. "On the other side of the swings. I like it here. I want to try everything."

We start across the playground.

"Boy, look at that," Daisy says. "One, two sandpits. Do you believe two sandpits?" I look. One sandpit is a small square, with steps going down it and a water table in the middle. The other is a spacious high sided oval. I am the daughter of reason, and for a beautiful foolish innocent moment I wonder why there are a dozen kids crammed into the small sandpit and only three kids in the big sandpit. And then I know.

"Hi, Daisy," a girl calls out from the big sandpit, a grubby cherub with hair even paler than my girl's.

Daisy waves at her, and the girl waves back, and the two boys in the sandpit wave. I do not wave.

"That's Sara," Daisy says. "And Jason and Matthew."

The bigger of the boys is holding out a silver shovel. The three mothers sitting on the high curved wall, tanned legs dangling, hold out friendly smiles.

I scoop Daisy up and start to run. I do not care that she is pounding my shoulders with outraged fists.

"I want to play with the kids!" she yells. "Bring me back to my kids!"

I run and I run and she keeps yelling and I suppose that I am screaming because the planet is theirs and no matter where I run she will always find Nora's children.

"A nearly purely bred, Arabian, chestnut mare bore a hybrid to a quagga; she was subsequently sent to Sir Gore Onseley, and produced two colts by a black Arabian horse. These colts were partially dun-coloured, and were striped on the legs more plainly than the real hybrid, or even than the quagga. One of the two colts had its neck and some other parts of its body plainly marked with stripes. Stripes on the body, not to mention those on the legs, and the dun-colour, are extremely rare—I speak after having long attended to the subject—with horses of all kinds in Europe, and are unknown in the case of Arabians. But what makes the case still more striking is that the hair of the mane in these colts resembled that of the quagga, being short, stiff, and upright. Hence, there can be no doubt that the quagga affected the character of the offspring subsequently begot by the black Arabian horse."

Charles Darwin
Variation of Animals and Plants Under Domestication, 1868

ACKNOWLEDGMENT

Dr. Douglas "Rigorous" Rowland of D Y Rowland Associates in Cleveland Heights, Ohio, kindly calculated mathematical probabilities for this book. Any flaws in interpretation are the author's own.

Bestselling Books

- ☐ 16663-6 **DRAGON STAR** Olivia O'Neill $2.95
- ☐ 08953-4 **THE BUTCHER'S BOY** Thomas Perry $3.50
- ☐ 65366-9 **THE PATRIARCH** Chaim Bermant $3.25
- ☐ 70885-4 **REBEL IN HIS ARMS** Francine Rivers $3.50
- ☐ 02574-9 **THE APOCALYPSE BRIGADE** Alfred Coppel $3.50
- ☐ 65219-0 **PASSAGE TO GLORY** Robin Leigh Smith $3.50
- ☐ 75888-6 **SENSEI** David Charney $3.50
- ☐ 05285-1 **BED REST** Rita Kashner $3.25
- ☐ 75700-6 **SEASON OF THE STRANGLER** Madison Jones $2.95
- ☐ 11726-0 **A CONTROLLING INTEREST** Peter Engel $3.50
- ☐ 02884-5 **ARCHANGEL** Gerald Seymour $3.50

Prices may be slightly higher in Canada.

Available at your local bookstore or return this form to:

ⓒ CHARTER BOOKS
Book Mailing Service
P.O. Box 690, Rockville Centre, NY 11571

Please send me the titles checked above. I enclose _____. Include 75¢ for postage and handling if one book is ordered; 25¢ per book for two or more not to exceed $1.75. California, Illinois, New York and Tennessee residents please add sales tax.

NAME_____

ADDRESS_____

CITY_____ STATE/ZIP_____

(allow six weeks for delivery.)

A-4

Bestselling Books

☐ 21889-X **EXPANDED UNIVERSE**, Robert A. Heinlein	$3.95
☐ 47809-3 **THE LEFT HAND OF DARKNESS**, Ursula K. LeGuin	$2.95
☐ 48519-7 **LIVE LONGER NOW**, Jon N. Leonard, J. L. Hofer and N. Pritikin	$3.50
☐ 80582-5 **THIEVES' WORLD,**™ Robert Lynn Asprin, Ed.	$2.95
☐ 02884-5 **ARCHANGEL**, Gerald Seymour	$3.50
☐ 08933-X **BUSHIDO**, Beresford Osborne	$3.50
☐ 08953-4 **THE BUTCHER'S BOY**, Thomas Perry	$3.50
☐ 78036-9 **STAR COLONY**, Keith Laumer	$2.95
☐ 11503-9 **A COLD BLUE LIGHT**, Marvin Kay and Parke Godwin	$3.50
☐ 24097-6 **THE FLOATING ADMIRAL**, Agatha Christie, Dorothy Sayers, G.K. Chesterton & others	$2.95
☐ 21599-8 **ESCAPE VELOCITY**, Christopher Stasheff	$2.95
☐ 37155-8 **INVASION: EARTH**, Harry Harrison	$2.75

Prices may be slightly higher in Canada.

Available at your local bookstore or return this form to:

C **CHARTER BOOKS**
Book Mailing Service
P.O. Box 690, Rockville Centre, NY 11571

Please send me the titles checked above. I enclose _____ Include 75¢ for postage and handling if one book is ordered; 25¢ per book for two or more not to exceed $1.75. California, Illinois, New York and Tennessee residents please add sales tax.

NAME _____

ADDRESS _____

CITY _____ STATE/ZIP _____

(allow six weeks for delivery)   A-9